Once Upon a Second Chance

Marian Vere

OMNIFIC PUBLISHING
DALLAS

Omnific Publishing
10000 North Central Expressway, Dallas, TX 75231
www.omnificpublishing.com

First Omnific eBook edition, November 2012
First Omnific trade paperback edition, November 2012

The characters and events in this book are fictitious.
Any similarity to real persons, living or dead,
is coincidental and not intended by the author.

Library of Congress Cataloguing-in-Publication Data

Vere, Marian.
  Once Upon a Second Chance / Marian Vere – 1st ed.
  ISBN 978-1-62342-915-7
  1. Romance — Fiction. 2. Fairy Godmother — Fiction.
  3. Contemporary Fairy Tale — Fiction. 4. Jane Austen — Fiction. I. Title

10 9 8 7 6 5 4 3 2 1

Cover Design by Micha Stone and Amy Brokaw
Interior Book Design by Coreen Montagna

Printed in the United States of America

To Scott

1

I stare blank-faced at the e-mail on the screen in front of me, praying I am misreading the first two words in the second paragraph.

Group memos like this one find their way into my inbox almost every day and are typically filled with nothing more than boring office news. An announcement about Sally-so-and-so's upcoming retirement, or a notice about Joe-shmoe's birthday next week. Nothing unusual or earth shattering. This particular memo started out that way, nothing worth panicking over. That is, until I arrived at the second paragraph and came to the two little words that currently have me in a chokehold.

Two. Little. Words.

Nicholas Kerkley.

Okay—dream or hallucination? If I'm expected to live until the end of this e-mail, it has to be one of the two.

A dream is easy enough to check, right? If this is a dream then something nonsensical or fantastic will be going on, like one of my co-workers will be Paula Deen from *Food Network* which, in my dream universe, will somehow make perfect sense. Or, I'll open the door to our office and it will lead into my grandma's kitchen. Then there's the ever popular—if not a bit cliché—one where I'll be naked.

I look around the office: no Paula Deen. The office door is open: no grandmother's kitchen. Last but not least, I glance down at myself, hoping—yes, hoping—to find that I'm only wearing underwear, but find myself fully clothed.

All right, not a dream.

So much for that, but dream or no dream, this still can't be real. It *can't* be. It must be some weird hallucination. I'll close my eyes, take some deep breaths, count to five, and everything will be fine.

One…(Breathe in…two…three…four…And out…two…three…four…)

Maybe it's the caffeine; I did have way too much coffee this morning.

Two…(In…two…three…four…Out…two…three…four…)

I should know better than to order a large when it's not decaf!

I continue my breathing exercise, but it's not helping.

All right, that's it, no more coffee, starting tomorrow.

Inhale. Exhale.

Please let it be the coffee…

Inhale. Exhale. *Dear God, please, please, please…*

One more breath…*Damn it!*

My screen still holds today's company memo for the Herstein Group, and Nicholas Kerkley is still the only name listed under "New Client."

I lean back in my chair and cover my face with both hands. This can't be happening. Why would he choose this firm? Does he know I work here? Does he even remember me? After all, it has been over eight years. Dear God…is he married? Does he have kids? This picture pops into my head: he has his arm around some twenty-something, blond-haired, blue-eyed beauty queen as they walk along the beach with half a dozen adorable children. All of them with her perfect hair and his gorgeous eyes…

"Jules?"

"Hmm?" My head snaps up, and I see Bree at her desk, staring at me as though I have a third eye. Only now do I realize I've actually been hunched over in my chair, face buried in my hands, practically hyperventilating.

"You okay?"

"Oh yeah, fine, just a headache. Face too close to the screen," I say with a smile I hope she buys.

Brianna St. Charles and I work for The Herstein Group, one of only four personal finance consulting groups at SMS Financial. Our boss (Margaret Herstein herself), Bree, and I make up the entire team. Bree and I met when I was hired over six years ago, and she's been one of my best friends ever since.

The only issue I have with her is the fact that it's incredibly hard on the ego to be anywhere near her in public or within sight of a mirror. She has huge, beautiful curls of strawberry-blond hair, silver-blue eyes, and a body a supermodel would kill for. She's a perfect, statuesque beauty, while I'm the even-more-mousy-and-plain-by-comparison friend.

You'd expect someone who looks like Bree to have the common decency to be flighty, or air-headed, or have some personality defect to balance it out. *Something* to keep the rest of us from just giving up altogether. But no, she's the sweetest, smartest, most down-to-earth person you could ever wish to meet. She's impossible not to love.

As Bree goes back to typing, I stand and make my way to the restroom with as calm a façade I can muster. The door shuts behind me, and I step into the large handicapped stall. Not only does it have extra space, but because it's the kind with its own private wash area. I walk over to the mirror and brace my hands on either side of the cold porcelain sink.

All right, deep breath. *You can do this.* It doesn't have to be that bad. After all, odds are I will never even have to see him. I'm just the admin; I hardly ever meet face-to-face with our clients, and there's no reason he should be any different.

Our clients are extremely wealthy individuals who come to us when they need help spending their money. We assist them in purchasing real estate, research business franchises, advise them as to which personal jet will have the highest resale value in five to ten years—stuff like that. They pay us to be the unbiased experts in whatever they're interested in. Over the past few years, our group has become the most successful one at SMS Financial.

That, however, has little to do with me and far more to do with Margaret and Bree. Margaret is the lead consultant (the boss), Bree is the junior consultant (her assistant), and I am the secretary (the nobody). Okay, I'm the *administrative assistant* if you want to be PC about it, but I have never been able to call myself that. "A rose by any other name would smell as sweet" is one of my all-time favorite Shakespeare quotes, but it works the other way too. Not that my job is awful—I love Margaret and Bree, and the work is fine, it just doesn't give you many good stories to tell at the bar. Margaret and Bree have stories, because everyone wants to hear about the heiress looking for her fifth penthouse condo just so she can piss off Daddy, or the multi-millionaire who wants a private house upstate so that he and his assistant can have some privacy for their frequent — *ahem* — business meetings. People are fascinated with how the other half lives. How the other half takes their coffee, not so much; that's the sort of stuff I know. I answer phones, sort mail, arrange meetings, and take notes. I have met a few of our current and past clients through conference calls or meetings where I took minutes, or the occasional intercepted phone call when Bree was away from her desk. However, none of our clients have ever *needed* to meet me, so there is no reason Nick — I mean *Mr. Kerkley* — will be any different.

I glance into the mirror and run my fingers through my unruly hair. It's not-curly-not-straight texture often causes me problems, and my struggle with it this morning is particularly bad. Though at the time, I hadn't realized my fight with the flat iron was actually a sign telling me that today would suck and to go back to bed.

Too bad I didn't get the message.

With a deep breath, I slowly make my way back to my desk. I arrive just in time to overhear Bree saying on the phone, "There she is, she just got back. I'll tell her. Okay, see you in a bit."

Must be Margaret. Good. She'll have a distraction for me; she always does. Margaret has been my boss since I was hired, and she has made my work life one big rollercoaster ride ever since. Not in a bad way, as she's one of the kindest, most caring people you could ever work for. She's just one of those people that is always running at full speed and never seems to slow down: the textbook definition of a Type A personality. Though I will say she has a great business head. There's a reason we're the number one group in our firm.

She keeps us busy, always blowing through the office, in — what Bree and I have affectionately named — a dizzy-tizzy, as she's passing out work and talking through schedules at a million miles an hour. By the time she blows out again, Bree and I usually have more than a day's work to do, and while we generally dread it, right now that's exactly what I need.

"Hey, Jules, that was Margaret," Bree tells me, coming over to sit on the edge of my desk, as is her habit if she has news or gossip to share. "Did you see the e-mail about our new client?"

I wince. No distraction then. "Yep, just a few minutes ago." Please let that be the end of it.

"Margaret just sent me his file. I was expecting the usual sixty-something divorcé or bald investor, but look at this." She hands me a small pile of papers. "Turns out he's only thirty-one, built this huge technical consulting corporation from the ground up, *and* he's worth over seventeen *billion* dollars! Can you believe it! We finally get to work with a hot guy!"

She is obviously thrilled. Good for her. Wait a minute…

"How do you know he's hot?"

"Oh, I went to one of his company's websites and saw a picture. Here, let me show you, he really is gorgeous—"

"No, that's all right," I say quickly, grabbing the mouse before she gets to it. My sanity can't handle pictures right now.

"Oh, okay then," she says, cocking an eyebrow. "You'll see soon enough anyway."

My heart freezes in my chest. "What?"

"That's what Margaret was calling about. He'll be here in an hour for our first meeting."

Please no, please no.

My throat closes like an allergy attack, and I ball my hands into fists to keep them from shaking. "B-But you never need me at those meetings."

"I know, but Margaret says this is a big one. An all-hands-on-deck sort of thing. Apparently there's a property up in Maine—"

"I can't make it," I interrupt, fishing frantically in my brain for an impromptu lie. "I have to leave early. Doctor's appointment." Weak I know, but it's the best I can come up with mid-panic.

"You do?"

"I told you yesterday, remember?" Wow, this is disturbing. Normally I don't lie this well. Amazing what the right motivation can do.

"Oh." She furrows her eyebrows, thinking back. "It must have slipped my mind. Oh well, no biggie. I can fill you in tomorrow. You're not sick are you?"

I see the worry on Bree's face, and my stomach sinks. Ugh, why does she have to be concerned over my lie? Don't I feel bad enough already? "No, no, just the yearly…you know." I give her the gynecology exam grimace, and she understands immediately.

"Oh…yuck."

"I was actually going to head out now," I say, gathering up my stuff and trying very hard not to analyze the fact that I'm being the very definition of a coward. I *like* to think of myself as a brave, confident person, but deep down inside I know that I haven't been brave or very confident in a long time. I try not to knowingly surrender to weakness, but at the moment, I have no other choice. This particular meeting would be far too much for me to handle.

"Oh, okay. Well, good luck I guess," she says, smiling sympathetically.

"Yeah, thanks." I throw my bag over my shoulder and all but run for the elevators.

My heart finally makes its way out of my throat as I lumber out the back doors and into the side alley. Normally, I would leave through the main lobby and out the front doors like a sane person. Today, however, I slip out the back because I, wuss that I am, decided at the last second to take the stairs—all fourteen flights of them—down to the main floor, as opposed to the elevator. Then in a further display of spinelessness, I avoided the lobby, took the side hall, and left through the unalarmed emergency door out back. All this, just in case *he* happens to be in the elevator, lobby, or anywhere in between.

God, I'm pathetic.

If I'm going to keep this up, I'll definitely have to come up with excuses that are more diverse than just a plethora of doctor's appointments, or eventually Bree and Margaret will think I'm dying.

I push up the sleeves of my blouse as I round the corner onto Chambers Street. It's the last day of August, but judging by the temperature, you would have no idea that fall is supposedly upon us.

I stop at a newsstand, hoping to find something to occupy my mind for the next few hours. My thoughts are currently nipping at the edges of memories that I've worked very hard to bury. I need a distraction. Something to read or, at the very least, flip through mindlessly. Anything—global news, celebrity gossip, how to lose ten pounds by the weekend. As I desperately scan the racks, Bree's words continue to fly around my head.

"*…he really is gorgeous…*"

Sigh. Yes, he is. I already knew that.

"*…he's worth over seventeen billion…*"

Knew that too. Seventeen point seven billion to be exact.

I've been following *Mr. Kerkley's* career almost since it began. I say "following his career" because it sounds much more normal than "I know everything and anything you could possibly want to know about his career, company, and business interests," which sounds like I am a telephoto lens and a pair of night vision goggles away from being a stalker. However, pathetic as it may be, I am something of an expert when it comes to Nick Kerkley's career.

He started his company with nothing—absolutely nothing—and built it himself from the ground up. The business and technological worlds took notice of his work almost instantly, and he has been a powerhouse ever since. His rise to the corporate elite has been documented thoroughly over the years. He's appeared in newspapers, magazines, special interest journals, and even the occasional television interview, which I could never bring myself to watch. For over seven years I've been collecting every bit of information I can find that deals with him in any way, and storing everything in a box under my bed.

Yeah…'cause that's normal.

Somewhere between paying for and finishing a chocolate bar, I decide to go and see my sister, Lisa. I need another person right now. I can't distract myself and normally I would call Bree, but in this situation, Lisa is my next best option.

For the past four years, Lisa has been the VP of Marketing for Century PR, one of the largest PR firms on the east coast. Her office is in SoHo and, as I'm in no mood to walk that far, I make my way down to the subway. I'm able to get a seat by the window as it's early in the afternoon and the rush-hour crowds are still hard at work. As the train jerks to life, I rest my head against the window and watch the hazy tunnel lights fly past.

Eight years. That's how long it's been. Eight years…

"Grilled cheese, fries, and a chocolate malt."

"White or wheat?"

"White."

"All right, it will just be a few."

"Thanks."

I was at Gerald's, the best diner in the city, and I ate there at least twice a week. That afternoon, I had just finished the last final exam of my senior year. It was Dr. Ortega's Advanced Financial Modeling, and I knew I'd aced it. I decided there was no better way to celebrate the proverbial weight of the world being lifted off my shoulders than a plateful of comfort food.

What a feeling! I was officially done with school and I had an amazing internship lined up for the fall. Everything I had been working so hard for was finally within reach, and I was on top of the world. It was as if I would never have to worry about anything ever again. I couldn't wipe the smile off my face.

I was so lost in my happy stupor that I jumped when the waitress placed a plate in front of me. A plate of…chicken salad melt and chips?

I looked up. "This isn't—" But she was gone.

Damn.

As I looked around to try to call the waitress back, I noticed an unbelievably hot guy sitting at the counter, watching me. When he caught my eye, he looked down at the plate sitting in front of him.

Ah, my food. This must be his.

He picked up his plate and walked toward my table. Dear God, he was gorgeous! Dark brown hair, and the most beautiful blue eyes I had ever seen.

"I take it this is yours?" he asked with a breathtaking smile, setting my grilled cheese down on the table.

Don't say something stupid, don't say something stupid. "Uh, yeah, thanks."

"No problem." He turned back toward the counter, and I let out the breath I'd been holding.

Uh, yeah, thanks? The hottest guy I would probably ever meet face-to-face, and that's all I could come up with? Why couldn't I say something witty or charming? Or at least something remotely intelligent like, "Yes it is, thank you, and this must be yours." You know, something a normal person would say!

I glared down at my plate, sulking over my first few fries. *Oh well, he's probably married. Or gay. That's the way it goes, right? Or—*

But my thought was cut short by the sound of someone sitting down in the empty seat at my table. A plate and drink suddenly occupied the space opposite me, and I looked up and into the amazing eyes I thought I'd never see again.

"Do you mind?" he asked, timidly gesturing to the seat he had just taken.

Holy crap! A hot guy wants to sit with me! Okay, okay, stay calm, be cool, don't blush like a twelve-year-old.

I grinned and nodded, not trusting my voice.

He smiled that same heart-stopping smile and held out a hand for me to shake. "I'm Nick."

"Julia."

The announcement of the Houston Street stop snaps me back to the present, and I'm both sad and relieved to be distracted from the memory. That's how my fairy godmother introduced me to my very own Prince Charming—or so I'd thought when I was still young and naïve. Since then, I've learned that fairy godmothers and magic wands are pretty pictures that people *in* love use to make a point. It's easy for people to talk when they're happy, doe-eyed, and blind to the fact that fairy tales are for children who don't know any better. But, when those same people find themselves out of love, suddenly that charming "We both happened to take the same subway even though he usually takes a cab, and I usually walk! I must have a fairy godmother!" story becomes "I should have known the minute I stepped on that disgusting subway not to talk to him! Only jerks and creeps try to pick up women on the subway. What was I thinking?"

With a sigh I close my eyes and sink lower into my seat. Yes, back then I thought I was on the way to my very own happily ever after. However, I discovered that what Fairy Godmother giveth, she could taketh away.

2

"The next time you get *anything* that says 'confidential' on it, you send it *straight* in to me, *understand?*"

"Yes, Ms. Basham."

"Now this all has to be redone because the seal has been broken! How am I supposed to explain this?"

"I'm sorry, Ms. Basham."

As I arrive at Lisa's office, I find her in the process of scolding her new receptionist. The poor thing doesn't look a day past twenty and, by the expression on her face, could very well be soiling herself as we speak. I really do feel bad for her. Don't get me wrong, Lisa is a wonderful woman who was born for the business world, and to know her is to love her. But even I can admit, *not* to know her is definitely to fear her.

I can't help but smile as I lean back and wait for the tongue lashing to end. Lisa is someone who tackles the business world with an iron fist, which is how she got to be where she is. All her employees and co-workers respect her as a focused leader, though fear comes inherently with that kind of respect. They all know Lisa is a great person, but they're also well aware that you don't want to cross her.

Even as a girl she was cutthroat. She was the first kid to be chosen for dodge ball and the last kid you wanted to play a board game with. Softball, swim team, debate club, spelling bee — everything she did, she was the best. Not because she was particularly talented in any one area, but because she worked for it. She was driven. It was no surprise that she graduated at the top of her class, or that she had no problem getting into Harvard Business School, or that she obtained the level of success she has now. If Lisa wants something, she doesn't stop until she gets it.

Luckily for me, this take-no-prisoners attitude not only applied to her competitive and professional endeavors, but to her family as well. She has always had a very strong belief in protecting one's own — namely me. Our father only passed away in recent years, but our mother died when I was six and Lisa had just turned ten. Since then, Lisa has really been both a mother and a sister to me. She packed my lunches for grade school, got me ready for my first day of high school, was there to help me pick out my prom dress, and she wouldn't let me stop until my college admissions essay was perfect. But more than just the trivial, she has always gone out of her way to take care of me emotionally as well, giving the advice and the guidance that she thought our mother would have given if she were here.

I try not to smirk as I think of her employees having the chance to meet *that* Lisa. The Lisa who was sweet and motherly, who took care of me when I was sick, and who used to tuck me in at night and read me stories. The Lisa who — though by no means perfect — really is the best sister anyone could ask for.

Lisa had just finished reading to me, and we sat curled up together in my bed.

"How will my fairy godmother know how to find me?" I asked, running my fingers over the picture of the sparkly dress the princess on the book cover was wearing.

"The same way Santa knows how to find you," Lisa answered matter-of-factly. "She knows everything. You see, she'll show up when you need her most, she'll know all about you, and know just how to help you."

"She'll know about me? Everything?"

"Sure, she has to. How else can she know who you should marry?"

"What about the bad stuff about me, will she know that too?"

"What bad stuff?"

"Like when I broke the picture frame and told Dad it fell over by itself, or when I don't finish my dinner?" I asked, holding the book tighter, as if clinging to the dreams my fairy godmother might take away because I didn't like peas.

"No, she won't care about that stuff." She smiled as I sighed in relief. "Her only job is to see that you get your Prince Charming."

"Will I get a pretty dress too?"

"I don't know. I guess if you need one."

"I think I'll need one."

"Then I'm sure she'll give you one," Lisa said, chuckling as she crawled out of my bed and pulled the covers up under my chin. "Whatever it takes so you can live happily ever after."

Lisa's bellowing continues to pour out of the office door, bringing me back to the moment. "This is payroll information! Employees' personal records! Do you have *any* idea what could have happened if it fell into the wrong hands? Do you have any idea how many lawsuits we would have been facing?"

I bite my tongue to suppress a chuckle. Yes, if only her employees knew how sweet she can be, everyone involved would probably keel over and die: the employees from shock — Lisa, of embarrassment.

I wait quietly by the door for the rant to end, pretending not to listen. After suffering another minute or so of berating, the watery-eyed receptionist slinks out past me with her tail between her legs. Deciding it's safe to enter, I step through the door into Lisa's enormous office.

"You know you wouldn't lose so many receptionists if you didn't scare the hell out of them their first week on the job."

"Jules!" Lisa looks up from her computer, obviously shocked to see me. "When did you get here? Shouldn't you be at work?"

"There was a big meeting this afternoon that I wasn't needed for, so I got out early." Not *entirely* a lie. "I came to see if you wanted to do dinner tonight."

"Sure, that'd be great! I have a conference call in five minutes, but it shouldn't be more than an hour. If you don't mind waiting you can hang out here, and we'll go after that."

"All right." I take a seat in one of the armchairs across from the desk. I look up to see Lisa staring at me, thinking. "What?"

"Nothing." As she turns back to her desk, she gets a mischievous glint in her eye. Before I can comment, she picks up her phone and hits two buttons. "Hi, Zach, it's Lisa."

Oh no.

Lisa has been trying to fix me up with Zach Connoray since he started as a copywriter at her firm over two years ago. The fact that he has a huge crush on me doesn't help things. He is all for the idea of us going out. Me, not so much.

"…so if you have some time…"

"NO!" I mouth to her, but she just smiles.

"…would you mind coming up to my office? Julia's here and I need someone to entertain her while I'm on a call."

"I'm gonna kill you!" I mouth again through clenched teeth, giving her the most menacing glare I can work up. Her shoulders shake with silent laughter.

"Great! See you in a few."

As soon as the receiver hits the cradle, I yell, "Why would you do that!"

"I thought you might like some company," she says innocently.

"I can *entertain* myself, thank you!"

"Oh come on, Jules, he's a great guy! You need to stop being so damn picky!"

"I know he's a great guy. It's not him; I don't date. That's not being picky."

"Come on, he's crazy about you. Just give him a chance. You need something to do for the next hour anyway. Speaking of…" She sits down and dials into her call, effectively ending my whining fit.

I walk out into the hall and wait for Zach to come up. Shouldn't take him long. Lisa is right; he's crazy about me. He is very nice, warm, funny, and charming—an all-around great guy. I am in no way going to deny that. I also have no doubt he will make someone a wonderful boyfriend. Just not me.

I don't date. Not since…well, I just don't.

I did try for a while. I went out with several guys — mostly setups by Lisa — and they were all great…except. That's just it — *except*. There was something wrong with all of them. One was too committed to work, one too attached to his mother, one too affectionate, one not affectionate enough, one too tall, one too short, and so on. Toward the end I came to terms with the fact that I was being insane, and gave up on the whole institution of relationships. The fact of the matter was that all my "excepts" were really only one thing. They were all great except they weren't *him*. I was going to find something wrong with anyone I tried to date no matter how wonderful they were, simply because they were not the man I really wanted. So, as opposed to leading on countless men for the rest of my life and being miserable in the process, I renounced all dating attempts and have since lived my own personal version of happily ever after. Maybe my version would be better described as *contentedly* ever after, but I'm fine with that. Happily ever after is overrated anyway. Contented can't be taken from you. Contented is good.

Right?

In any event, I am not about to lift my relationship embargo just to stomp on the hopes of a great guy like Zach. Anything more than friendship between Zach and I would never work because, honestly, I wouldn't let it. He would just end up getting hurt. Better to let him have a crush on me, and eventually someone else will catch his fancy and I'll be old news. For now, all I have to do is smile and be as friendly as possible without giving him any ideas.

Just when I sit on the couch in the waiting area, Zach turns the corner with a big grin on his face.

Here we go.

After an hour and twelve minutes in Zach's office, twenty minutes in Lisa's office waiting for her to get off a last minute call, and a nine-block walk to the restaurant after giving up on a cab, Lisa and I finally sit down to dinner. We had decided on Marino's, an Italian place only a few blocks from my apartment. Great food, great service, great atmosphere, great…wine. I start draining another glass and Lisa eyes me suspiciously.

"So what's going on? Why are we lushing this evening?"

"I'm not *lushing.*"

"That's your third glass and we've been here twenty minutes. Plus *you* were the one who ordered the whole bottle. You're depressed." It wasn't a question.

I reach for a piece of bruschetta without looking up. "What was the deal with your receptionist today?"

She rolls her eyes at my blatant change of subject. "Oh, nothing. We've had some payroll issues lately. Someone down in accounting may be stealing money. I'd sent for the accounts payable invoices so I could look them over, but I had to have them redone, as Becky decided to open a file marked 'confidential.' No biggie. She won't do it again," she added with a slightly evil grin.

"Someone in payroll is stealing?"

"Possibly. Now stop avoiding the subject," she says, done with my diversion tactics. "Spill."

I take another sip of wine, then stare down at my plate. "Our group was assigned a new client today."

"Okay…"

"A thirty-one-year-old entrepreneur who is currently worth over seventeen billion dollars." I pause, taking a deep breath. "Mr. Nicholas Kerkley." I see her eyes widen.

"As in…"

"Mmhmm."

"And this meeting you weren't needed for today…"

"Mmhmm."

"Ah. I see."

An awkward silence follows. After a few moments, Lisa reaches for the wine bottle and tops me off, giving me a sympathetic half smile. I return it—though I'm pretty sure my smile comes off more as a painful grimace—and look back down at my plate.

"So," she says, not-so-subtly changing the subject, "why aren't you a consultant yet?"

I roll my eyes and glare at her. She's obviously trying to piss me off. Maybe she thinks anger will be a good emotional distraction.

"Really? You're going to go there? We've been over this, and nothing has changed." I try to keep my cool and thwart her plan. "Margaret is the consultant, Bree is the junior, and I am the admin."

"Who could be the junior," she says, adding her own ending to my sentence.

"Bree got the position. I didn't."

"Because you didn't try. You could have had it all over Bree, and you know it."

"She is better suited for the job than I am, that's all. She's got the personality."

"That's about the lamest excuse I've ever heard. Personality my ass! She graduated from community college with a degree in *general business*. You interned at Stauncher House for God's sake! You should be leading your own group by now!"

I rest my elbows on the table and rub my eyes. "Next topic please."

"You sure?"

"Yep."

"You're not going to like it."

"Got to be better than this." I take another drink. "Try me."

"How did it go with Zach?"

Damn. I glare at her. "Yeah, still gonna kill you, by the way."

"What did you two do?" she asks, undeterred by my threats.

I sigh, rolling my eyes. "We discussed how Zach's assistant needs to dye her hair back to brown, talked about the television lineup, then watched a plethora of stupid videos on YouTube. It was magical."

"Sounds like it," she says, with an obvious ooh-la-la inflection.

"Give it up, Lis."

"Oh, lighten up. I'm just trying to help you."

"I don't need help. I'm fine."

At my declaration, she leans back in her chair and crosses her arms. "You mean to tell me you want to be alone forever? That you don't at all miss having a night out, or the occasional…bed partner," she whispers.

"*Bed partner*…seriously? What is this, Victorian England?"

"What would you prefer? Booty call?"

"Actually—" I smirk "—I think I would."

"*Anyway*, I just want you to be happy, that's all."

"So you're saying I need a man to be happy? This coming from the woman who has proclaimed to God and anyone else who would listen, that she's going die happy and alone?"

"Yes, and that's me. I've never wanted marriage, or kids, or the picket fence." She waves her hand dismissively. "I'm not a happily ever after kind of person."

"Neither am I."

"You used to be."

She's right; I used to be. But that was before.

"Regardless," Lisa continues, "I'm not talking about love or anything like that. I'm not trying to marry you off; I just want you to have a little fun. Hell, even I go on a date every now and again."

"Well, you enjoy yourself." I raise my glass in a mock toast before taking another swig.

"All right, all right, I get it," she says, lifting her hands in mock defeat. "I'm just saying, having a man can be fun when you give it a chance."

The waiter comes back with our food just in time, and I concentrate on my ravioli. Unpleasant as the conversation has been, I know she's at least somewhat right. I probably could have my own group by now if I wanted it.

I *had* wanted it.

I used to be ambitious.

But that was before.

She was right about another thing too. Having a man *can* be fun.

"Well, that's two hours of my life I'll never get back."

"Just be glad we waited to rent it and didn't see it in the theaters. Then it would have been two hours and twenty bucks you'd never get back," I said with a laugh, as Nick reached across the couch, grabbed me from behind, and pulled me up against his chest. I laid my head back onto his shoulder and closed my eyes. "After all, it couldn't have been that bad. I was with you," I added sarcastically.

He turned his head and lightly brushed his nose up and down my cheek. "You, my love, are the only thing that kept me from throwing my shoe at the screen."

"Why, because I was with you, or because it's my TV?" I asked, goose bumps rising on my arms.

"Yes," he breathed, then kissed the hollow under my ear.

We had been together for a month and a half, and I was totally and completely in love. I had become one of "those people." The ones that single folks can't stand to be around, because we're always in a lovesick daze. I knew it was totally cliché, but I couldn't help myself. He was perfect.

And he loved me.

Really loved me. There wasn't anything he said or did that didn't have those three little words hidden behind it. He was sweet and affectionate, but not in the annoy-the-hell-out-of-you clingy way, but more like the makes-you-feel-like-the-center-of-his-world way. By day he was absolutely devoted to me, and by night…well…wow.

I was in heaven.

We were at my apartment, like usual. His was tiny, and had little more in it than some clothes and a bed. He was currently working in a local bookstore, and—as his apartment would suggest—not making much money. It didn't matter though because he was the sort of guy who didn't need much. He and his sister, Cathy, who I had yet to meet, grew up on very meager means, their parents having been public school teachers. Then both parents died when Nick was just out of high school, leaving him and Cathy with even less. They each had enough money to go off to college, where she graduated with a degree in social sciences, while Nick took a few years off, then began a major in information technology.

He stuck with it for almost three semesters, but withdrew of his own choice the year before we met. He claimed school just wasn't his thing, and planned to go into business for himself. He already knew a lot about different technological services and wanted to start his own consulting company. He had spent the past few months testing the waters, but was finding it hard to land reputable clientele when he had no name and no diploma.

None of that bothered me though. Not his lack of money, or his thus far failed attempts in the business world. I knew he would make it. He had all the right stuff—personality, drive, skill—it was just a matter of time.

Speaking of…

I reluctantly pulled myself off the couch and made my way over to my laptop which was sitting open on the table. Just one more read through…

"Not again," Nick groaned.

Ten days ago, I found out that Jill Fabian, VP of Personal Finance Management for Stauncher House, would be taking an intern.

One intern.

Ever since then, any thought that passed through my mind was in some way, shape, or form connected to the letter on my laptop, which was currently begging me to come over and read it over just once more.

My internship would be starting in a few weeks, and all the interns had been told during orientation that we would be assigned to a mentor. Our potential mentors would look over our résumés and qualifications, and then choose who they wanted to work with. Typical stuff, nothing we hadn't expected. The blow had come the previous week, when I'd been at the Stauncher building for the preliminary tour. During our lunch break, I had been in the ladies room and, completely by chance, happened to overhear that Jill Fabian had just lost her secretary and had decided replace her with one of the new interns.

I flipped out—silently, because I was hiding in one of the stalls at the time—but there was much rejoicing.

Ms. Fabian was one of only three Stauncher House VPs. Having her name on my résumé—not to mention her knowledge and guidance—would land me any job I could want anywhere in the country. She had more seniority than practically anyone else in the entire company, which meant she would get to choose her intern first.

She *had* to choose me.

I had made up my mind then and there that I would do anything to make sure my name was at the top of her list. That, however, meant that she had to know my name, and the only way for that to happen was for me to let her know what it was. I decided to approach her. Not in person, as that would be impossible with her schedule, but I could send her a letter. An eloquent and professional letter, stating who I was and what I wanted. That was the best way for me to make myself known, show her my ambition and my drive, not to mention get a leg up on my competition. I was the only one who knew she wanted an intern, and I had to make the most of my advantage.

Ever since that fateful trip to the restroom, I had pretty much spent every waking moment working on my letter. I had gone through over thirty different drafts, and made Nick read it so many times he was probably seeing it in his sleep—which undoubtedly is what made him insist on a laptop-free movie night.

"Yes, again," I said.

"Don't make me restrain you…"

I giggled and made a run for it, but he was too quick. His arms came around me, pinning my back to his chest just before my fingers reached the keyboard. I tried to wriggle free but it was no use.

"No you don't," he growled, playfully biting my neck. "You promised."

"I know, but it has to be perfect."

"It is perfect," he said, turning me to face him. "It was perfect two days ago, it was perfect this morning, it was perfect two hours ago, and will still be perfect tomorrow—that is, if your constant obsessing and overanalyzing doesn't inadvertently end up ruining it."

Hmm…I hadn't thought of that.

"You see," he said triumphantly, seeing the truth of his words register in my expression. "Enough. You can send it tomorrow, then feel silly when it gets lost in the mail, so she never gets it, and then chooses you anyway simply because you're amazing."

I rolled my eyes, but his lips came down on mine before I could argue with him.

After a long moment he broke the kiss and looked at me—a mischievous glint in his eyes. "Now then, Miss Basham," he said, his voice low and gruff. He leaned forward and brushed his lips against my shoulder, making me shiver. "It looks as though you need a distraction." His lips slowly made their way up my neck. "If only there was something we could do…"

I turned my head and caught his lips with my own. "I love you," I said after a delightfully languid kiss. He didn't say anything, but the look in his eyes said more than his words ever could. His mouth came down to meet mine again, this time hungry. I leaned against him in an obvious invitation that he wasn't slow in accepting. The next thing I knew, I was in my bedroom being thoroughly…distracted.

$$3$$

It's only nine thirty in the morning, and already this day is beyond repair. I overslept (too much wine last night), have a terrible headache (way too much wine last night), and forgot to clean my black skirt so I had nothing to wear this morning but old dingy khakis. Now I'm finally walking into the office forty-five minutes late.

Awesome.

I sit down at my desk, slump over, and hang my head in my hands. I'm going to need more aspirin.

As I reach into my bag for the bottle, Bree comes running around the corner.

"Jules! There you are!"

"I'm late, sorry. I got stuck on—"

"No, don't worry about it, it's fine. I'm just glad you're here." She runs to her desk, grabs two folders and tosses one to me. "Come on, Margaret is waiting for us. We have to go."

"Go where?" I ask, caught slightly off guard. She seems to be a little hyper for this early in the day—though that could be the hangover talking.

"Up to the conference room. Mr. Kerkley is here for his meeting."

My stomach rolls over. It's a good thing I didn't have time to eat this morning or I would probably throw up. "W-What?" I stammer. "I thought the meeting was yesterday."

"It was supposed to be, but he got stuck in a different meeting and couldn't make it. Oh my goodness, Jules, he is so nice!" she gushes as she pulls me to my feet and starts towing me toward the hall, while I concentrate all my energy on remaining conscious. As the elevator doors close behind us, she continues. "So yesterday after you left, we were waiting for Mr. Kerkley when he called and said he was caught up, and wouldn't be able to make it. And he insisted on taking us out to dinner to apologize for keeping us waiting! How sweet is that?"

"Hmm," I say, barely hearing her. I watch the lights on the elevator slowly go up as we approach the conference level—the knot in my stomach grows with each passing floor.

"I swear," she goes on, "he has got to be the nicest man I have ever met! The three of us talked all through dinner, and not once about business. He insisted we save all the work talk for the meeting today, and just enjoy the evening. It was unreal! You'd have thought we were all old friends."

"Wow," I croak out.

"Working with him is going to be wonderful, I can just tell! He is so friendly, and obliging, and sweet. You have no idea!"

Actually, I do.

The doors slide open and we step out into the empty hall. Bree leads the way to the room while I follow behind, my feet suddenly weighing a ton each. I can't even hear her as she continues to gush over our newest client, due to the panicked thoughts flying through my head.

What do I say? *Hopefully nothing.*

What will he say? *Hopefully nothing to me.*

Should I act like I know him? *No need, as I won't be talking.*

Does he even know I work for this group? *Yes? No? I'm not even sure which one to hope for.*

If he does, did he say we had met before? *Probably not, or Bree would have mentioned it.*

Okay, so we're strangers. I can do strangers. Can't I?

Sure…

My hands start to shake as we round the corner and the door to the conference room comes into sight. I can barely breathe over the lump in my throat, and all I want to do is run into the nearest bathroom and cry. Oh God, this can't be happening. Why did I even bother coming in today? Why didn't I stay in bed?

"And just wait till you *see* him!" Bree whispers as we approach the door. "He is *unbelievably* hot!"

I am two seconds away from darting the other way down the hall, but before I can make an excuse, Bree pushes the door open and steps inside, leaving me no choice but to follow.

"There you are," Margaret says to Bree, smiling. "We can get started." She sits near the end of the long wooden table in the center of the room. I lock my gaze on the table leg, determined not to notice the second figure sitting at the table. "Oh, Julia, you *are* here, wonderful!" Margaret adds as she sees me standing behind Bree, silently calling upon every ounce of dignity I can muster. I'm frozen in place, every muscle in my body rigid as ice. Margaret stands and makes a gesture toward the only other occupied seat in the room.

Oh boy, here we go…

"Mr. Kerkley, this is Julia Basham, our admin." I drag my gaze over to the chair holding a figure with dark hair and a light green shirt.

It's him. My God, it's really him.

Not that I didn't know it would be, but I guess there was still some little part of my mind that was hoping it might be some other Nicholas Kerkley. But no, it was Nick. My Nick. I fix my stare on his collar button.

Don't blush, don't blush, don't blush…

"Julia," Margaret continues the introduction, "this is Mr. Nicholas Kerkley."

Blush.

DAMN!

"Nice to meet you," he says, nodding stiffly. He doesn't stand or offer to shake my hand, for which I am eternally grateful. I don't think I can move. I open my mouth to reply, but my *"Nice to meet you too"* catches then dies out in my throat when I see that he has turned away from me and back toward the table, as though he didn't even expect an answer. "Shall we start?" he asks Margaret with a smile.

With that, Bree and I take our seats and Margaret begins the meeting.

That was it. It's over.

After eight years, Nick and I are officially in the same room, and it's as though we are complete strangers. He greeted me like someone he has never seen before and may never see again.

Like a nobody.

I fight the lump in my throat and concentrate intently on the cap of my pen. Of course he treated me like a nobody—what did I expect? A hug? Yeah, right. A "Hey, it's been a while"? Honestly, I'm glad he didn't because I don't think I could have answered.

The meeting continues and I sit quietly, not paying nearly as much attention to the discussion around me as I should. Eventually, I realize we are talking about a piece of real estate somewhere in Maine. I assume he must be looking to buy it, though I haven't been listening close enough to any of the specifics to know for sure.

I direct my eyes down to my notepad, idly wondering how hard I would have to stare to actually burn holes through the paper. I fix my gaze, determined not to look up for the remainder of the meeting. Well, that may have been my plan, but after a few short minutes I realize it's not going to happen. No matter how hard I try, every so often I can't help but glance over at him. At this point he's looking at some paperwork with Margaret, so thankfully my glances go unnoticed.

He is still the same old Nick: dark hair, blue eyes, dimple in his chin. Yet, he's definitely changed. It isn't a physical change—nothing you could put a name to—but there is an overall difference. Something beneath the surface, spelled out in the experience in his face and the wisdom behind his eyes.

He has grown up.

What's more, with his adulthood, I can no longer agree with Bree's assessment of his looks. He's not hot. Not anymore. He's beyond that—he's *handsome.*

"I've already been in contact with the executor, and he will have the house open for us tomorrow." Margaret's words snap me out of my daze. "Will anyone else be joining us?"

Damn, what have I missed?

"My sister and brother-in-law"—*Brother-in-law? Cathy must have gotten married*—"will be coming up with two of my best friends, so with your team, the total will be eight," Nick tells her.

Wait, "with your team"? What the hell is going on? Where are we going? Damn it, why wasn't I paying attention!

"Great, we will drive up tomorrow then," Margaret says.

Suddenly it hits me. He *is* looking to purchase property, and we are all going to a showing. That's what this is about.

Property showings for the rich aren't like showings for the rest of us. You don't spend millions of dollars on a home you've simply walked through a few times and seen some pictures of. No, no…you move in. You pack a bag, bring family and friends, and test drive the property to make sure it is a good fit for you. You would also bring a personal advisor to oversee the inspections, or (if you have one) a financial planner, and (if he or she has one) their team.

I feel sick.

I look over to Margaret and Bree who are packing up, and also notice that Nick has walked to the corner of the room, his back to us, having taken a phone call.

"I'm going to run to the restroom," I whisper over to Margaret.

"Sure, go ahead. We're just wrapping up."

I grab my notebook and make a beeline for the door. Luckily the restroom is right next to the conference room, and once inside I take a deep breath, lean over the sink, and wait for the room to stop spinning.

Go away with him, with his family and friends, stay in the same house as him for God-only-knows how long—could this possibly get any worse? I have never even met his sister! Does she know about me? Do his friends?

I turn the faucet on and let the cold water run over my hands and wrists. All right, there has to be a way out of this. There has to be a story I can come up with. But no more doctors. I need something original this time.

Wedding?

No, it has to be something last minute.

Reunion?

No, Bree knows I never go to those.

Death?

No, that's just…wrong.

It's useless! I could come up with the perfect story, but it still wouldn't matter. He saw me. He knows I know about the showing, and he knows I am supposed to be there. If I don't go, it will be obvious that I'm avoiding him, which is just as embarrassing as going.

I'm totally stuck.

I can't take this anymore and I have to get out of here. I peek out the restroom door and see that Bree, Margaret, and *Mr. Kerkley* are still in the room. I run to the stairway entrance, burst through the door, fly down the stairs to my floor, and collapse into my desk chair before consciously taking a breath.

I rest my elbow on the desk and lean my head in my hand, huffing and puffing.

Did I really just do that? Seriously, can I be more of a wuss? Why can't I handle this like an adult? It shouldn't be that big of a deal, right? We are just two people who used to see each other, and…

…and…

Sigh. Okay, maybe it is a big deal.

I approached our designated meeting spot at River Terrace, and I could already tell something was wrong. I saw Nick in the distance, his elbows on the fence, hunched over, looking out over the river. He had gone to see his sister that day to talk about ideas regarding his business plan. By the looks of it, it must not have gone well.

I came up behind him, wrapped my arms around his waist, and rested my cheek on his back. I felt his shoulders relax as he brought one of his hands up to cover both of mine and sighed.

"I love you," I said, sensing he needed to hear it.

Without answering, he turned in my arms, took my face between his hands, and kissed me. When our lips parted, he kept his eyes closed, and rested his forehead against mine.

"What happened?"

He let out something between a groan and a growl. "Oh, nothing really. Met Cathy, told her my thoughts, and spent the rest of the time listening to her tell me that all my ideas are horrible, that I'm not using my head, that I should give it up, that I should grow up, that I should go back to school, et cetera, et cetera."

Ouch. "I'm sure she didn't mean it the way it came across."

"I know she's trying to look out for me. I get it. She even said she would support me no matter what I decided, but she also made it perfectly clear that she thought I was deciding wrong."

He walked a few steps over to a bench and sat, running a frustrated hand through his hair.

"Well, the only thing left to do is show her she's the one who's wrong," I said, sitting beside him.

"And you really think I can?"

"Of course. Why? You're not having doubts, are you?"

"No, not at all. It's just that you seem to be the only one, other than me, who believes I can do this."

"I know you can." I smiled and kissed his cheek. "Now we just have to prove it to everyone else."

He caught the back of my head and pulled me into his chest, holding me tight. "Thank you," he whispered into my hair. "You don't know how much it means." He didn't finish the thought, but I knew. After several quiet minutes, he let me go and I sat up to find his eyes burning into mine. He took a deep — if not a bit shaky — breath.

"Do you know how much I love you?" he asked, not breaking his gaze.

I nodded.

"And you know I would do anything for you?" He raised his hands to either side of my head, lacing his fingers into my hair.

"I know."

He closed his eyes for a moment, holding perfectly still. When he finally opened his eyes again, there was something new in them. Fear? Hope? And then…

"Marry me."

My heart jumped to my throat. "What?" I said, although I didn't think any sound actually came out.

He took my hands and slid off the bench onto to his knee, never taking his eyes off mine. "Julia Lee Basham, will you marry me?"

I sat unmoving for a moment and trying to find my voice, scared that the overwhelming happiness I felt might be enough to kill me. I smiled slowly and the fear in his eyes dissipated.

"Yes, *yes!*" I threw my arms around his neck. He stood, lifting me with him, and kissed me breathless. When we finally parted, it was only at a hand's length. He beamed.

"This wasn't at all how I planned on asking. I don't even have a ring."

"I don't care, this is perfect," I said, still trying to catch my breath. "Wait, you had been planning on asking?"

"Oh, sure," he said with a wry smile. "I even told Cathy this afternoon. That was the more pleasant half of the conversation." He kissed my forehead, and I buried my face in his chest. "She can't wait to meet you."

I couldn't speak, and for the moment it didn't seem that he could either. Though it didn't matter, as there was nothing to say. He simply held me, resting his cheek on the top of my head. My mind was hazy with happiness, and the only coherent thought I could produce was that this was it—this was the beginning of our happily ever after.

"There you are!" I look up to see Bree beside me. "We were wondering where you went."

"Sorry, I thought you would have been back by the time I came down."

Yeah, right.

"How exciting is this! It's like a paid vacation!"

"Yep, I know." Margaret goes on showings like this a few times a year, but this will be a first for Bree and me. Under any other circumstance I would be thrilled. I smile, feigning enthusiasm.

"What's wrong? Aren't you excited?"

"Sure, I'm fine, just…" I pause, looking for the right word.

"Overwhelmed?" she asks, her inflection implying it was a good thing.

"I guess." *You have no idea.*

"It will be so great! And we get to go together!" She was practically busting.

"So where in Maine is this?" I ask.

"Not sure. On the coast somewhere. I'm not familiar with the town. It's not too far from Bangor. You have a friend up there, don't you?"

"I do. Susan. I wonder if we will be anywhere near her."

Susan Tinder was one of my best friends growing up. We lived just down the road from each other as kids in Hamilton, New York, and were practically inseparable. We had sleepovers almost every weekend, campouts in the summer, and neither of our sets of parents were surprised to see an additional mouth at the dinner table most evenings. We both went away for college—she to Duke and me to NYU—and haven't seen much of each other since, but we e-mail a few times a month. The last time I saw her was at her wedding three years ago. It was held at her and her husband's new home on the Maine shore, which her mother and extremely wealthy stepfather had bought them as a wedding gift. Maybe I would get a chance to see her. That would be at least one light at the end of this tunnel that isn't a train ready to hit me head-on.

A moment later, Margaret appears with two black portfolios in her hand.

"All right, ladies, here are your dossiers. This is everything we have on the estate as of this morning."

As Margaret continues to ramble, I slip the folio—just another piece of the nightmare—into my bag, determined not to look at it until I absolutely have to.

Two hours later I stumble into my small apartment, drop my bag on the floor, and fall onto my couch. Margaret, Bree, and I had spent the better part of an hour hammering out the details of tomorrow's trip. Margaret reserved a company suv, and we are scheduled to meet her outside the sms building at four tomorrow morning to drive up.

Yay.

Since we had to be up so early, Margaret told us both to take the rest of the day off to pack and get ready. We would be in Maine for four days, arriving on Thursday and leaving on Monday. And of course, we would all be staying in the house on the Marston Estate. Our dossiers included—so I was told, as I hadn't opened mine yet—not only pictures, floor plans, and maps of the house and property, but also a list of inspections and appraisals Margaret, Bree, and I would need to be present for.

This is, after all, a work trip.

I roll over, pick up my laptop from the floor, and turn it on. Margaret had mentioned that the estate was in Toulston, which is only two towns away from where Susan lives. I type up a quick e-mail to her, letting her know I will be in the area.

I shut my laptop and wander into the kitchen. A lengthy internal battle ensues on whether or not to open a bottle of wine. My practical side argues that it is only two o'clock in the afternoon, not to mention I still have the remnants of a headache from last night's wine-fest, while my emotional side argues inarticulately, "To hell with it all, I need a drink!" I finally decide a bowl of ice cream is the healthier way to go.

How sad is your life when ice cream is the *healthiest* option.

I take my bowl of Moose Tracks into the bedroom, pull out my suitcase, and reluctantly begin packing. I start out thoughtfully selecting outfits, thinking about the occasions for each, but by the end I mindlessly pull things out of my closet and throw them into the case—my thoughts are somewhere else completely.

Somewhere specific, actually.

The dossier.

I slump down on the edge of the bed and look down the hall at the black tri-fold sticking up out of my work bag. Why is it scaring me so much? Is "scaring" even the right word? It's a few pieces of paper, nothing worth getting my panties in a bunch over. Preparing to bite the bullet, I take a deep breath and will my feet to carry me over to the bag. A moment later I am looking at the specs for Marston Estate:

52-Acre Property

Main House Square Feet: 26,515

Main House Built: 1938

Expanded: 1942, 1955, 1958, 1969, 1983

Fully Refurbished: 2009

Bedrooms: 11

Bathrooms: 13 full - 5 half

Guest House Square Feet: 5,238

Guest House Bedrooms: 4

Guest House Bathrooms: 3 full - 1 half

Asking Price: $47,000,000.00

Dear…Sweet…God…

It's four a.m., and Bree and I are outside the SMS Financial building with our pillows and bags, waiting for Margaret to come around Chambers Street with the company SUV.

It would be wrong of me to complain about having to get up at three a.m. due to the fact that "getting up" would imply that I'd slept. I'd tossed and turned all night, so dreading today's trip that by the time three o'clock finally rolled around, I was actually happy to have an activity to distract myself.

We have been standing out here for going on fifteen minutes, but of course as soon as I decide to unload my arms and take a seat on the curb, Margaret pulls around the corner in a brand new black Escalade.

Wow.

Pretty impressive for a company car, though they're primarily used for escorting clients, and I guess you can't drive multi-millionaires around in a soccer-mom van.

"Here we are, girls," Margaret says as she hops out and pops the back hatch open for our stuff. "Nice, isn't it?"

I nod, while Bree can only muster a yawn.

We pile our bags in the back, and climb into the very roomy, coffee-scented interior. I crawl to the last row of seats, while Bree claims a spot in the middle row. The front passenger seat is filled with huge to-go coffees and a box of doughnuts.

Ah, Margaret.

Bree and I get settled while Margaret climbs back into the driver's seat. "Okay, now everyone have some breakfast." She hands back the doughnut box. "The GPS says it will take eight hours, but I bet I can get us there in seven. That will give us two hours to unpack and relax before our preliminary walkthrough."

"What time will Mr. Kerkley and his family get there?" Bree asks between bites of doughnut.

"They are set to arrive around three."

"Oh, so they won't be there for the walk through?" Bree asks. Does she sound...*disappointed?*

"No, I told Mr. Kerkley not to bother. We can handle it and fill him in later."

With that, we all settle into our seats and I try my best to get comfortable enough to sleep. I end up propping my pillow against the window, figuring it'd be too juvenile to sprawl out across the entire back row.

After an hour or so of unsatisfying catnaps, I feel an arm on my shoulder.

"Jules, are you awake?" Bree whispers.

"Yep." I yawn, stretching my back. "I gave up on sleep a while ago. What's up?"

"Can I come back and sit with you?"

"Sure." I kick my small bag on the floor to make room, and Bree crawls back and sits cross-legged on the seat next to me. She looks almost worried, which is odd considering how excited she's been.

"Bree, what's wrong?"

"I think I have a problem. I don't know what to do. It's wildly inappropriate," she whispers, leaning in.

"Okay," I say, trying not to sound amused. As if Bree could ever be inappropriate.

"I think I have a crush on Mr. Kerkley."

Amusement gone. "What?"

"I know, I know, it's crazy, but I can't help it! He is just so..."

Perfect, handsome, kind, sweet, compassionate?

"I don't know what to do. It's wrong, right? Isn't it wrong?"

Oh, great, what the hell am I supposed to say? I suddenly get a weird vision of a cliché cartoon angel and devil that both look like me, floating in the air by my head. Do I side with the angel and tell her no, it's really not that big a deal? It's really not, especially considering Angela, one of the junior consultants from a partner group actually *married* one of her clients about two years ago. They've since moved to the Hamptons and, if rumors are to be believed, now have twins. She would obviously have to be discreet about it, but this is Bree we're talking about. She's never exactly been the type to take every client to bed with her—and believe me, there are those who do. If she and Mr. Kerkley were to start a low key, mutually agreed upon relationship, I highly doubt anyone would bat an eye.

That's what I should tell her. That's the truth. However, my possessive, territorial, selfish side wants to tell her that it's a huge deal, she will probably get fired, and that she should stay away from him. Then maybe hiss or click my tongue at her for good measure. Basically, be a catty bitch. And for what? So I can keep imaginary possession of a man I have absolutely no right to claim in the first place?

I look over into her overly concerned face, and realize I have to do the right thing. Or at least mostly the right thing. "Well, it's only a crush right? I mean, are you actually planning to do anything about it?"

Please say no…

"Oh, I don't think I ever could. I am way too shy. I just feel so guilty for some reason."

Okay, don't be a bitch, be a good friend, don't be a bitch, be a good friend…

"I wouldn't worry about it. If something were to happen where he approached you, you could ask Margaret, but otherwise, it's just a crush—no big deal. Besides, you were the one who said how different he is compared to all our other clients. He is the first one you could even think about actually being with, or even seeing in that sort of a light. I'm sure that's all it is. Just take a deep breath, and see how it plays out. No need to panic yet."

No need to panic.

"Yes," she agrees, visibly relaxing. "You're right, I'm overreacting. Still though—" she smiles, and gets dreamy-eyed "—if he approached me…wow, how amazing would that be! You really don't think Margaret would mind?"

"She always says 'whatever it takes to keep the client happy.'" I say it with what I hope is a believable smile. Bree giggles.

"Who knows," she sighs, resting back on the seat. "Maybe I have a fairy godmother who will make it all magically work out."

She is obviously kidding, but the knot in my chest gives an unpleasant squeeze. Sure, why not—a grandma with a wand shows up and makes me watch while she gives my Nick away to another woman—sounds about right.

"Oh." Bree sits up. "That reminds me. Why didn't you tell me you already knew him?" My stomach turns over. "Yesterday when we were leaving the meeting, Margaret apologized to Nick for not having had much of a chance to meet with you, and he said that the two of you were already acquainted. He said you had met the last time he was living in New York, a few years ago. Why didn't you tell us?"

Oh God. Okay, make something up.

"Oh, um, I guess I didn't realize it was him."

Wow, lame.

"I figured it was something like that. After all, yesterday was the first time you actually saw him, and he said you hadn't known each other well."

Wait, what? "He said we didn't know each other well?"

"Not in so many words, he just said that if he hadn't have seen your name, he wouldn't have recognized you, so I figured you weren't close."

What?

Bree yawns and leans back in her seat, turning to look out the window while I try to control my breathing.

Wouldn't have recognized me?

What the hell was that supposed to mean? I haven't seriously changed that much, have I? Was he just trying to insult me? No, that couldn't be it; it's not like him. But what, then? For God's sake, I could pick him out of a crowded room in less than a second, and he *wouldn't have even recognized me?*

Suddenly there is a painful squeezing in my chest, and a lump closes my throat.

So it's true, then. He has moved on and forgotten me.

Of course he has. What did I expect?

I turn to the window and lean my head against the glass so Bree can't see my nostrils flare or my eyes water. No wonder he greeted me the way he did yesterday. It's exactly how you would expect a person to greet someone who means nothing to them.

Unfortunately, the trip to Maine doesn't go as smoothly as we had hoped. We hit traffic in Connecticut, which led to us needing to stop for a lunch break, which made us hit more traffic outside of Bangor, which led to us arriving at the estate exactly fifteen minutes before our scheduled walkthrough.

As we make our way down the seemingly endless driveway, we see the executor, Mr. Clifton, waiting for us.

"Oh, my gosh, this is so embarrassing!" Bree says, gesturing to the fact that she and I are still wearing pajama pants and ratty T-shirts. "We were supposed to get here early enough to change!"

"Don't worry, we're parking at the guesthouse. Maybe he will have it open and you girls can run in," Margaret says, pulling up to a gray stone house with a long, white front porch. She hops out and greets Mr. Clifton, confirms that the guesthouse is open, and that we are more than welcome to use it to freshen up.

Mr. Clifton takes Margaret around back to show her the guest-house garden while Bree and I grab our bags and run inside. As we step into the entryway, our mouths drop.

"This is the *guest house?*" Bree whispers.

It is *huge.*

After a few moments of gawking, Bree finds a bathroom just to the left of the entry and goes in to change. I continue to look around in awe, feeling a bit queasy. The house is spectacular. It has to be as large as most of the East Hampton homes we normally help clients purchase, easily selling on its own for two to three million.

I wander down the hall, looking for a guest room to change in, instead finding a sitting room with a private washroom attached.

Yeah, because most sitting rooms have their own bathroom. Sure, why not.

I change quickly and step back out into the sitting room. There is a huge bay window on the wall opposite the door, which is covered by a thick embroidered curtain. I pull one corner of it back so I can peek out—and almost fall over.

There it is.

The main house.

It's practically a castle. Gray stone like the guesthouse, peaked roof, columned entry, three stories tall, and big as a hotel. Yet somehow, it's not overbearing, gaudy, or garish. It is welcoming and happy.

And it's all going to be his.

"You can't be serious, Jules!"

"Damn it, Lisa, you're supposed to be happy for me!"

I was furious. I'd gone to Lisa to tell her about my engagement and get her support, but she was treating the whole thing like a joke.

"I would be happy for you if you were using your God damned head!"

"You said you liked him!"

"I do, but…" She let out a long sigh and reached across the table to take my hands. "Listen, honey. I'm sorry to be so blunt. I didn't mean to yell or upset you. You just caught me off guard. I do like Nick. He seems like a nice guy, and I know you like him a lot, but that doesn't mean you should marry him."

"We love each other."

"Of course you do! You've been together for three months! It's puppy love, and everyone goes through it! He's the center of the universe, he's perfect, all the songs on the radio are about him, you can't imagine life without him, so on and so forth. I get it, really I do. The problem is, that's not real love."

"You don't know that."

"He's the first guy you have ever been in love with! What do you have to compare it to?"

"Just because I can't compare it to anything doesn't mean I don't know what love is."

"Okay, fine, let's say for the sake of argument that it is love. Don't you see that's not even the real problem here? Do you honestly think love is all a marriage needs?"

"Yes, actually I do."

"Jules, listen to me. Now you're going to get mad at me for saying this, but the fact of the matter is—"

"What?"

"You can do so much better than him!"

She was lucky she still had hold of my hands or I might have hit her. "How can you—"

"Listen to me for a second, okay? Just hear me out." Satisfied that I wasn't going to interrupt, she continued. "You can talk till you're blue in the face about his dreams, and ambitions, and all his wonderful ideas for this fabulous business, and all the great things he's going to do. That's all well and good. The fact remains that you can't build a future on what *might* be. You can only go on what *is*, and at the end of the day, he is a college dropout, with no money, no real job to speak of, and a bunch of pie-in-the-sky dreams with no foundation. And now, with nothing else in his life in order, he wants to get married!

"On the other hand, you graduated top of your class, have an amazing internship that will lead to an amazing job where you'll be making a lot of money. Do you think he's the only person out there with no real prospects, mooching—"

"He's not mooching!"

"Fine, relying on his friends and family? Friends and family who he has talked into believing that he will someday 'make it' and pay them all back? I'm sorry, but as it stands right now, he's going nowhere, Jules."

"I believe in him. You don't know him," I said quietly, feeling my resolve begin to sway. Did she have a point? She had always been a no-nonsense person, cutting straight to the heart of the matter, and she was so sure what I was feeling wasn't real. Was it? It certainly felt real.

"No, honey, I don't, but neither do you, not really. And that's my point. I'm not saying he's a bad guy, or that he is deliberately misleading you. I'm sure he's not. I'm just saying he isn't marriage material for someone like you."

"I've already said yes. I *want* to say yes!"

"Tell him you've thought about it and changed your mind about marriage, but you still want to stay together. Maybe things will work out later."

"Oh yeah, 'cause that works. We would never be happy after that; it would always be between us."

"Make it out to be your fault. Tell him you just aren't the marrying type, or you're worried about your own career right now, or something like that."

"He'll never buy that. He knows me."

"Well…then maybe it's not meant to be," she said, and I felt the tears welling in my eyes. "Listen, honey, you know I'm right. You came here to get my support, but if you were absolutely sure about all this, you wouldn't have needed it. Most of the wisest decisions aren't the easiest, but you have to have the guts to make them. Yes, it'll hurt for a while, but you have to believe me, it's for the best."

I bowed my head and closed my eyes, letting the tears roll down my cheeks. Maybe I was only thinking with my heart and not my head. After all, a lot of what she had said was true. Besides, I didn't know if I could do something that my sister was so strongly against. She had always guided me, and I wanted her approval.

Maybe this is what I needed—a rational voice to put things in perspective without sugar coating it. Lisa had always known best. I didn't agree, but that didn't mean she was wrong.

Maybe she was right.

5

My initial assessment of the main house and surrounding grounds is right on the money. It is the most beautiful place I had ever set foot in. If the outside of the manor is gorgeous, then the inside is transcendent. Hardwood floors with high crown molded ceilings, a grand double staircase surrounding the foyer, floor-to-ceiling windows in all the bedrooms, an enormous two-story gourmet kitchen, a formal dining room, plus it's listed to be sold fully furnished.

The surrounding park has been well cared for and would be a nature lover's paradise. The flower garden is lovely, the wooded areas have trails, and there's even a small produce and herb garden to use for the kitchen.

We spend almost three hours on our tour, walking through room after room of gorgeous furniture and art. I am particularly impressed with the library as it is incredibly-well stocked. The only part of the day I opt out of—claiming a need for the restroom—is the tour of the master suite. I really don't need to have an actual mental image of the rooms he'll one day share with his wife.

My imagination works well enough on its own, thanks.

Margaret pours over every small detail, making lists of what would need professional inspection, what would need fixing, and what should be appraised. Once the preliminary evaluation is complete, we gather back in the foyer to debrief.

"That should be all for today," Margaret says, shaking Mr. Clifton's hand. "Thank you so much for coming out."

"Not at all. It was a pleasure to meet you ladies. I'll come back tomorrow for the plumbing and structural inspections. Just leave me a message with the times."

After another round of good-byes he was gone, leaving Margaret, Bree, and me to go to our separate rooms to relax and unpack. My room is amazing, though having seen the rest of the house, this doesn't really surprise me. I throw my suitcase on the bed, pondering whether or not to unpack. I really don't want to spend the next four days living out of my tiny suitcase, but looking around at the ornate furniture in my room, I'm almost afraid to take anything out. Stupid as it sounds, I have this mental image of the elegant solid oak armoire repelling my jeans and plain cotton underwear like an opposing magnet. The doors and drawers will then all lock tight and a little sign will pop out that reads "No designer tag, no service."

With a huff, I sit on the edge of the bed, rest my face in my hands, and rub my eyes. Why am I here? All I want to do is go home or, at the very least, crawl into bed, sleep away the next week, and pretend none of this ever happened. Afterward, I can get on with my mundane, humiliation-free life. Is that really too much to ask?

I stand, groaning, and shuffle over to the window. Dear God, look at all that space. What would I do with all of this? This land, this house—all too big. Maybe everything has been for the best. Come on, I could never live in a place like this. I'd get lost going to the bathroom. And how many bedrooms are there? Eleven? What would I do with eleven bedrooms? Hell, I don't even have eleven friends!

I begin counting on my fingers: Lisa, Bree, Susan…Margaret…

…um…

Susan's husband, Matt, though he would obviously share a room with Susan, so I guess technically he wouldn't count, but for the sake of padding my numbers, he's going in…And that nice guy who lives across the hall from me that let me watch TV with him when I locked myself out of the apartment that time. I think his name is Tom. Oh, and I guess I could count Zach, but only if I'm desperate.

There, what was what, seven? Barely half. See, this life would definitely never work for me.

Definitely.

The bedroom door opens with a bang. I whirl around to see a startled and embarrassed man with a suitcase.

"Oh! I'm sorry, I thought…I'm s-sorry," he stammers, trying to quickly pull his bag back through the door. "I didn't know." He yanks on the handle of his roller bag without aiming, causing it to hit the doorframe and pop open, spilling his stuff all over the floor. "Damn it!" He scrambles to grab everything back up.

"Easy, easy," I say, going over to help him. He's actually a good-looking guy. Tall with blond hair, green eyes, and red, red cheeks—though I'm pretty sure that last one has less to do with looks and more to do with his current extreme embarrassment. Not sure why though; it's not like I'm naked. "Here, let me help."

"I'm so sorry. I thought this was my room. I didn't know you were in here." He flushes even more, if that's possible.

"It's fine. Don't worry about it." I smile, hoping to ease his mind. "This place is enormous, so I very well may be in the wrong room," I add to reassure him. I know very well this is my room; he just looks so upset. He must be an extremely shy person to worry so much over something so innocent.

"It is huge, isn't it?" he says, his shoulders relaxing a bit.

"I'm Julia," I say, as we pick up his clothes.

"Chris." He gives me a shy smile. "Are you a friend of Nick's?"

Wince. "No, I'm here with the financial team." Ah, so he must be one of the friends Nick—Mr. Kerkley brought with him.

"Oh, right. I guess you must stay in houses like this all the time."

"No, actually, this is pretty rare." I'm exceedingly glad for the quick change of subject, and he seems to be relaxing.

"Yeah, I wouldn't know what to do with all this space."

"I was just thinking that same thing!" I blurt out, but then remember that I'm here for a client who is not paying me for my opinion, or to vocalize to his friends that I think his choice of house is excessive. "But to each their own."

He smiles and we finish repacking his bag. He seems sweet. Incredibly shy and obviously a bit awkward, but nice.

He stands, taking his bag again. "Well, I guess I should go find *my* room. You wouldn't happen to know—"

"I do actually." I lead him out the door. "There. You were close, it *is* the first door on the right, but down *that* hall." I point to the hall adjacent to mine, which had been designated earlier during our tour as the wing for the client and his guests.

"Great, thanks. It was nice to meet you, and sorry again." Some of the pink returns to his cheeks.

"Nice to meet you too, and I'm sure I'll see you later."

He heads off down the hall, and I resume my unpacking efforts. Once I confirm that the furniture will in fact allow my less-than-posh clothes entrance into their keeping, I put all my stuff away, then make a temporary workstation at the desk by the window. After I set up my laptop, I realize that we have a working wireless signal.

Of course. After all, what castle would be complete without the Internet? What *was* I thinking?

I open my e-mail and see that Susan has sent me a reply.

> Julia,
>
> Matt and I will be leaving to see my family on Saturday, but I am free all day Friday. It would be so great to see you! We can meet at the Ryce Commons Shopping Center, it's just about halfway between us, and it should only take you fifteen minutes or so to get there. I have attached directions for you. Just let me know what time you can get away.
>
> Talk to you soon,
>
> - Susan

Suddenly I feel a wave of relief. It will be so nice to see her again, and I desperately need someone to talk to.

> Susan,
>
> I won't be needed here until noon tomorrow, so how about breakfast? Maybe around 9:00? Can't wait to see you!
>
> - JB

Good. At least *something* to look forward to.

It's a good thing I set my alarm to wake me up for dinner, or I probably would have slept straight through to breakfast. I stare up at the ceiling, listening for nearby activity, but hear nothing.

Everyone must be downstairs.

I am also suddenly aware that, as it's almost six, Mr. Kerkley will have arrived by now.

In an attempt to ignore that last thought — and the knot of panic it brought with it — I get up, throw on jeans and a blouse, and take a look in the mirror. Happy with what I see, I step over to the door, but then hesitate.

I could open this door and he could be standing there.

No, damn it, stop it! You can't keep doing this! Act normal, for God's sake. You're on your way to dinner, everyone will be there, and you can't show up freaking out like an idiot! Pull it together!

You can handle it.

Try as I might, I start to lose it. My hand, which is currently frozen on the doorknob, begins to shake.

How am I going to do this? What will I say? Will I even have to talk? There are plenty of people here now; surely someone else — who preferably hasn't slept with the client — can do the talking. That way I can sit quietly in a corner and count the seconds until we leave.

I let out a long breath and lean my forehead against the closed door. What is wrong with me? I can't keep doing this. I have to grow up and handle this like an adult. If he can reach a point where everything that was between us means nothing, and can casually co-exist with me as though I'm not even there, then damn it, so can I. I'm done hiding, and done with awkwardness and shame. Starting now, I'm taking my life back! From this moment on, he is nobody. Just another client, just another account. Nothing different, nothing special.

Sure. I can do that. Why not? He seems to have no problem, so why should I?

With new determination in my step, I walk out into the hall, chin held high, and head down for dinner. I find the massive staircase and start down with extra bounce in my step. This will be nothing! Why didn't I come up with this earlier? I'll treat him the way I treat every other client I have dealt with. Maybe I will even strike up a conversation with him, just to show him how okay I am with all this. Nothing too personal though, maybe something about the house? Or the grounds?

No! No, I'll come up with it on the spot. If I plan out what I am going to say it will sound staged. It has to be natural. After all, I talk to people every day without planning out conversations, so he will get the same treatment.

I reach the bottom of the stairs and hear voices. I make sure Margaret is one of them before tracking them to the kitchen, stopping just before the arched entryway and taking a deep breath.

All right, here we go. You can do this. Operation Take Your Life Back begins now.

I take the last confident step into the large kitchen and survey my surroundings.

Off to my left, Margaret is talking with Chris and another man. He must be the second friend Mr. Kerkley invited. Further down, I see a man and a woman—Cathy and her husband, I assume—looking over some paperwork.

However, I don't see Bree, or Mr. Kerkley.

I walk over to greet Margaret, and meet the man she is talking to. Sure, why not? If I am going to be indifferent and friendly to him, I have to be indifferent and friendly to his guests as well. Besides, I would like to talk to Chris again.

"Julia," Margaret says when she sees me beside her. "This is Mr. Derek Ross, and Mr. Chris Langston, friends of Mr. Kerkley. Gentlemen, this is Julia Basham, the other member of our team."

Mr. Ross is a tall man with light brown hair who seems very pleasant. He greets me with a warm smile, while Chris, I notice, stays back.

I extend a hand. "Nice to meet you, Mr. Ross."

"Derek, please." He warmly shakes my hand.

"Derek," I repeat politely.

See, this isn't bad at all.

"And Mr. Langston and I have already met," I add, smiling kindly at Chris. He smiles back, but says nothing. It's now clear that he had not actually been a part of the conversation between Derek and Margaret. He had been hanging back and listening quietly, his shyness seeming to have gotten the better of him.

"Is everyone here then?" I ask Margaret, still noting the absence of Mr. Kerkley.

"Yes, everyone's here. Over there is Mr. and Mrs. Rob and Cathy Dewitt, Mr. Kerkley's sister and brother-in-law."

"Where is Bree?"

"She and Mr. Kerkley stepped out to look at the garden," she says with a knowing smile that makes my stomach twist.

"Oh." I try to ignore the sharp pang in my chest.

I'm disappointed, but only because I can't approach Mr. Kerkley and show him how fine I am with this whole situation as soon as I had planned.

That's all.

Yeah…

Margaret turns and continues her conversation with Derek, while I step over beside Chris.

"So did you find your room?" I ask with a grin.

"Yes, thank you."

"No random women this time?"

"No." He laughs, blushing slightly. "Too bad," he adds, his flush deepening.

A few moments later I am vaguely aware of the outside door opening as Bree and Mr. Kerkley rejoin the group.

Sure, *vaguely.* We'll go with that.

"Excuse me, everyone," Mr. Kerkley calls out, effectively ending everyone's conversations. "Just a few things real quick. First, since there is no food here yet, I had Cathy call for pizzas. I hope that's okay with everyone."

Only then do I look over and see Bree still standing next to him.

Like *right* next to him.

Not that it matters.

"And secondly," he continues, "Miss St. Charles and I have had an idea."

They've had five minutes together in the garden, and already they're talking in plurals?

Not that it matters.

"Since there are no inspections scheduled for Sunday, and the weather is supposed to be nice, what would everyone say to a trip to the beach?"

An excited murmur indicates that everyone thinks it's a great idea, while I try to muster a believable smile. Mr. Kerkley moves to join his sister and brother at the far counter, but not before resting a hand on Bree's arm and giving her a heart-shattering smile. The knot twists in my chest.

Great, a whole day at the beach where we can all watch Bree and Mr. Kerkley frolic in the sand.

No, wait…take a deep breath.

It's fine. Everything's fine. It will be fun.

No big deal.

Stay the course, damn it!

Though it does look like I will need to buy a swimsuit at the shopping center tomorrow. Speaking of…

"Margaret." I turn to her. "Would you mind if I went out for a few hours tomorrow morning before the inspections? I have a friend who lives nearby, and we would like to meet if it's all right."

"Sure, no problem. If you need to take the car, the keys are in the console."

"Great, thanks."

Just as I turn to walk away, Bree joins us, all aglow.

"So how was your walk?" Margaret asks with a hush of confidentiality.

"Great," Bree says, trying to be blasé, but then gives herself up by blushing furiously.

I smile at them both and turn back to Chris, again fighting off that damn knot.

"Come on, Nick, your turn, tell everyone about Chuck Hoster!" Derek says over the roar of laughter.

"No way, not a chance! That's where I draw the line," Nick laughs, as he downs the last of his Coke. "But I'm sure they would all love to hear about *Michelle*." The way he says her name implies that this is a—*ahem*—romantic encounter, and the rest of the group is instantly eager to hear the tale. Derek, however, is less enthusiastic and pales slightly.

"N-No one wants to hear about that. How about we tell them about the time—"

"Oh, but it's a great story," Nick interrupts, smiling at his friend's discomfort. "I'll tell it for you. You see—"

"Nick, I swear to God," Derek growls at him, though he is smiling now, chagrined.

Nick continues as if Derek hasn't spoken. "We were at a bar on the Upper West Side one night, The Dead Poet I believe—"

"*Nick*," Derek groans, leaning forward onto the table and resting his head in his hands.

"And there were a few women there we had never seen before."

Derek has given up the fight, but moans slightly as his ears begin to turn red.

"Our illustrious Derek," Nick continues in a terrible medieval English accent, "picks out one of the ladies and makes it his personal goal to take the fair maiden home with him that night."

"Poor girl," Rob adds with a laugh.

"Go to hell, Rob," Derek mumbles without lifting his head.

"So all night he is after this woman, whose name we come to find is Michelle, and all night he is shot down. Finally, persistent little bugger that he is, he's able to get her to talk to him, and eventually leave with him."

Derek lets out something of a whimper, his ears almost purple.

"He leaves the bar and gets her home, only to find out that his *Michelle* is actually a *Michael!*"

The group erupts into laughter, while poor Derek sinks his head to the table in mock defeat. Nick reaches over and ruffles his hair, receiving a playful punch in the shoulder in return.

Isn't this nice. Everyone is laughing, telling stories, and having a ball while I sit here in my own little slice of hell. I don't think I have ever felt more awkward and out of place in my life. My smile is so forced it feels like my entire face is carved out of granite—it probably looks more like I have gas than like I'm enjoying myself—and I am doing what I hope is a natural-looking gaze rotation: look down at my plate, over to Margaret, across the table to Derek, over to the four half-empty soda bottles standing in the middle of the table, back down to my plate, wait a few moments, repeat.

Luckily, everyone else is having too good a time to notice that I have become some sort of socially inept robot. I have never seen Margaret this way. She is laughing so hard, she may very well fall off her chair. As for Bree…it's hard to say. About fifteen minutes ago she was sitting next to Mr. Kerkley, drinking up every word he said with wide-eyed wonder. He was more than happy to reciprocate her interest and rested a hand on the back of her chair, at which point I removed her from my rotation. I haven't looked back since.

There has to be a way out of this nightmare. If I could just find an excuse to leave the room. Maybe I could say that I received a phone call from home and have to leave right away. I know the reason would have to be something serious, but I'm fine with that. Hell, at this point, I'm not above putting Lisa in the hospital with an imaginary illness if it gets me out of here. Extreme, I know, but I'm desperate and I can apologize to her later. After all, I'm sure she'd understand. I'll even owe her a fake hospital trip for her next awkward social situation if that would make her feel bett—

"What about Miss Basham? You're awfully quiet."

Hearing my name yanks me out of my mental evacuation plan and back to the faces around the table, which are all looking at me waiting for an answer to a question that I didn't hear.

Oh, please don't make me talk.

My hands instantly start to shake in my lap, and blood rushes to my cheeks. "Yes?" I ask, hoping for a repeat of whatever was asked.

"War stories? Bar fights? You haven't shared yet. Whatcha got?" Derek asks, a friendly, teasing smile on his face. He must think I want to be included. Little does he know I want nothing more than to crawl in the nearest hole and never come out. Yes, crawling and hiding go completely against my "show Mr. Kerkley I don't care" plan, but right now that is the farthest thing from my mind. I'll get back to that later, preferably when the entire party isn't staring at me.

"Sorry." I shake my head and rejoice that my voice didn't squeak.

"Well, if you aren't going to go, then I will," Margaret says. "I was doing a walkthrough last year…"

Ah, the bathroom sex story. Margaret was walking a client through a penthouse uptown. When they got to the master bath, they opened the door to find the owner and the maid going at it in the tub. God bless Margaret. If that story doesn't take the focus off of me, then nothing will.

With a small sigh of relief, I glance to my left to see Chris sitting quietly, looking down at his hands folded on the table. If I'm going to get through this evening, I need to at least *try* to talk to someone—for the distraction if nothing else—and, seeing that he looks about as comfortable as I feel, I decide Chris is my best option. I slide one seat to the left so that I am directly adjacent to him.

"Hi," I say.

"Hi."

"So, you hate this as much as I do, don't you?" I ask in a low voice no one else would be able to hear.

"Pretty much." He smiles. "I don't do well in groups."

"I know the feeling. If you don't mind my asking, why did you come up?" I figure he had to know from the beginning that this would be an uncomfortable situation for someone as introverted as he is.

"Nick asked me." He says it so matter-of-factly, like there could be no other reason. It is really…sweet. He is willing to make himself uncomfortable to help his friend. He may be the epitome of shy, but those three simple words proved something else about him — he is extremely loyal. I am suddenly fiercely happy that Nick has such a good friend. What an odd thing to feel.

"So," I ask, recovering myself, "shall we be awkwardly out of place together?"

"Sure." He seems genuinely relieved at the idea, despite his ears going a bit red.

"Where do you live?" I ask, already relieved to have found a way out of the general group discussion without being blatant about it. It is also nice to have someone I am genuinely interested in talking to.

"Manhattan. I grew up in Queens."

"Really? Where in Manhattan?"

"East Village. You?"

"Midtown West," I tell him.

"I looked there, but I couldn't find anything open."

"I sublet from my sister. My old studio wasn't in the best neighborhood, and she had been on me forever to move, but I couldn't afford it. When she got a place uptown, she basically forced me to rent her old place from her at a fraction of what it should actually cost."

"She forced you?"

"Well, not so much forced as gave me an ultimatum that I couldn't refuse."

"Which was?" he asks with a grin.

"Either I agree to the move and the low rent, or she would spend whatever money she made on the sale of the apartment to hire me a live-in bodyguard."

"Sounds like she takes good care of you," he chuckles.

"She does. She doesn't always know best, but she tries." I glance over at Nick before I can stop myself.

No, she doesn't always know best.

"So, how do you know Mr. Kerkley?" I ask as casually as possible, secretly hoping to steer the subject away from Lisa.

"Through Derek, actually. Derek and I were roommates at NYU. During our senior year, he went to London to study abroad, where he met Nick. They kept in touch after Derek came home, and when Nick came back to the States, they reconnected and have been tight as brothers ever since."

"Oh, I guess I assumed you both worked with Nick at some point."

"Well I do, but that's coincidental. I'm a systems administrator for Sytsaff, which Nick's company now owns, and Derek is an attorney for City Hall."

Our conversation continues pleasantly, and sooner than I would have thought possible, dinner is officially over. Everyone makes their way to their individual activities. For Nick and his family and friends, it's a movie in the media room. For Margaret, it's a call to her husband and a chance to organize the paperwork for tomorrow's inspections. For Bree and I, it's bed, since we have both been up since four a.m. I've left out the part where Mr. Kerkley invited Bree to watch the movie with him and his guests, because I've decided I didn't hear that.

After refusing Mr. Kerkley's offer — *ahem,* I mean, after I don't know what because I wasn't paying attention — Bree and I head upstairs to turn in. She practically floats up the stairs.

"So, the beach on Sunday! That should be fun," she says, as we reach the first landing. I mentally added in the "with Mr. Kerkley" that she left out, but was obviously thinking.

"Sure, though I'm going to have to get a suit," I say, hoping to steer the conversation in a new direction.

"Oh, you didn't bring one? I have a spare you could borrow. I think it would fit."

"No, it's fine; I'm meeting Susan tomorrow morning at some shopping mall. I'll get one there. Thanks, though." I give her one of the first smiles of the night I don't have to fake.

"Oh, good!" she says, as we stop in front of her door. "Well, goodnight!"

"Night," I say as she steps into her room.

I look down the hall toward my room, but instead of heading in that direction, I go back to the large bay window across the hall from the top of the stairs. I look out across the enormous back lawn, and sigh in spite of myself.

Even at night it's beautiful here.

As I gaze lazily out over the lawn, my mind wanders back to dinner tonight. I didn't have the chance to approach Mr. Kerkley and prove my okay-ness like I'd hoped, and I can't quite figure out if that makes me sorry or relieved.

Maybe both.

Not that I think I can't do it, or am afraid — not at all. It's just that alone in your room is probably the easiest place to be brave.

Suddenly, I hear footsteps behind me and I turn to see a man standing at the top of the stairs.

Oh God.

Mr. Kerkley.

I stare blankly at him, praying it's too dark for him to see that my face is ridiculously red, while he looks back, his face locked in an unreadable expression.

Okay, now is your chance, say something.

Silence.

Say something, idiot! Don't just stand here like a boob!

Nothing.

"Goodnight," he finally says with a slight nod.

I open my mouth to reply, but no sound comes out.

He turns down the hall toward his room without looking back.

DAMN IT!

I run to my room and shut the door behind me before even taking a breath.

What the hell is wrong with me?

Here I have this great casual indifference scheme, and I can't even say goodnight? God, if he didn't think I was an idiot before, I've certainly cleared that up for him!

Embarrassed and thoroughly disgraced, I undress and slump onto my bed.

Okay…maybe it's time for a new plan.

6

"Oh my gosh, it's so good to see you!" Susan says, giving me a tight hug.

From across the parking lot I'd seen the brown wavy hair that I would recognize anywhere, and had all but run up to greet her.

"I know!" I'm embarrassed how close I am to tears.

But it *is* good to see her. I can't think of anyone who knows her and doesn't love her. She's always been the kind of friend you can tell anything to, and not worry about being judged or criticized. She isn't dramatic or petty like so many women are. Even when she was younger she didn't take to gossip or rumors, which was comforting when you needed someone to talk to or confide in. It's rare to have a friend who you know will always be there for you when you need her, but that's exactly who Susan is. One of those friends who—no matter how long it's been since you last saw each other—when you meet up it's like no time has passed at all.

God, I need her right now.

"So, do you want to go eat?" I ask, realizing we're still in the parking lot of this ridiculously nice outdoor shopping mall. When I pulled in I was immediately glad I was driving the Escalade so that I could at least *pretend* to fit in—though even the Escalade wouldn't turn any heads next to the auto-elite of this parking lot. In the back of my mind I wonder if I'll be able to find a bathing suit here that's within my price range.

"Well, the place I want to take you to doesn't open until ten, so do you mind walking around until then?"

"Actually that's perfect. I need to buy a bathing suit." I cringe.

"Sure, there's a great place just down the way."

After two stores — the first was a juniors store with no tasteful options — and countless racks of suits, I'm at my wit's end.

"Where are the normal suits?" I huff, leafing through yet another rack.

"Well, that depends on what you mean by 'normal suits,'" Susan says, smiling at my tone.

"Normal as in — just because I am relatively thin and have a decent rack doesn't mean I want to look like a hooker — suits."

"I think we passed that aisle — " she giggles " — but have a look at these." She motions to the display of cover-ups.

"Cover-ups, good. The more we cover up, the better."

"Why? You look great in a two piece."

I picked up a yellow sundress and held it against myself. "No, it's not that, it's just that the last thing I need is to look like I am trying to solicit male attention."

"You mean Sunday, or in general?"

"Sunday."

"Any particular reason?"

Sigh. "Yeah, but I'll tell you later. For now, just suffice it to say, no hooker suits."

"Okay. Well, maybe you can de-hooker one of the suits with something like this." She holds up a two-piece, thin-linen, drawstring pant and top ensemble.

It actually isn't half bad. The pants are relaxed, and the jacket-style top has loose, elbow-length sleeves, with a drawstring closure just under the bra line. It's pale green, and matches a pink and green two-piece suit I had not entirely hated.

"All right. Sold."

We take my purchases, and — now that it was well past ten — head to breakfast. The restaurant she leads us to is really nice, and has a great menu. When we get inside, I see a door leading to a deck that has tables overlooking the large lake that borders the shopping center. Only one table out there is occupied, and that couple is ready to leave.

"Could we possibly sit outside?" I ask the hostess. I really did want to tell Susan about my situation, and would feel infinitely more comfortable in a secluded area.

"Oh, sure. Right this way. Rocky will be thrilled. No one seems to want to be out there today."

"You don't mind do you? I know it's a little cool today," I ask Susan as we are seated.

"No, this is nice. I've never been out here."

"Rocky" turns out to be our waitress, and after we place our drink order, Susan eyes me with a concerned look.

"Is everything all right? You seem distracted."

"You could say that."

"Work?"

"Sort of. Our new client, the one we're here for."

The ill-attempted fairy tale between Nick and I had happened while Susan was studying overseas. We only spoke once every few months during the years she was away. The first conversation I had with her after meeting Nick didn't happen until after it was over between us. To this day I had never told her. Actually, I had never told anyone. Lisa was the only one who knew about him when we were dating, so obviously she knew when it ended, but other than that I had kept the story of those three precious months to myself.

Susan looks at me quietly. She doesn't pry or try to force anything from me. She simply waits patiently, knowing I'll talk when I'm ready.

"Well, I guess it started eight years ago…"

I tell her everything. How Nick and I met, dated, fell in love. About his dreams and plans, the proposal, all of it. By the time our breakfasts come, I had reached the part of the story where Lisa finds out about the engagement, and her less than subtle reaction.

But that is as far as I go.

That was as far as I had ever gone. Even just in my own mind.

Over the years, I had mentally relived all the moments Nick and I had spent together countless times, but had never consciously allowed myself to think beyond the proposal. It's like there's a black hole of time in my life, starting from just after that evening to about a week later, when I awoke from my deluded haze of denial and found myself alone.

As much as I don't want to bring all those memories to the surface again, I want to tell her. Somewhere in me, there has always been a need to tell someone. Lisa had asked of course, but I could never bring myself to talk about it. I was always too afraid, terrified that if I let the memories out of the box I have so carefully kept them in, they will totally consume me.

I don't know how long I have been staring down at my half-eaten strawberry waffle when Susan asks, "So what did you do?"

For a moment I don't move. She's probably wondering if I heard her. Finally I whisper, "I broke it off."

"Here you are! Where the hell have you been, I've been worried sick!" Nick said, hurrying into my apartment. "You were supposed to meet me at five."

"Oh," I said, my voice dry. "I guess I forgot."

I hadn't forgotten; I just hadn't realized the time. I had been sitting at my kitchen table for the past two and a half hours, sipping a glass of wine and staring off into space. My mind had been in complete turmoil: raging, debating, planning, re-planning, and deliberating. I'd analyzed everything Lisa had said to me the day before about marriage to Nick, and I had finally come to a decision.

She was right. She always was.

Even if I didn't agree with her at the moment, I would someday.

It would hurt, but it was for the best.

I had to end this.

I had been thinking for the past hour or so — since the moment I made the decision — about approaching him. How it would be best, what to say, and so on. I was basically attempting to prepare myself for what I knew would be a horrible encounter.

Horrible, but for the best.

All I had to do was remain constant. Once it was done, it would be done, and I could relax and move on. I just had to get through it. And the best way to ensure that was to be numb. If I could shut down my emotions for the next few minutes, it would all be fine.

Numb I could do.

"What's wrong?" he asked, suddenly sensing the change in me and looking concerned.

I took a deep breath. "I can't do this."

He glanced quickly sideways then back to me, his eyebrows pulling together in confusion. "Then we can just eat here."

"I can't do this," I said again, though a bit quieter.

His face paled as he realized I was talking about something much more serious than dinner.

"Can't do what?" he asked, a new edge to his voice.

"I'm sorry, Nick, I just—"

"Can't do what?" he asked again, cutting me off.

I looked down and pushed the horrible feeling welling up inside me off to the side.

It's for the best.

"The wedding. Us. This. I can't." I looked back up at him, which was a mistake. The rest of the color drained from his face as hurt and shock took over his expression.

"What…why—" He swallowed and tried again. "Where is this coming from?"

I stood from the table and took a few steps, neither closer nor further away from him. "I've just been thinking and—"

"Lisa," he cut me off. "You went to see your sister yesterday. Is this her talking? What did she say?"

"She just…it's not that…I…" I stammered, looking down. I didn't know what to say to that. I should have realized he'd guess that Lisa had basically been the reason for my decision. Before I could think of something to say, he closed the space between us and took my hands in his.

"Jules, we don't need her. I know how much her opinion means to you, but we can show her she's wrong. We can get married anyway, and I promise she will be fine with it eventually. It may take time, but it will work out."

He looked so hopeful all of a sudden, I just couldn't…

No, it's for the best.

I slowly shook my head. "I can't."

He let my hands drop and stepped back, running his hands through his hair. "So what, then?" He began to pace back and forth. "Lisa's going to run your life from now on, is that it?"

"No. I've just realized this isn't what's best for either of us. I really think that after a while you'll see it too."

"I'll see?" He stared at me with in disbelief. "What I see is the woman I love, the woman I want to marry and spend the rest of my life with! We will have a good life together, Jules. I'm going to get things running for myself, I know it! You know it. Please tell me you still believe that."

After a moment's hesitation I said, "I do. I just…" But I didn't know how to finish the sentence.

The disbelief in his eyes turned to shock, and then terrible hurt. "You just…" he whispered, mentally filling in the part where I said I actually don't believe it any more. The part I had left out.

Because it wasn't true.

"Nick, I'm not trying to —" But I stopped talking as he came toward me.

He took my face firmly between his hands, and I could see the tears in his eyes.

"We are the only ones who know how we feel. You say you want this to end? Then look me in the eyes and tell me you don't love me."

He didn't think I would do it. He thought he had found the one weak spot in my armor, and honestly, he had. He knew I loved him, and would hold me to it until I convinced him otherwise.

Oh God, I couldn't…

No! Don't buckle now. Stay strong, it's almost done. Numb.

It's for the best.

He continued to hold my face, wet eyes boring into mine. I kept my face clear of any emotion and took a deep breath.

"I. Don't. Love. You."

For a moment he was still as ice, almost as if I hadn't spoken. The only movement at all was the tears brimming in his eyes, then spilling down his cheeks. He slowly released my face and let his arms hang by his sides. Without a word he turned and walked to the door. He reached to open the door but hesitated, resting his hand on the handle as he looked back at me one last time.

And that's when I saw it.

The face that would haunt my dreams for years to come.

The face that would wake me from sleep in a cold sweat.

The face that would cut my very being into shreds.

A face of hurt, pain, heartbreak, and worst of all…betrayal.

A moment later, Nick turned back toward the door, opened it, and stepped out into the hall, closing it softly behind him.

I stood motionless for several minutes, staring after him.

That was it. It was done.

I had done it.

I had held my own, taken charge, and followed through.

It was hard, but necessary.

As I stood there, gathering the strength to move, a thought came hurtling at me. A thought that I had somehow failed to consider throughout this whole decision making process.

I would never see him again.

Oh my God.

My throat closed as I stumbled back into the chair I had spent the last two hours in. My hands began to shake, and I couldn't tear my eyes from the door.

I…would…never…see…him…again.

What had I done?

From that moment on, "my life" began a not-so-slow spiraling transformation into "my existence."

I tried for a while. I continued on with my life, trying to get back to normal, but it was no use. Now, the only thing I wanted was the only thing no amount of ambition, schooling, or work could get me.

Nothing seemed to matter all that much anymore. Nick had somehow become the driving force in my life without my even realizing it, and now that he was gone, so was my momentum. I continued to work at my internship at Stauncher

House, but I'd lost my drive. After a while I tried to start dating again, going out on Lisa's fix-ups, but I'd lost my passion. My internship ended with praise for my work, but no job offers. And we know how my love life ended up.

Don't get me wrong, I'd never been bitter or resentful. How could I be?

It was all completely my fault.

Everything that my life became was entirely my doing.

I hear someone sniffle, realize it's me, and look around in surprise. The dishes have been cleared away, and somehow there is a caramel cappuccino in front of me. I glance up at Susan who looks at me with sad sympathy and offers me her napkin. Only then do I realize tears are running down my face. I had gotten so lost in the memory; I wasn't even sure how much of it I had actually verbalized for her.

I take the napkin, lean back in my chair, and wipe my face with a heavy sigh.

"So, that's it," I say.

Susan opens her mouth, but closes it again.

"Go ahead." I wave my hand in a "nothing you could say is going to bother me" gesture.

"You obviously regretted it immediately. Why didn't you try to apologize?"

"I thought about it, but by the time I came to my senses, it was too late. I did regret it instantly, but there was still part of my brain trying to convince me it was all for the best. A week or so later when I let myself realize how wrong I'd been, it was too late. Besides, what could I say? It was all too much; I couldn't possibly ask him to forgive me."

"Broken hearts can still forgive."

"I know. And if it were only his broken heart I might have risked it, but it was more than that. I *betrayed* him. I was the only one who believed that he was going to make it. Believed he was going to go somewhere. Even his sister thought he was crazy, but I was there for him. And when I said what I did…I became just like everyone else. I let him down."

"And, did you actually have any doubts?"

"I wish I could say I did! Then what I did *might* be considered understandable! But no! I knew he would pull it off! I knew he would end up being a huge success! But I let Lisa plant an illusion of doubt that was never *really* there."

"So you blame her?" There was no accusation in her voice, just simple curiosity.

"No. I know what she was trying to do. She really did think it was in my best interest to let him go. By the time she realized how wrong she had been, it was too late. She tried to make up for it in her own way, which was basically by setting me up on countless dates with countless guys, hoping I would be happy with one of them. I know she blames herself somewhat, but no, I can't blame her. It was me. I did it. She might have convinced me, but then I *let* her convince me. I can't blame her for that."

We sit in silence for a few minutes, Susan more than likely trying to wrap her mind around everything I'd told her.

I had done it. I'd relived the one memory I had been hiding from for almost a decade. As horribly depressed and low as I feel, there is also something else that feels oddly pleasant. It's as though I could breathe a little deeper and exhale a little more fully.

"And you still love him," she suddenly states. I twitch my lips into an un-amused smile for a second, and then take another sip of my drink.

Of course I still love him. I'd never stopped loving him. Even during those hours when I was convincing myself that I didn't want to be with him, I was *never* trying to convince myself that I didn't love him.

"Why don't you talk to him?"

"And say what exactly?" I give her a sad smile. Bless her heart, I knew she would try to find some way to make it all better. Unfortunately, this is beyond anyone's help. Especially mine.

She seems to realize this as she considers my question.

"Besides, this is *my* problem, not his. He's over it. He's moved on. I have too…at least, as much as I'm ever going to be able to. And the sickest thing of all is that part of me doesn't even *want* him to forgive me. It's as if I'm getting what I deserve. I don't know." I sigh as I slowly spin my cappuccino cup on the saucer. "Maybe I have some inner masochist or something."

"Maybe you should focus your attention somewhere else. What about that Chris you were talking about? He seems nice."

"Yeah," I chuckle in spite of myself. "Dump a guy, go eight years without seeing him, then start macking on one of his best friends. That's classy."

"Well, when you put it like that," she says, with an amused eye roll.

"Anyway, he's not my type. He is really nice, but *really* shy. Wouldn't surprise me if he's never been on a date in his life."

We sit silently for another moment until I think to look down at my cell. It's eleven ten, and I have to go. I'm in a weird daze as Susan and I walk out to the parking lot. On one hand I'm more depressed than I have been—or rather have *let* myself be—for years. On the other hand, it's almost like I have a new lease on my mental freedom. I've been avoiding memories for so long, afraid that they would take over, when actually they had already taken over and what I really needed was to set them free.

"Why don't you come out to Mom's ranch with us?" Susan says as we reach the cars.

I smile at the idea, truly wishing I could. "I have to work."

"Well sure, for the next few days. I mean after that. Take a week or two off, I'm sure you could. When was the last time you took a vacation?"

That's true. I hoard vacation time like nobody's business. Hell, I could stop going to work altogether, and still get paid for a year.

"Besides," she continues, "you would be doing us a favor. I need someone to drive my car down."

"Your car?"

"Matt and I need to drive down together to wrangle the boys, but one car is never enough while we're there. You could bring mine down and stay a while. You know my mom would love to see you."

I'm sure she is making the car situation up for my sake, as I have to imagine that her mother and stepfather have a slew of cars that they would be more than willing to loan her if need be. However, since I'm tempted to take her up on the offer, I let it go. After all, I need something to get me through this weekend.

"All right," I say, "but only if you are *sure* it won't be a problem for your mom and the rest of your family. I don't want to impose." She smirks. "All right then, I'll see if I can take the time."

"Yay!" She throws her arms around my neck. "It will be great! You'll see, it's just what you need!"

"Maybe it is."

7

Okay, so time for a new plan.

I drive down the secluded road that leads to the estate, enjoying a new outlook. Breakfast was wonderfully relaxing and incredibly emotional at the same time, but it's given me some perspective — I'm an idiot. I never should have tried to convince myself that I could play off this whole situation like it's nothing. It is something — to me anyway — and I was naïve to think I could avoid that fact. Furthermore, the bold step I was going to take in talking to Nick and convincing him I'm fine with all of this isn't going to happen, but that's all right. It would have been a lie anyway. And yes, I've decided to call him Nick, as "Mr. Kerkley" only makes me more depressed.

I'm not fine.

I realize that, but that doesn't mean everyone else has to. I did well last night, talking and being friendly with everyone. I behaved like a professional, and that is what I'll continue to do. I'll be friendly with everyone when it's required and quiet when it's not. I just have to make it through the next few days, then it's off to Susan's for two weeks — provided I can take the time off.

There is one major change from the last plan to this one, however. No contact with Nick. Not unless absolutely called for. It will take a huge weight off my mind, and it's not like he's made any effort to seek out my attention, so I will do the same. If I don't have to constantly fear a conversation with him, I'll be able to think more clearly. The day at the beach might be harder, but I can deal with that when it comes. For now, if I stick to the new plan, I just might be able to get through this.

I *will* get through this.

The rest of the afternoon passes quickly and quietly. Both inspections go well, with only one minor repair to be scheduled. Margaret, Bree, and I spend the later hours reviewing work orders and making phone calls.

The rest of the guests went out after lunch to visit the town and surrounding areas. I'm not even aware they've come back until I'm in the kitchen that afternoon, fighting with the coffee maker, and am suddenly joined by Cathy.

"Oh, hello," she says, as my breathing catches for a moment. "I didn't realize anyone was in here." She sets her bags down on the counter and comes over, offering me her hand. "I don't think we have actually been introduced yet."

No, no we haven't.

"I'm Cathy Dewitt."

"I'm Julia. It's nice to meet you." I shake her hand, feeling unnecessarily awkward. She turns back to her bags, which I now see are groceries, while I continue to battle with the filter tray.

"I picked up some food for the beach on Sunday."

"Oh, great. It should be nice." I'm trying not to let my frustration with the coffee maker show in my voice.

"Do you need some help with that?" She comes over and takes the filter from me. "These ones can be a pain." She flips the tray, fixes the pot, throws the filter in, and turns it on like it's nothing at all. "There we go," she says, smiling.

"Wow…that was easy."

"I have the same kind at home," she tells me.

She's nice. One of those people who just gives off a happy energy. The sort of person who could make you feel better just by being around. It makes me sad I was never able to meet her when—well, anyway, she's nice.

"You know you shouldn't put me to shame like that. Getting coffee is pretty much what I get paid for," I joke with a wry smile.

"Oh, I'm sure you do much more than that! But regardless, you don't have to feel too bad; it took me a week to learn the first time."

We laugh, and I step back over to the counter with her and help with the groceries.

"Oh, you don't have to—"

"Don't worry about it." I cut off her attempt to keep me from helping. "I've got nothing to do until the coffee's ready."

"Well, thank you. Actually, I do have a question for you, if you don't mind."

"Sure." I am suddenly sweating. Does she know about me? I mean, I know she knows what happened with Nick all those years ago—she would have to—but does she know it's me?

"I hope I'm not being rude, I don't mean to be. I'm just curious."

Gulp. "What is it?"

"What *do* you do, exactly?"

Thank God.

I chuckle (hopefully not hysterically) as I drop a bag of lettuce into a crisper drawer. "I assume you mean my group, as all I really do is take notes, answer phones, and—" I wave toward the brewing pot "—get coffee."

"All very important jobs," she says, in a very dignified tone, "but yes, I did mean your group. Nick says you are financial planners, but I thought they handled things like stock trade, and all of that."

"We do some of that, but if that's all someone needs, our firm has large groups devoted to stock investments and managing income. What our group does is more on a personal level. We research all the major factors involved with large purchases, like estates," I say, gesturing around us, "or business franchises. Things like that. Instead of hiring separate people to advise you in different areas, real estate, inspections, codes, et cetera, and then put it all together and try to make sense of it on your own, we do it for you. After all, not many people have a lot of experience buying homes like this one. We do the leg work, go to meetings, supervise inspections, and other annoying stuff so our clients don't have to." I take the now full pot of coffee off the burner and pour it into the waiting mugs. "Basically," I say with a smile, handing her a steaming cup, "we help wealthy people spend their money in the wisest and most productive way, with as little effort on their part as possible."

We exchange a giggle and clink our coffee mugs in a mock-toast.

"Well in any event, I know Nick is glad you're here."

Ha…now I know you're referring to the team.

"So, does the house have your approval?" she asks between sips.

"Well, nothing seems disastrous so far, but we will have to wait for the inspection reports. All the renovations have really done wonders; you would never know how old this place actually is."

"I know, it's amazing! My parents would be shocked."

I look up from my mug. "Your parents?"

"Mmm." She nods, taking a drink. "They both passed away years ago, but they were actually married here, back in the late sixties. Nick and I have never been here, but they used to talk about it all the time. When Nick found out it was up for sale, we both thought it would be worth a look."

Ah…

"That makes more sense now. I've been wondering why he's interested in a place like this. He's not extravagant…that is to say…he doesn't strike me as an extravagant person." *Oh, yeah. Good save.* "In this line of work it gets pretty easy to tell," I add, hoping to help cover my slip.

"No, he's definitely not. It doesn't have much to do with the house itself." She grins.

I smile back and go to take another sip of coffee, but no sooner does the mug reach my lips then Nick appears in the doorway. My heart is suddenly in my throat, and I have trouble swallowing the coffee in my mouth. I turn to the other two mugs on the counter and pick them up, preparing to run—I mean, preparing to calmly leave the room, because Margaret and Bree are waiting and the coffee is done now, and for no reason other than that.

Head up, damn it! Don't be a coward!

"I should take these over," I say, looking at Cathy.

"Okay, I'll see you later," she says warmly, placing a hand on my shoulder.

I walk straight toward the door, not looking at Nick, but not looking away from him either. I'm actually praying he will move aside and we won't accidentally touch, as this is definitely the closest we have physically been since this whole screwed up reunion began. I hold my breath as I slide past him, and he steps aside without looking at me.

After I round the bend, I stop and release my breath. There, that wasn't so bad. Just two more days, nineteen hours, and—

"She's really sweet," I hear Cathy say from the kitchen.

Oh, God…

"Yes, she is," Nick answers after a moment.

My heart jumps.

Sweet? He thinks I'm sweet? Really? Did he say that just for her sake? He didn't even hesitate.

I tiptoe closer to the kitchen, but still out of sight.

"She doesn't seem to think much of her job, but I'll bet she's one of those people who runs the whole office without realizing it. The kind the boss says they couldn't do without. She seems the type."

"She is," he says softly. "Or, she seems like she would be," he adds quickly.

My cheeks catch fire, and I take a step nearer to the door.

"What?" Cathy asks after a pause.

"Nothing," he says.

"What?" "Nothing"? What was that? Was he making a face? Was she asking what was wrong, or what he's thinking? What is he thinking?

"Were there more bags in the car?" Cathy asks.

"Just one, hang on and I'll get it," Nick answers, his voice getting closer.

Shit!

I run down the hall toward the room Margaret, Bree, and I have been using as a temporary office, hoping with everything in me that I'm fast enough, and he won't actually catch me eavesdropping, or running away for that matter. I am in such a hurry, I run headlong into Margaret, almost spilling the coffee.

"Oh, God, I'm sorry!"

"Whoa, easy there! Where's the fire?" she asks, grabbing my shoulders to steady me.

"Here you go." I hand her the coffee. "Sorry it took so long. The machine here sucks," I tell her, realizing I am out of breath.

"No problem, we just wrapped up. There are a few write-ups on your computer that need to be entered into the log, and that should be it for the day."

She grabs her briefcase and leaves, giving me a much needed moment to think. He had been talking about me. Granted, he didn't start the conversation, but he didn't end it. What had happened? Did he actually make a face? What did it mean?

I let out a heavy sigh, lean back in my chair, and look up at the ceiling.

Get a hold of yourself. It more than likely meant nothing, just like he said. Hell, odds are, it wasn't about me at all. He probably saw something weird in the refrigerator while Cathy was putting the rest of the groceries away, and grimaced.

And here I am, getting all worked up over nothing!

Not that it matters. Professional, friendly, passive, remember?

As I bring my computer back to life, Bree runs in the room in a tizzy. She makes a beeline for her seat and grabs her bag, not noticing me.

"Whoa, what's up?"

"Oh! Jules, I didn't see you! Oh my gosh, oh my gosh, oh my gosh," she says, skipping over and taking my hands. "Guess what?"

"What?"

"I just ran into Mr. Kerkley in the hall, and he asked me to take a walk with him down to the lake!"

"Wow, that's great!" I say, straining to control my face.

It should be great. She's my friend I should be happy for her. I am. It's great.

It's good anyway.

Okay, maybe a little bothersome.

And just a little upsetting.

It's terrible.

Down right, God damned, gut-wrenchingly, horrible!

She pulls me into a quick hug. "Wish me luck!" she says, and skips out the door.

I fall back into my chair, fighting the urge to cry.

The remainder of that afternoon is quiet, which is mainly because I spend it alone in my room. If I had gone out into the rest of the house and attempted to be social, I'm sure I would have spent most of the time watching and waiting for Nick and Bree to come back from their walk. Then I would have analyzed every look, word, smile, and gesture between the two of them until I drove myself out of my mind.

Not the best way to spend an afternoon.

Instead, I hide — or that is, *rationally decide to stay* — in my room, reading a magazine I brought with me, re-folding my clothes, showering, and actually taking the time to do my hair, which is usually too unruly to bother with, unless it's a special occasion. I'm sure that fighting with the brush, blow-dryer, straightener, and curling iron will take up at least an hour or so.

By the time I walk down to dinner, I am fifteen minutes later than I had planned to be, but my hair looks spectacular — so spectacular in fact that I had no choice but to pull it back. Sure, that was over an hour and a half of work for nothing, but I can't have people thinking I'm *trying* to impress anyone.

I walk into the kitchen, and the first thing I see is Nick, Bree, Cathy, and her husband sitting on the stools at the counter, chatting and laughing like a happy little foursome.

Wince.

Good for Bree; *her* fairy godmother obviously showed up to work. I should go over and check her shoes — they're probably glass.

No way is the happy family the group I'm going to approach, so I look around frantically for Margaret…who's not here yet. Damn. Now what? I can't just stand in the doorway like a wallflower. Thankfully, I notice Chris sitting by himself against the far wall.

"Mind if I join?" I say, taking the seat next to him.

"Not at all," he answers with a shy but warm smile.

Every time I talk to him, I become more and more grateful that Chris was invited up here. He has been invaluable to my overall mental state, having saved me from what could have been two awkward situations already. Luckily enough, he also seems to enjoy my company, which makes me feel a little bit better about monopolizing his time the way I have.

"How was town?"

"It's a town." He grins. "Nothing special. Though the restaurant we had lunch at was pretty good. Derek actually saw someone he knows."

"Really?"

"Some lawyer who used to work with him at City Hall. The guy retired up here I guess. You should have seen his wife!" he adds with a smile, leaning in and lowering his voice.

"Yeah?" I grin.

"I guarantee you, he has kids older than she is!"

"Really?" I giggle in spite of myself.

"If he hadn't actually introduced her as his wife, I would have sworn it was his daughter!"

We chuckle again, and I am so thankful that Chris is here that I could kiss him! I have almost forgotten the man sitting at the counter.

Almost.

We talk for a good twenty minutes about this, that, and the other, while I studiously avoid looking at the counter. I do a good job, slipping up only once when, from the corner of my eye, I swear I see Nick staring over at Chris and me. I glance over — just a reflex — to check, but he's deep in conversation with his group. Great. Now I can add paranoia to the list of issues I'll have by the end of this trip.

"Come and get it!" Derek calls from outside.

I turn to look out the window, and see him standing by a grill on the huge stone deck out back, a beer in his hand. Margaret sits on the stone wall nearby.

We all file outside to eat. Derek is a whiz at the grill, and everything looks amazing. While everyone gets food, I catch up to Margaret.

"I was wondering where you were."

"Oh, well." She leans in confidentially. "When I came down, Bree and Mr. Kerkley were alone in the kitchen talking. I didn't want to interrupt," she says with a grin and a wink.

Wince.

"Right," I say, and go back to filling my plate, though now I'm queasy.

Looks like I'll be adding paranoia *and* stomach ulcers to the list. Awesome.

That night I can't sleep. I lie in bed, thumbing through my magazine again, hoping it will put me to sleep, but it's no use. Too many "Nick and Bree" visions dancing in my head. Normally, reading is a good distraction for me, but tonight all it seems to be doing is adding unnecessary fuel to the fire that is my ramped imagination. All the articles about love and relationships take on new meaning when I start to unwittingly imagine Mr. Kerkley and Bree in the scenarios they describe. "10 Things He's Thinking When He Sees Your Lingerie" becomes "What Lingerie Will Bree Look Fantastic In." "The Surefire Way To Land A Second Date" becomes "The Surefire Way To Land Your Best Friend's Ex." When the photo of the half-naked spooning couple under the heading "Better Sex For Both Of You" actually *becomes* Nick and Bree, I've had enough. I toss the magazine into the corner of the room and roll out of bed with a growl. Time to find something else to do.

I slide on my slippers and stick my head out into the hall. No one's around, though it's past midnight, so I guess that would make sense. I silently make my way downstairs to check out the library. I've wanted to take a closer look at it ever since the first walkthrough, and now seems as good a time as any. The large wooden doors groan when I open them, but as all the bedrooms are on the upper levels, I don't imagine that anyone heard.

I step inside and am awed by the number of books. The shelves go from floor to ceiling, and there doesn't seem to be an empty spot left on them. For a long while I casually scan the shelves, realizing that the books are in alphabetical order by author. Austen, the Brontës, Dickens, Poe, Shakespeare, Thoreau—it doesn't look like anyone has been left out. From Dante Alighieri to Edgar Rice Burroughs, everyone is accounted for. Some are older and leather bound, while others are newer paperback editions, and everything in between. And Bibles! There is an entire shelf full of them; some look to be older than the house itself.

One book in particular catches my eye. It is a larger, leather-bound volume with an ornate gold-leaf rose down the spine. I pull it out and read the title. *The Complete Anthology of Folklore and Fairytales: Illustrated and Unabridged.* I leaf through it, admiring the colorful artwork. Not only are there pictures depicting characters and scenes, but the text itself is beautifully done. It is just like those old religious books from the Middle Ages, where the first letter of a chapter takes up half the page, and is ridiculously elaborate with scrolls and flowers over it. Very impressive.

My casual reading is interrupted when I come across a beautiful watercolor-style illustration. It is of an older woman in a robe. She has translucent wings and it looks as though light is spilling out of the tips of her fingers. There is no caption, but I don't need one — I know who she is.

She's the Fairy Godmother.

She is the woman sent to solve all of poor Cinderella's problems, as that's wh —

"Never liked that picture, not my best angle."

My head snaps up and I almost drop the book in surprise as I suddenly find myself looking at a woman in a long, sky blue robe, leaning casually against one of the bookshelves. She's older — in her sixties maybe — but she isn't the plump, happy, grandmother type. She is thin and drawn, with a raspy voice, deep set wrinkles, a frizzy beehive hairdo, and way too much makeup: the sort of woman you picture sitting in the corner of a dingy diner with coffee and a cigarette, yelling at the waitress about the coffee being cold.

"Admit it," she continues, "it makes my ass look big."

I look slowly down at the book in my hands, then back up to her. "This is you?"

She gives me a look that says my question is too obvious to deserve an answer. "So," she says, waving her hand in the air in a let's-get-on-with-it gesture, "what do ya need?"

"Sorry?" I ask, totally at a loss. What the hell is going on? Who is this? Did she really just appear out of thin air? That's not possible; I'm standing right next to the only door to the room. There is no way I could have missed her coming in.

"I'm waiting." She drums her red-lacquered nails against the bookshelf, obviously annoyed at my lack of response.

All I can do is stare.

"Look, you called me, do you need something or not?"

"I…I didn't…"

"All right, I've got about thirty more appointments tonight, so if we're done—"

"No wait!" I call out, stepping forward as she turns to leave. "Don't go." She turns back and looks at me, hands on her hips, eyebrows raised, waiting for me to speak.

This is all crazy. She can't really be my fairy godmother, can she? How can I be sure? Does she have a badge or something I can ask to see?

Suddenly, a memory stirs in my mind and I hear Lisa's voice in my head, *"She'll know all about you."* The echo of Lisa's words gives me an idea.

"What's my middle name?" I ask, looking her square in the eye.

"What?"

"My middle name."

"You're quizzing me now?" she asks, with something between disbelief and censure in her tone.

"That doesn't sound like an answer," I say, trying to fake some bravado.

"Lee," she answers, doing nothing to hide her irritation as she folds her arms across her chest.

"What's my cat's name?"

"You're allergic to cats."

Impressive, but I should probably give her a question in her field. "Who was the first guy I wanted to marry?"

"Super Grover from *Sesame Street*, but as I'm pretty sure we can't really consider him a 'guy,' we'll have to go with Danny from New Kids on the Block."

Whoa…

"Are we done yet?" she sighs, growing frustrated.

No—no, it's not possible. But then again, she seems like the sort of fairy godmother I'd get. In any case, I can't let her leave. "I'm sorry, this is just…" I trail off. After a deep breath, I try again. "I…I want a second chance." The words are out before I even know what I am saying.

"A second chance? What the hell do you think all this is?" She waves her arm around her. "You've got your second chance. You just don't have the guts to do something about it!"

"I do, I just…" I look down at the book that I'm hugging against my chest like a shield.

"You just…"

I don't know what to say, so I make an excuse. "I haven't been able to talk to him alone." Weak, I know, but I have to say something. I haven't been scolded like this since I was ten; I have to at least *try* to stand up for myself.

"Oh, so you need some alone time with him do you?" she says with mock sweetness, not hiding the cynical edge to her tone. "All right then…go!"

With that, she disappears before my eyes into a cloud of dingy gray smoke. In the same moment I hear the door behind me groan, and I spin around to find Nick standing in the open doorway.

"Oh," he says, surprised and little embarrassed. "I didn't think anyone would be in here."

I can only gape at him, frozen in place. Somewhere in the back of my mind a little voice yells at me to speak up and say something—anything. The rest of my body, however, refuses to comply.

After a few more awkward moments he says, "Goodnight," and turns back into the hall, closing the door behind him.

The sound of lazy applause coming from behind me pulls me out of my stupor. I turn, tearing my eyes from the door, to see the old woman sitting in one of the oversized armchairs on the other side of the room. She stands and walks toward me, still clapping a slow, mocking rhythm.

"Bravo," she says. "I have never heard such a heartfelt speech. How *does* he keep his hands off you?"

My cheeks flush in embarrassment. "It was too sudden. I wasn't ready," I snap, not able to meet her eyes.

"Right. I'm sure if I'd have warned you, it would have gone much differently."

Her patronizing sarcasm makes my eyes sting, but I refuse to give her the satisfaction of seeing me cry. "I—I just," I say, trying to swallow the lump in my throat.

"You just, you just, you just. You just need a second chance, you just need some time alone with him, you just need some warning." She stalks toward me, and I step back until I'm up against the wall. "I'll tell you what *you just*. You just want someone else to blame, you just want someone else to swoop in and solve all your problems, you just want to reserve the right to bitch and moan about everything you are too scared to try to change—"

"Stop it."

She continues as though I hadn't spoken, "That is why nothing will ever change for you—"

"Stop it!"

"That is why you will never truly be happy again—"

"Stop!"

"And that is why you will die miserable—"

"Stop it!"

"And alone!"

"STOP IT!"

My eyes fly open, and I find myself looking up at the ceiling over my bed. My heart pounds, my blankets are balled up in my fists, and the magazine lies open on my chest. I toss it on the bedside table and roll over with a huff.

Two more days, seven hours, and twenty-seven minutes to go…

8

S unday dawns with the promise of a clear, beautiful day.
Outside.

In my room, however, you'd think a hurricane had struck. Work
files are strewn over my desk; there are water bottles on the floor, a
tipped-over bottle of aspirin on the bedside table, an empty plate
and cereal bowl on the dresser, and a bed totally in shambles. All
products of one of the worst nights ever.

Yesterday had been a disaster. Oh sure, the work aspects of the
day were fine; all the inspections had gone smoothly. It was the rest
of the day that was hell. I had to suffer through three meals and two
hours of after dinner socializing, all the while enjoying a front row
seat in *America's New Cutest Couple*, starring Bree and Nick. All day
long the two of them were talking and touching and giggling, while
I did all I could to keep from screaming.

On top of that, the one portion of the day that shaped up to
be tolerably pleasant ended up ruined. It was after dinner, and Nick
had suggested we all play a card game. The one he suggested was
called Spoons, basically musical chairs with cards and silverware.
Everyone sits around a table, passing cards counter clockwise — as
quickly as possible — trying to be the first to collect four of a kind.
When you get your four, you grab a spoon from the center of the
table. Once the first person claims their spoon, everyone else must
grab one of the remaining ones, but there's always one fewer spoon
than there are players. If you don't get a spoon, you're out. It's a fast,
rowdy game that I wasn't particularly in the mood for. Chris seemed
to share my opinion, so the two of us decided to take the spare set

of cards and play Rummy over in the corner. The Spoons war raged across the room and resulted in a torn shirt, several bent spoons, and one snapped clean in half, while Chris and I sat, played, and talked, having an all-around nice time.

It didn't last. At one point, I felt the need to look over at the other table. Everyone except Nick was absorbed in the game. He was looking over at our table, but not just pleasantly glancing, mind you. He was glaring to the point where my skin started to crawl, and my hands got all sweaty. What the hell had we done? So we didn't want to play his stupid game, was it really that big of a deal? I suddenly felt so uncomfortable, I had to fight the urge to run out of the room. I turned back toward Chris and resumed our game, making absolutely sure not to look over to the other table for the rest of the evening.

The only remotely enjoyable part of the day was seeing Susan's car parked by the estate garage. I had called her the night before, after speaking with Margaret, and told her that taking the time off wouldn't be a problem — in fact, Margaret seemed even more excited than I was. You know you work too much when even your boss is thrilled you finally want some time off. I told her Susan was planning on joining her at the ranch if it was still all right. She said that of course it was and the easiest thing to do would be to drop off her car for me on their way out today. Seeing it sitting there, ready and waiting for me, was a happy little reminder that this would all be over soon.

I had gone to bed that night and tried to sleep, worried that my dreams would once again be haunted by the "anti-godmother." However, the images my mind seemed to be stuck on were of a far more real and disturbing nature: a happy, flirty, Bree and Nick. Every look, every touch, every laugh the two had shared that day replayed itself over and over again in my head. What's worse, the harder I tried to picture something else, the clearer and more detailed my imagination became. I could actually see Mr. and Mrs. Nick and Bree Kerkley living happily ever after in this gorgeous house, with their ten blond-haired, blue-eyed kids, smiling, playing, and riding off into the sunset. I've never been so nauseated by such a pretty picture.

So I gave up on sleep altogether and spent the rest of the night trying to occupy my mind in any way I could. Somewhere during the early morning hours — after 4:08, because that's the last time I remember consciously looking at the clock — I passed out into a thankfully dreamless semi-coma.

And now it's eight a.m., we're leaving for the beach in a half hour, and I can barely move. This day is going to be hell. Much worse than yesterday anyway, because I won't even have work to distract me. I'm heading straight into a nonstop beachside Nick and Bree flirt-a-palooza.

I hope someone brings alcohol.

Somehow I drag my ass out of bed, get ready, pop two more aspirin, and lumber downstairs to meet that evil, harpy bitch called karma.

Two hours later, we arrive at Sand Beach in Acadia National Park. The beach itself is tiny, less than a quarter mile long, but it is the most beautiful beach I have ever seen. White sand with rolling waves and rocky cliffs—it's like a piece of heaven. It's mid-September, which puts us a few weeks past tourist season, so it seems we'll have it pretty much all to ourselves. There is only one other person in sight, and he's on the far side near the cliffs, fishing in the calmer waters. The sky is as clear as I've seen in a long time, and the sun is warm without being overly bright. The water looks warm, and the air is perfect.

I take a deep breath and look out over the horizon. Maybe today won't be so bad. I can enjoy the scenery, take a nap, maybe talk with Chris for a while. As long as I can find some way to studiously ignore the flirt-fest, maybe I can make myself enjoy this.

"Oh my gosh, it's beautiful!" Bree says, coming up behind me and resting an arm across my shoulders.

"It really is."

"So, are you okay?" she asks, concern thick in her voice. "You've seemed down the past few days. This really isn't your sort of thing, is it?"

What? Watching my ex-fiancé, who I am still madly in love with, flirt and fawn all over you? No, not my thing.

Obviously I can't say that, nor do I even want to imply that this is her fault, so I simply say, "Not really."

"Yeah, it's pretty easy to see."

"It is?" I'm suddenly worried. Miserable as I am, I've been doing my best to make sure no one else knew about it. I guess I'm not doing such a great job.

"Oh, don't worry," she says, feeling my shoulders stiffen. "I'm sure no one else has noticed. I meant it's easy for me to see."

"Good."

She makes a sympathetically sad face and brings her other arm up, hugging me from behind. I know she has no idea what is actually going on, but at the same time, it feels like she really understands. I want so badly to be able to talk to her the way I did with Susan. It would be so nice to have someone here with me who knows what I'm going through. I always tell Bree everything, and if it were anything else I could—but not this.

After another moment she lets me go, and we walk back to the cars and help Margaret and Cathy carry all the towels and bags down to the beach. The men follow with the coolers, food, and anything else deemed heavy. We set up our little camp as close to the water as we can without having to worry about the tide or larger waves. I spread out my towel and start to set up my own area.

"Anyone up for a swim before we eat?" Nick asks the group, as we all organize our stuff.

"I am!" Bree says without hesitation, taking off her cover dress. Chris, Rob, and Derek join too, and all the guys start to pull off their shirts. I drop my eyes to the towel below me, praying I don't blush, while realizing how depressingly juvenile it is that I even need to worry about it. The five of them head down to the water, leaving Margaret, Cathy, and I to relax.

I lie back on my towel and watch them. Bree looks incredible, as always—and in a one piece no less! She doesn't even need a bikini to turn heads. Good thing she didn't wear her two piece, or the men may not have been able to function. I watch Bree and Nick walking side by side. Nick leans in to hear something Bree says, placing a hand on the small of her back. They step into the water, which is apparently much colder than it looks—there are some shocked faces as they get their feet wet. Finally, I see Nick reach out and take Bree's hand and lead her in behind him.

I shut my eyes and let a stream of profanities run through my mind, directed both at me for deliberately watching the two of them, and at Nick and Bree for being so disgustingly perfect! Really, I think that might be what bothers me the most—the fact that they are absolutely perfect for each other. Suddenly, without a conscious command for my brain to do so, I picture Bree falling in a sand pit, being sucked out to sea, and a number of other disturbing images.

My God, my imagination is actually trying to kill her? What is wrong with me?

She's one of the nicest people on earth, not to mention one of my best friends, and here I am subconsciously wishing a spontaneous shark attack on her! Well, that settles it—I am definitely going to hell.

"So," Cathy says quietly, leaning in toward Margaret, "I see my brother has taken a liking to your girl."

"Yes, I noticed the same thing. You don't mind, do you? I can certainly tell her to stay away if you would rather…"

"Oh no! Not at all," Cathy insists. "I'm thrilled. It's nice to see him interested in someone again."

"Again? An attractive, sweet boy like that? I would have thought he had women lined up just waiting."

Cathy chuckles. "You would think, but no. Actually, it's sad. He had a terrible break up a while back, and I don't think he's dated much since."

Oh no.

I stare down at the towel, pretending not to hear them.

"Really?" Margaret says, sounding genuinely upset. "Oh, that's a shame."

"It was back when he lived in New York the first time, oh, eight years ago now I guess. He met someone, they dated for about three months or so, and he told me he wanted to marry her."

My heart is thumping so hard in my chest that my vision actually pulses. I can't just sit here; I have to do something. I turn around and focus my attention on the picnic bags behind us, and start unpacking and organizing them. At least this way if I start crying they won't see.

"The next thing I hear," Cathy continues, "is that they are engaged, and he is on top of the world."

I go through the bags, trying to ignore the lump in my throat.

Oil and vinegar go with the salad; ketchup and mustard go with the buns…

"Then, out of the blue, a few days later he comes to stay with me. He says the wedding is off, he canceled the lease on his apartment, and that he is moving to London! He left the end of that week."

Ice tongs in the cooler…

"What happened between them?" Margaret asks.

"I don't know. He wouldn't talk about it. All I could get from him was that she called it off and didn't want to see him anymore."

"Oh my."

Serving spoons with the dishes…

"He was *devastated!* The few days he was with me he wouldn't talk, he wouldn't eat, and he spent most of his time alone in his room. I was scared to death; I had never seen him like that before."

I tried to read the bottle in my hand through the tears in my eyes.

"Oh, the poor thing. He must have really loved her."

"He did."

"Well, maybe it will all turn out for the best."

"I hope so. Though I can tell you there is nothing I'd like more than to give that girl a piece of my mind."

I want to run away. I want to run all the way back to my apartment, lock the door, and never come out again. Do I need this? Really? Am I seriously not feeling bad enough?

Sensing the conversation has ended, I blink several times to clear away the tears so I can turn back around. I lie down on my towel and close my eyes. Maybe I can sleep this day away. Or maybe I'm already asleep and this is all just some ridiculous nightmare. I know the odds are pretty slim, but hey, a girl can dream.

I do doze off for a while until Margaret's sudden shout jerks me awake.

"Oh!" she cries, pointing out toward the water.

Nick is carrying a limp and very pale Bree.

Oh dear God, my shark fantasy! I killed her!

We run down to the water, and are joined by Derek and Chris, with Rob pulling up the rear. As soon as Nick lays Bree down on the sand, everyone starts loudly talking over each other.

"What happened?"

"Is she breathing?"

"What do we do?"

"Does anyone know CPR?"

"Was she pulled under?"

"Can't she swim?"

"Nick, what happened?"

Nick hears this last question and attempts to answer, though he is out of breath and almost beside himself. "I don't know! She said something cut her, then she started wheezing, and couldn't stand…"

Cut her? I look her over for blood and don't find any. What I do find are red welts in a vein-like pattern up the front the side of her right leg. I recognize it immediately: jellyfish sting. Her trouble breathing must mean she's having a reaction to the venom.

Not as bad as a shark, but still…

I turn and run back to our camp, trying to think. Lisa was stung once when we were kids, and my dad had used his shaving cream on it. I know nobody brought shaving cream with them today, but I remember the doctor saying something about vinegar.

I take the vinegar and the ice tongs from the cooler, grab the first wallet and cell phone I see, and run back down the beach, dialing 9-1-1. As it rings, I find it odd that no one else has thought to call an ambulance. Everyone is still grouped around Bree, yelling over each other, panicking, calling her name, and a slew of other things that aren't going to help in the least.

"*9-1-1, what is your emergency?*" a man on the other line says. However, I reach the group and can barely hear him over the racket.

"Can everyone keep it down for a minute?"

No one hears me.

"QUIET!" I shout, in no mood to be polite. Everyone is instantly silent and staring at me in shock. "Yes," I say into the phone, "I am at Sand Beach, and I have a woman who has been stung by a jellyfish. She seems to be having a reaction. We are going to need an ambulance."

"*Is she conscious?*"

"No." I open the vinegar and pour it over the sting as I talk.

"*How is her breathing?*"

"Labored but audible."

"*And what is your location? Are you near the road or on the beach?*"

"We will be at the road," I tell him, knowing it would be best for the paramedics.

"All right, we have called it in. An ambulance is on the way."

"Thank you."

As I hang up, I look around and see everyone still staring at me, stuck in some sort of stupor. I realize if anything is going to get done, I'm going to need to start giving orders.

"Derek, Chris, Cathy, go pack everything up. Margaret, go and open the backseat of the car and clear out anything that is in there. Nick, Rob, when Margaret's done, you carry Bree up and lay her in the back of the car. Make sure you don't touch her leg."

Everyone obeys immediately and without question. While we wait for Margaret to prepare the car, I take the tongs and begin removing the tentacles from Bree's leg. The vinegar seems to have done its job, and they come off easily. When that's done, I scrape over the sting with a credit card — hence the wallet — to make sure it is totally clean. As soon as I finish, I look up and see Margaret waving us up to the car.

I glance over at Nick, expecting him and Rob to already be lifting her, but he's looking at me with a strange expression in his eyes. Appreciation? Admiration? Whatever it is, it knocks the wind out of me, and had the situation been different, I would be blushing like crazy. However, this is about helping Bree — not impressing Nick. I simply nod in her direction, which seems to snap him out of his train of thought, and he and Rob begin to pick her up.

They make their way up the beach as I grab the vinegar bottle, the phone, the wallet, and the tongs — AHHHH!

GOD DAMN SON OF A BITCH!

I look down at my hand and realize I wasn't careful enough with the tentacles. There must have been one left on the tongs and it's now wrapped around my index and middle fingers. I furiously shake it off and bend down to rinse my hand off in the seawater. Luckily no one is looking my way, so I swallow the pain, bite on my tongue, and run up the beach, leaving the tongs behind.

As I reach the parking area, the ambulance pulls up. The paramedics jump out and administer an injection to Bree, for what I can only assume is the allergic reaction. The next few minutes are a blur of questions, most of which I answer, before they load Bree into the back of the ambulance. Nick immediately speaks up when they ask who will be going with her, and the rest of us begin to pile into the cars to follow them to the hospital.

Just before I climb into the Escalade, I feel a hand on my shoulder. It's Nick.

"Come with me," he says quietly, but with incredible intensity—his blue eyes are practically begging. "Please."

I nod, utterly shocked. "I'm going in the ambulance. We'll meet you there," I call to Margaret in the driver's seat. With that, Nick and I climb through the large red doors, they close behind us, and we take off.

The atmosphere is much calmer as one of the paramedics checks and records Bree's vitals. After that, he starts an IV and then confirms that her allergic reaction is under control. He crawls up to the front cab so that he can call in Bree's information to the hospital, and Nick takes the now-vacated seat next to Bree. He looks horrible: pale, sweaty, and obviously sick with worry. But of course he would be; they were practically dating. I turn my head and swallow the lump in my throat. As ridiculous as it is, I feel so guilty. Not twenty minutes before the accident, I'd wished her harm. Well, maybe not wished it per se, but close enough.

And why? Because I was jealous of her relationship with a man I had no claim over? Because I resented the fact that they could be happy together? Isn't that what I should want? I love them both; shouldn't I want them to be happy, even if it is with each other?

After a few minutes of self-loathing, I hear Nick sigh as he leans back against the ambulance wall and stares off into space. I notice something else in his expression. Something beyond the worry—guilt? Of course. It was his suggestion to go swimming, so he's going to blame himself for anything that happens during said suggestion, even though I was actually the one mentally spouting voodoo curses. That would be just like him. He closes his eyes, and I feel so bad for him that I want to cry. He just looks so young and helpless. I have to fight the urge to throw my arms around his neck and assure him that everything will be all right.

"Jules?" he says quietly without opening his eyes.

"Hmm?" Just hearing him say my name sends a bolt of lightning though me, and I struggle not to seem as overwhelmed as I am. This is the first time he's spoken directly to me since our short hello back in New York.

He turns toward me with such a powerful look in his eyes that my throat constricts and it takes everything in me to meet them and not drop mine to the floor. "You really—"

"Okay, guys," the paramedic cuts in, "we're here. You two are going to have to get out first so we can pull the stretcher out."

No, damn you! Go away! I really… what?

The back doors open and Nick and I hop down, and once Bree is pulled out, we follow the stretcher into the ER.

The moment is lost.

A half hour later, we are in one of the beige-walled ER triage rooms, and I feel like the proverbial third wheel. Nick sits beside Bree, holding her hand, and I'm sitting over by the door in the only other chair in the room. Everyone else had followed us to the hospital, and arrived just after we did. They sat in the waiting room for a while, but once it was determined that Bree was doing well and would be able to leave in a few hours, they decided to go back to the house and wait there. They left us a car, and told us to call with updates.

Bree woke up shortly after we got here, and she and Nick have been talking almost nonstop ever since. Their conversation consists of Nick asking her how she is, if her leg hurts, if there is anything he can do, telling her how sorry he is, then starting all over again from the top. Bree actually did seem comfortable enough, which was most likely due to the massive amount of numbing cream they put on her leg when we arrived. On the other hand, my fingers are stinging like a bitch, and have grown to the size of sausages. I probably could get some cream if I speak up, but I am not about to make a fuss over something so small. I can deal.

A moment later the doctor comes in. "Well, Miss St. Charles, how are you feeling?"

"All right," she answers with a smile.

"I'm going to have the two of you step out to the waiting area for a few minutes while I examine her. I'll come to get you when I've finished," he says, looking at Nick and me.

Nick takes a last look at Bree, squeezes her hand, and we walk down to the waiting area in silence. There are only a few other people there, and we find a small couch on the far side of the room that no one is using. Nick all but collapses on it, leans his elbows on his knees, and rests his face in his hands. I sit next to him and again feel the overwhelming need to comfort him, though I'm not entirely sure how to do it. As opposed to telling him the reason this was all my fault, and looking about as crazy as the day is long, I decide to go in another direction.

"It's not your fault you know," I whisper. I can't let him continue to torture himself.

He doesn't move for a minute, then slowly leans back against the couch and lets his hands fall in his lap. "Yes it is," he answers just as quietly. "I called her out there. She was talking with Chris nowhere near me. She came because I asked her to."

"That doesn't make it your fault."

"She wouldn't have been out there if it wasn't for me. Besides, it was my idea to swim in the first place."

"We were at the beach. I think the general idea was to go in the water. Someone else would have suggested it if you hadn't."

"I was in deeper water, I should have…"

"It doesn't matter where you were," I say, taking advantage of his pause. "Jellyfish travel in huge groups; there were probably hundreds out there. We were all going to be in the water at some point today, so someone was bound to get stung. None of that is your fault. Bree is a big girl, and she wouldn't have gone out to you if she didn't want to."

We lapse into silence, but he does seem to relax a little.

"Thank you," he says after a few moments. I glance at him, and he looks steadily back at me. "For today, I mean," he says, ashamed. "You were amazing. We were all useless, and you…you were incredible. How did you know what to do?"

"Lisa was stung once when we were kids. I remembered my dad using his shaving cream on it. I knew no one had that, but I remembered her doctor saying something about vinegar. The rest, cleaning it and all, was the same."

Even as I'm talking, I realize how strange this is. For the first time, there is no weirdness between us. We're actually having a normal conversation, with no awkwardness or embarrassment. I expect no less from him, as I'm more than aware he's over the whole "us" thing, but for me, this is new. New, and unbelievably nice.

"Well, you were great. I don't know what we would have done. Thank you." He reaches out and takes my left hand in his, giving it a gentle squeeze. My heart jumps.

Oh God, I love him, I love him, I love him…

Okay, weirdness back, awkwardness back, embarrassment back.

I look down at the floor as my cheeks begin to flame, and I'm acutely aware of the fact that I have seen this man naked. But before I can thoroughly embarrass myself, the doctor appears. Nick sees him and stands, letting go of my hand.

"How is she?" he asks.

"She will be just fine. Who cleaned her leg? Do you know what they used?"

"I did," I say quietly. "It was vinegar."

"Oh, it was you? Very well done. So well in fact, that had it not been for her reaction, she would not have even needed to be brought in at all."

"Thank you," I say, as I catch Nick looking at me out of the corner of my eye. What's that expression in his eyes? It looks like — but it can't be — affection?

Affection?

"She's dressing now," the doctor continues. "I have given…" He stops suddenly, having caught sight of something. My hand.

Shit!

"Why didn't you say anything?" he asks me with a disapproving look.

"What?" Nick asks, looking back and forth between us, confused.

"Did it happen when you were cleaning Miss St. Charles?"

"Yes," I say, timidly. No use in denying it now.

I glance over to Nick and see the change in his face as he finally sees my hand. "Jules!" he says under his breath, glaring at me.

Even when he's mad it sounds beautiful.

"Here." The doctor hands me a tube of something and gauze from his pocket. "Put this on it, and wrap it. You can get tape from the reception desk. The swelling should go down by tomorrow."

"Th—"

"Thank you," Nick says, cutting me off and taking the tube and gauze from the doctor.

"Miss St. Charles will be out in a moment. I have given her a prescription, and she will be walking with a cane for a day or two, until the swelling goes down. Otherwise, she is ready to go."

Nick thanks him again, and shakes his hand. Once he is gone I turn to Nick. "It's really not a big deal—"

"Sit," he commands, with a still pissed off "don't even try it" look in his eye.

I sink down to the couch, giving up. He sits next to me, takes my hand carefully in his, and begins to dress my fingers. "You should have said something," he says, with less anger and more worry as he sees my fingers close up.

I don't answer. I stare quietly down at his work, never once lifting my eyes to his face. I'm afraid if I do, I'll cry. As he gently cares for my sting, something I have avoided for a very long time becomes painfully evident—how much I've missed him. I've been pushing the feeling away for so long, that the open realization of it is almost more than I can handle.

He finishes my hand, and places it gently in my lap. I raise my eyes and they lock with his; for a moment I almost can't believe what I see. It's as if all my current emotions are there staring back at me: longing, pain, affection, hope, *everything*. It stops my breath and makes my pulse race. Could this possibly be real? Deep down I know it can't be, but my heart wants to believe it is.

Over his shoulder, I see Bree come around the corner and I reluctantly break our gaze to greet her. Nick rushes over to her side while I drag behind in a daze. We help Bree out to the car, and Nick hands me the keys. I climb in behind the wheel, while Nick helps Bree into the back where there is more room, and takes a seat next to her. I glance back at them in the rearview mirror before pulling out, but for the first time, I don't feel the stab of jealousy I normally do every time they touch. I don't need to, because…because I saw something.

I don't know what, but it was there—in his eyes. My head is still spinning, and I don't care how impossible it is. All I know, is it couldn't have been my imagination. It was real. I know it was.

9

It's quarter to one, and I'm unable to sleep for the second night in a row. At this rate, I may need surgery to get rid of the bags under my eyes.

Today, as I'd expected, had been a total disaster in almost every way. I got to watch Bree and Nick hold hands and frolic in the waves, heard a firsthand account of how much I had hurt Nick all those years ago, got stung by a jellyfish, and Bree almost died due to an allergy she had no idea she had.

Oh yeah, what a great day.

Though oddly enough, none of those events are what's keeping me awake. Through all the chaos and mayhem, something else had happened. Something that I had honestly never thought would.

Nick and I talked.

Talked like regular people, alone, just the two of us. Talked without any awkwardness or tension. More than that, we had shared something. Something unspoken, but powerful. Something communicated only through his eyes. It's that nameless, obscure, emotional thing that is currently raging an all-out war in my head.

This mental war is basically the familiar forces of practicality and sensibility battling it out with the evil empire of emotion. My practical and sensible side knows that anything I saw in Nick's eyes today was completely my imagination. I know that I am over analyzing, and turning the whole situation into something it isn't. I'm making it what I want it to be, simple as that.

He was grateful for my help and is a compassionate person. No less than that, but certainly no more.

Unfortunately, no matter how many times I try to make that case, my emotions won't listen. All they can think about is the tenderness he used caring for my hand, when he easily could have left me to wrap it myself. Or the way he had practically begged me to come with him in the ambulance. "Come with *me*," he had said, not "Come with *us*." He wanted me there for his sake, not Bree's. That *had* to mean something, didn't it? People don't beg strangers for comfort during difficult times; they turn to people they trust. He could have just as easily asked Derek or Cathy to go with him, but he didn't. He asked me.

I always listen to my practical, sensible side, but for some reason, I just can't make my mind obey tonight. Doesn't *that* mean something? It has to! I can't just ignore all these signs; this could be fate! Maybe deep down, somewhere inside me, there is a part that knows that my sensible side is wrong, so…

Sigh. All right, calm down.

I take a deep breath and sit up slowly, rubbing my face with my hands. I pull my legs up under me, staring out the window into the night sky and wondering idly if the moon is full, as it seems unusually bright outside. After another deep breath, I let out a long sigh.

Okay, what am I saying here? Am I actually suggesting that Nick still has feelings for me? After all, it's easy to talk about abstract things like a look, or a gesture, but when I actually think about it like that, the whole thing becomes almost absurd.

For God's sake, I dumped the man flat, broke his heart, and betrayed his faith! He has no reason to feel anything for me! *I* should be the one left to suffer with feelings like this the rest of my life, not him! He is totally innocent in all this! He owes me nothing! And now, when he has moved on — something that I will obviously never be able to do — I feel the need to drag up the past, simply because of a few harmless little details! And, if we're being realistic, these details mean nothing at all.

Did he ask me to come in the ambulance with him? Yes. Was that because he felt some emotional need for me? Probably not. More likely he wanted me there because I had been the only one who was of any help during the initial panic, and he was worried he wouldn't have been able to answer all of the questions the paramedics might have asked.

Did he wrap my hand? Yes. Would he have done the same for anyone else? Probably. He obviously didn't like seeing me hurt, but that's his nature. He would have done the same for Margaret, or Cathy, or anyone else in my place.

Was there actually affection for me in his eyes? Probably. Was it love, or anything even remotely close? Probably not. Far more likely it was appreciation mixed with emotional exhaustion, which could be confused for a lot of things. Especially when the observer is incredibly biased.

But still…what if…

Ugh!

I throw the covers back in a frustrated huff, get out of bed, and storm over to the window. Why does this have to be so hard? Why can't I have a little help? Where's *my* fairy godmother? Bree seems to get one, so where's mine? Not the creepy bingo lady my subconscious seems to think I deserve, but a real one. I needed her to slap some sense into me eight years ago, but she didn't show. Where's the bib-bity bobbity do-over for all the schmucks like me who botched it up the first time around because we were on our own? That's what a fairy godmother is supposed to do, right? She shows up when you hit rock bottom, and gives you everything you need to "land your man." She might not hand you everything on a silver platter, but it's her job to give you the proper tools, if you will.

Take Cinderella. She just happened to need a shower, some pumps, and a chauffeur—which wouldn't do me a whole lot of good right now—but I'm sure it's a customizable program. All *I* need is a nudge in the right direction, or maybe the ability to read minds for an hour or so. Come on, after Cinder-needy-ella, is that really too much to ask?

I cross my arms with a groan and lean my forehead against the glass. What's the use? No one is coming to help me. No happy grandma with wings, no wand-wielding fairy, not even the boorish, beehived harpy from my dream. Scary as that last one was, even I can admit she had a point: say my fairy godmother did pop up and tell me exactly what to do—would I trust her? Honestly, probably not. Let's not forget, I *did* have a fairy godmother eight years ago. I gave Lisa the job, whether or not she realized it, and her advice pretty much ruined my life. Unintentionally of course, but does that really matter? If I'd followed my own instincts and not asked for help, I wouldn't be in this situation.

So, what then? Is the answer to follow my own instincts? Currently I have two sets, and they are still at war. It would be easy to fall back on my usual choice of practicality and sense, but there is another factor here. What if he really *does* still have feelings for me?

I know, I know, just hear me out.

Ever since my time with Nick, I've lapsed into a life of the practical, the sure, the sensible, and the boring. It was never a conscious decision per se; I just gradually started to shy away from anything risky or passion-driven, because those were the things that could ultimately lead to more pain. However, there was one conscious decision I did make, and that was to never allow what happened with Nick to happen to me again. To never again let something that wonderful slip through my fingers due to my own indecision or stupidity. Up until now, the answer had been simple: don't ever want anything that much again. But this is *Nick*. I will always want him, and always love him. There is nothing I can do about that—and God knows I've tried. So, what if I'm right and he does still have feelings for me? Can I really just ignore it all and walk away? Can I allow myself to blow what could be a second chance? I promised myself I never would, though promises like that are easy to make when you don't actually think you'll ever have to worry about keeping them.

If only there's some sort of sign…

No sooner does that thought cross my mind than something outside catches my eye. I look down to see a figure sitting on the stone railing of the steps leading off the porch. Middle of the night, two stories up, and over fifty feet away and still I have no problem seeing that it's Nick. He's facing away from me, looking out over the yard, chin resting in his hand.

All my thoughts and worries from a moment ago vanish as I look down on him. This is the first time since arriving that I have been able to simply watch him without having to worry about being caught and embarrassed. It's a strangely liberating feeling. The longer I watch, however, I'm more certain that something is bothering him. It may seem strange considering the physical distance between us, but for me it's as clear as if he were sitting next to me. True, I can't see his face, but the way his shoulders are hunched—not to mention the late hour—tells me more than his face ever could.

He's lonely.

An unexpected wave of emotion comes over me as I feel a strange connection to him. He has his sister and brother-in-law and his friends, and probably countless others I'm not even aware of—but he's somehow as alone as I am.

With that realization comes another: I have to do it. I have to take the leap.

As he hops off the rail and walks back into the house, I feel like an invisible weight has been lifted off my shoulders. I've made the decision; the war is over. Emotion has won the battle. I'm going to take a risk, and chance my happiness. I have to. If I don't, I will always regret it.

I go back to bed and lie on my back, staring up at the ceiling. Now I can actually do some constructive thinking. My first thought is that I need to strap on a pair of wings this time. Disturbing as the creepy godmother of my dream had been, she had a point: I have to take advantage of the opportunity I've been given and stop waiting for my problems to fix themselves. If someone is going to mess up my life, it might as well be me.

Suddenly, I feel empowered, like nothing can take me down. Almost like I can walk down the hall and knock on his door, right now!

On second thought, maybe not the best idea.

First things first—I need a plan. A *new* one, actually. What is this, number three now? Oh well. Love is a process, not a science.

I should probably start off slow, and take the less-is-more approach. There's no need to make this more embarrassing than it needs to be. I'll start out observing, to see if his demeanor toward me has changed at all. Shouldn't be hard to pick up on; his overall behavior has been the textbook definition of passive. I'll wait for a change in *him*. If I don't see one, I'll abandon the whole idea. Moreover, I'll strictly stick to observing without analyzing. Analyzing can get way out of hand, and that will lead to trouble. I'll simply gather up observations, and then systematically analyze them as a whole.

Luckily, I'll have all day tomorrow to focus on my observations without having to worry about anything work related which, ironically, is all thanks to Nick. When we got back today, he absolutely insisted we push back the inspections and any other work until at least Tuesday, to give Bree some time to heal.

My stomach hits the floor. Bree.

Damn! I'd forgotten all about her. All about *them*.

I start to panic as practicality and sense rear up, threatening to rip off my wings and crush my new plan before it even gets off the ground.

Okay, calm down. I may have made more out of situations than there really is. Maybe that's true of the whole Bree and Nick thing too. Maybe in this case, instead of seeing only what I want to see, I am seeing only what I *don't* want to see. It's possible, right? I'm sure mental blocks don't just work in one direction.

Have Nick and Bree been flirting? Yes. Has it been enough to make the people around them take notice? Yes again, but not to a horrible extent. Not to the point where people don't want to be around them, or feel annoyed or nauseated by their presences. Well, other than me, but that is obviously a special circumstance.

Now that I think about it, maybe it hasn't been flirting at all. They have been together a lot and seem to enjoy each other's company, but Nick is a friendly, charming guy, and who else is there for him to turn his attentions to? Derek, Rob, and Chris are guys, Cathy is his sister, Margaret is much too old for him, so who's left? Other than me, Bree is the only one. Why wouldn't he show her special atten-tion? She is great company. I'm sure, had I not been so engrossed in my thoughts, I would have realized that Nick hasn't been paying any more attention to Bree than he has Margaret or Cathy. I've just been so focused on him and Bree, considering her to be my only—for lack of a better word—competition, that I didn't notice.

I almost laugh at myself. How stupid can I be? There's nothing between them at all! What have I been thinking? Have I really been letting my imagination run that wild? I was even dreaming about their *kids* for God's sake!

I roll over, feeling much better and utterly exhausted. This will work. It has to. Tomorrow will be the beginning of a new Julia. A risk taking, future making, magic wand-waving chick, who is done waiting around for her life to fix itself.

Julia Lee Basham: Personal Fairy Godmother.

An image of myself in a sparkly dress and wings pops into my head just before I fall sleep.

10

The next morning is dreary and overcast, but I couldn't care less. This is the first day of my new life. A life where I take the reins, make my own curfews—no "by the stroke of midnight" for me, thanks—and make my own dreams come true. I can't remember the last time I felt this good. It's like there's been this ominous dark cloud made up of regret, self-loathing, mundane aspirations, and other random depressing crap floating over my head for years, and this morning it's finally gone, leaving me with my first glimpse of clear blue skies. The sun is bright, the birds are chirping, and there's nothing but proverbial clear skies ahead.

Okay, so maybe I'm exaggerating a little. Don't get me wrong; I'm confident in my new plan, and I do feel liberated and excited, but that doesn't mean there are absolutely no doubts in my mind. It's funny how an idea can seem totally flawless at night, while the next morning…not so much. Maybe it has something to do with the sun; I'm not sure. All I know, is I am definitely more nervous about all this than I was at one in the morning. However, doubts or no doubts, I'm not going to let anything sway my decision. My happiness is up for the taking, and I plan on doing just that. This fairy godmother is ready to roll!

I start to get ready, and realize I still have the bandage from yesterday on my hand. I take it off and look at my sting for the first time since the ER waiting room. Not bad. The swelling is almost gone, and the sting itself has faded to a dull pink. At any rate, I don't think anyone will notice. I brush my hair, throw my clothes on, and make my way down the hall to Bree's room.

I knock lightly on her door. "It's Julia."

"Come in!" she calls. It almost sounds like she's laughing.

I open the door to find her sitting on the seat of her bay window with…Chris?

"Good morning," I say, slightly surprised. Nick seems to have left her side for a moment, which is a nice change of pace. "I guess you don't need help down to breakfast after all." I smile at Chris who nods a hello.

"Nick had to go out this morning, and he asked Chris to look after me while he's gone."

Ah.

"How are you feeling?" I glance at her leg. "It looks like some of the swelling has gone down."

"It has." She pulls her pant leg up a bit. "It feels much better. Hurts to the touch and it's hard to walk, but otherwise the pain is almost gone."

"Good," I say with a smile, knowing they gave her some serious painkillers.

"Shall we go down?" Chris asks, standing. He turns to Bree and helps her up, while I get her cane from the foot of the bed.

"Just let me use the restroom first." Bree steadies herself and hobbles toward the bathroom.

"Do you need help?" I ask, pretending not to notice Chris blush at the idea of me helping Bree pee.

"No, I think I can handle it. I'll call if I need you."

Chris and I both take a seat on the edge of the bed.

After a moment, he asks, "How's your hand?"

I look up startled. "How did you know about that?"

"Nick told me last night."

Nick was talking about me? Why? Where was I? Was he concerned? Does concern equal feeling? Okay, calm down. Remember, no analyzing, just observing.

"Oh, it's fine," I say, forcing myself back to the conversation. "The cream the doctor gave me was good stuff." I hold out my hand for him to see. "It doesn't even hurt anymore," I add, just to make sure he didn't feel the need to tell anyone else about it. Though with Chris, that was a shallow worry.

"You were really great yesterday on the beach. We were really lucky you were there."

"Thanks, but it was no biggie. My sister was stung once when we were on vacation as kids, and I remembered what to do. So how did you get put on babysitting duty?" I grin, trying to change the subject.

"I offered. Nick and Derek were on their way out this morning when I heard Nick saying how bad he felt leaving with Bree hurt. I told him I would keep her company until he got back. I think he feels really bad about all this."

We hear the toilet flush, and a few moments later Bree comes limping out. "Okay, let's go!"

As we help Bree down the stairs, I can't help but smile to myself. Chris has unwittingly told me exactly what I wanted to hear. One, that Nick had spoken — and thereby was thinking — of me yesterday, and two, he confirmed that Nick felt guilty about the incident. Granted I already knew that, but it only proved that his current attentions toward Bree were guilt, and not romantically driven.

Yay!

When we get downstairs, we find Derek in the main hall, coming from the direction of the kitchen.

"You're back? That was fast," Chris says.

"Yeah, the office was closed. We brought coffee though." Derek motions toward the kitchen, then turns to Bree with a smirk. "How are you feeling, hop-along?"

"Good, just a little sore. Nothing I can't handle."

"Good to hear. You should probably sit though. Don't let me stop you."

"Aren't you coming?" Bree asks, as he continues toward the front door.

"Just a few things to get from the car. I'll be back in a minute."

"You need help?" Chris asks.

"You help Bree to the kitchen. I'll help him," I say, turning and following Derek outside.

One of the cars is pulled up to the front of the house, and I see several bags across the backseat.

"Thanks," he says, handing a few of the bags to me.

"No problem."

"So, hot chocolate over coffee?"

"What?"

"Your drink order. No offense, but I always assumed that Starbucks only carried hot chocolate for kids."

What the hell is he talking about?

"Okay, you've lost me…"

"When Nick ordered the drinks this morning, there was a peppermint hot chocolate. I asked whose it was, and he said it was yours. Wasn't it?"

"Oh…yes, sorry. You caught me off guard, so I didn't follow. Yep, that's mine."

Oh my God…he remembered my drink.

I haven't even seen him since last night. He never asked me what I wanted, and he remembered! It is completely ridiculous that this little detail could make me so happy, but it does! He remembered! As I follow Derek back into the house, fuzzy butterflies are fluttering in my chest. We file into the kitchen and find everyone there, talking and sipping their drinks. I place the bags on the far counter, and turn my attention to the to-go drink trays sitting on the table. There is only one drink left, a grande peppermint hot chocolate. I grin and bite my lip as I feel my cheeks go red. I take a slow sip immediately as I turn and sit at the table, so at least my hands and the cup are covering half of my face. I quietly, listening to the conversations going on around me, and feeling better and better about my new plan. Maybe it's only because I'm consciously looking, but I can already see a definite change in Nick. Before I can think too much into it however, I stop myself. No analyzing, that was the rule. I'll analyze later. For now I just have to sit back, observe, and enjoy my peppermint hot chocolate.

I climb into bed that night, totally and completely on a love high. You heard me, love high. The kind of blissful, floaty happiness that radiates from every inch of you. You can feel it in your eyes, on your skin, in your smile—everywhere.

Today had been wonderful. It was the first day since I found out Nick was to become our new client that I have been totally relaxed.

Something was different. He was different. I was comfortable being in the same house with him. I didn't have to fear meeting him in the hallway or getting stuck next to him in a group. He was friendly. Granted he's been nothing but wonderful with everyone else all along, but not with me. With me he had been aloof and passive, where today he was warm and sociable. Oh, yes, there was definitely a change.

That change is what has put me in an amazing mood. That change is what made up my mind to talk to him tomorrow. That change is the very best thing of all, because it proves I was right yesterday. There *had* been something in his eyes, it *wasn't* all in my head, and this new, risk taking fairy godmothering plan *was* the right decision to make.

Risky, emotional instinct: 1

Boring, risk-less security: 0

Yay!

The only thing left to do now is figure out how this confrontation was actually going to happen. First things first, I will need to get him alone. Luckily, Margaret has taken care of that one for me; she has already asked Nick to meet her in the library after breakfast tomorrow to go over some estimates with her. All I have to do is beat her there and I can steal a few minutes with him. Even if I don't have time to say everything I would like to right then, I can at least ask to talk to him alone later in the day. Then I can tell him how sorry I am, how wrong I was, and so on. I don't want to plan out a speech exactly; it will only sound contrived and forced, when it should be heartfelt and natural. I'll leave it to spontaneity. After all, risk and emotion have gotten me this far; no need to stop now.

Before I even realize I have fallen asleep, my alarm wakes me up. The weather is just as horrible as it was yesterday, with the added pleasure of rain. For a split second I wonder if the weather could possibly be a bad sign, but I squash those thoughts immediately. No thinking like that allowed in my new life. Maybe a few days ago, but not now. Now I make my own luck.

Breakfast is already started by the time I make my way down to the kitchen. The typical morning spread of bagels, fruit, doughnuts, and coffee is laid out on the island, and everyone is sitting, eating, chatting, and enjoying the morning. I slowly make my way over to the food, grab a jelly doughnut and a coffee, all the while casually scanning the room for Nick. I don't find him, but I do see Margaret sitting alone in the corner, going through some paper work. Nick is probably already in the library waiting for her.

My heart starts to hammer in my chest as I realize this is it. This is the chance I need. I set my coffee and doughnut down on the counter while my feet take me out of the kitchen and toward the library before I'm even aware of it. As the door to the library comes into sight, I begin to panic. Can I really do this? What if he laughs at me?

No! Don't wuss out! This is the plan, no backing out now!

My hand is frozen on the library door handle, and I can't seem to will it to move. Suddenly, I hear a voice approaching the door from the other side. My heart leaps to my throat and I take off running down the hall, through the foyer, and out the front door before even taking a breath. My heart pounds a mile a minute, and I stagger over to one of the huge white columns marking the main entry to the manor and slump against it.

Great. Just great.

I decide to take control, I make a plan, then when the perfect time comes to follow through, I run away like a spooked rabbit! I punch the column with a growl, thoroughly frustrated with myself.

The rain seems to have let up for the time being, so I slowly walk down the steps to the driveway, taking a few deep breaths of the cool damp air. So much for my unwavering commitment to my new philosophy on life! One scare, and I'm right back where I started! God, what if he *saw* me!

I make my way around the house, staring at the ground, trying to come up with a new plan. Or better yet, come up with a way to salvage the old plan. As lame as that last move was, it doesn't mean that I have to give up altogether. I can go back to the house a little later and try to catch him after his meeting with Margaret. Or maybe I could get him alone for a minute or two later tonight after dinner. Sure, why not. There are still plenty of opportunities. The real question is how do I keep myself from losing my nerve again once another opening arrives? As much as I hate to admit it, the anti-godmother from my dream was right about one thing: I'm not the best at taking advantage of the opportunities that are given to me.

Lost in my thoughts, I turn onto the path that leads around the back, where there is a small bench tucked against the side of the house—basically somewhere I can sit and hide for a while. I turn the corner, look up and stop short, heart once again in my throat.

Nick.

He's sitting causally, eyes closed, in the very spot I was making for, leaning back against the wall of the house. His arms are crossed across his chest and shirt, which is the same ice-blue color as his eyes. A slight breeze ruffles his dark hair and he sighs softly, almost as if he's sleeping.

God, he is beautiful!

His eyes open suddenly.

"I-I'm sorry," I half whisper, choking over the dry patch in my throat. I start to back away. "I didn't know anyone was…I'm sorry."

"No, no, it's fine." He sits up, looking a bit awkward.

For what seems like the hundredth time this trip, I am waging an internal war. Part of me—the old safe and boring, duck and cover, no-risks-no-gains Julia—wants to run. A second and much louder part of me that still has an ounce of pride left refuses to take off like a wimp twice in the same day. However, there is a third part of me—my recently discovered fairy godmother part—that tells me that this is my chance. More than a chance: it's a sign. I am *supposed* to talk to him. The situation couldn't be more perfect—we're alone, hidden away with no chance of being overheard or interrupted, every aspect of this meeting practically custom designed for my plan.

So why can't I speak?

All I seem to be able to do is stand and stare, listening to the voice in my—

"Do you like it?" Nick asks, throwing me off guard. He looks down at the ground in front of him, still sitting on the bench.

"Like…what?" I ask confused, but trying not to seem rattled.

"This." He glances around him. "The house, all of it. Do you like it?" Something about the personal tone in his voice gives me a warm feeling in my chest. He is asking me, not as a member of his financial team, but as someone he trusts. As a friend.

"It's amazing," I answer timidly. "Don't you?"

"Sure. I mean I do, but it's…I guess it's not what I thought it would be."

There is a sad undertone to his voice that draws me toward him. "What did you expect?" I sit down on the other end of the bench a few feet away from him.

"I don't know." He sighs, looking up to meet my eyes. After a pause so long that I think he won't say any more, he continues. "My parents were married here. They used to talk all the time about what a wonderful place it was. How beautiful it was in the fall. How it was almost its own world being so far out of the way from everything else. How there was no other place like it anywhere they'd ever been. Cathy and I used to dream about coming here to Marston when we were kids. After years of listening to our parents talk about it, we'd built it up in our heads to be this amazing place, like something out of a movie." He stands and begins to absently pace slowly back and forth. "Mom used to tell us that she and Dad would take us one day. That sort of became our dream. That one perfect place that we would go *one day*. For most kids it's Disney World or Hawaii, but for Cathy and me—" he gestures around him "—this was it. Silly as it sounds, for us this was better than Disney World because it could really happen. Disney World was impossible for people like us with no money, but here…for some reason it seemed accessible, you know? Like it was more than just a dream because it was actually within reach." He stops pacing and leans against the wall of the house with a sigh. "I don't know what I was thinking. It's just not at all the way I pictured it, but at the same time, I don't know for sure what it was that I pictured. Somehow still it's disappointing. I know that doesn't make any sense…"

He seems so sad and let down that it takes everything in me not to run over to him, throw my arms around his neck, and tell him that it's okay. That everything will be all right. I know him well enough to see that he needs it, but I could very possibly be the last person he would want affection from, so I stay where I am.

"It does make sense," I assure him quietly. "I understand. It's like…going back to Chuck E. Cheese's as an adult." He chuckles at my analogy while I look down at my hands to hide my blush. "You expect it to be just as great as you remember it being as a kid, but it never is. The games that used to be so much fun are sort of lame, the crawl-through tubes that used to be huge now only come up to your shoulders, the ball pit that was the size of an ocean is really about as big as a bathtub…It almost makes you wonder why you ever thought it was so great to begin with. It's disappointing, but in the end it doesn't matter. What matters are the memories. The ball pit was an ocean when we were kids and we needed it to be. We needed to have a place with amazing games and gigantic tubes to dream about at night and look forward to for birthdays and special occasions. That's what Marston is for you. Coming here and seeing that maybe it's not so different from anywhere else doesn't have to change what it's meant to you. This place was amazing and wonderful and perfect when you needed it to be, and you'll always have that." I pause a moment before asking, "Do you still see yourself living here?"

"No," he says, staring at the wall of the house without really seeing it. "Honestly, I don't think I ever did." He turns to me and runs a frustrated hand through his hair. "But I feel like if I don't take it I'm…I don't know…giving up on…something."

"Your parents." It isn't a question; I can see that's what he means. It's clear to me because I know him. Eight years or not—I know this man. His only response is to bow his head. "Just because you don't see yourself living here doesn't mean you have to give up on it altogether. There are ways to honor the memory without making yourself unhappy. You can still buy it, but instead of moving in, why not rent it out for weddings? Let other people get married here. That way, they'll have somewhere special and amazing and perfect to tell their kids about."

There is a long pause, which makes me wonder if he's still listening to me. I glance up to see he is standing completely still, arms crossed, looking down. "How do you always know what to say?" he asks me suddenly, lifting his head to meet my gaze with eyes so wistful and tender that it takes my breath away. He takes the four steps separating us, and sits down next to me. The smell of his aftershave gives me goose bumps. He lifts his hand and gently places it on my upper arm. "Thank you." His voice is only a rough whisper.

My heart rate jumps through the roof as I look in his eyes and realize…

He's going to kiss me!

It doesn't seem possible, but I can just tell. Any second now, he's going to lean in and—

"Nick!"

Nick drops his hand to his side and stands as we both turn to see Derek coming around the corner of the house.

Damn!

"There you are," he says to Nick, then nods in my direction. "Hey, Julia." Turning back to Nick he says, "Margaret is looking for you."

"Right, thanks," he says, then looks back at me. "I've got to—"

"Sure," I say, cutting him off.

As though he doesn't know what else to say, he turns and follows Derek back toward the front of the house, leaving me on the wall in an emotional stupor.

Yes.

Yes!

He wanted to kiss me, I can feel it!

I was right!

This really is going to work!

It is unbelievable! I feel like I'm going to float off the ground, like nothing will ever bother me again. All is well with the whole world.

We talked. *Really* talked, just like we used to. It was so wonderful just to be needed by him again, even in this small way. To be appreciated. To be able to help. It's such a little thing, but at the same time, so huge!

Huge and exactly the confirmation that I need—he wants me, too!

I'm dying to talk to him. Itching to run up to the house and tell him everything I had planned to tell him this morning. But, due to my poor planning, I'll have to wait until after his meeting with Margaret. Though even that can't wipe the smile from my face. I'm on cloud nine!

I force myself to wait all of fifteen minutes before I make my way back into the house. I had planned on twenty but the rain started up again, giving me an excuse to go in early. I'm practically skipping by the time I get to the front door. Once inside, I start to make my way up to my room to freshen up and kill a few more minutes, when I see Margaret walking down to our temporary office.

"Margaret?"

"Oh, hello, Julia," she says, looking up from the document she is reading.

"I thought you had a meeting with Mr. Kerkley."

"We just finished."

"Oh." My pulse suddenly races. "Is he still in the library?"

"I believe so." She steps into the office, lost in her document once again.

I turn on my heel and head straight to the library. As the door comes into sight, my hands begin to tremble, but I am committed. I reach out and grab the door handle, this time with a strange combination of fear and pride. The fear part is obvious, but the pride is somewhat unexpected. It is a strange moment to realize I'm proud of myself, but I am. I'm proud that I have taken matters into my own hands, taking charge, going after what I want, and not running away.

You never expect the turning points in your life to be obvious to you until after they've happened, but I can tell this moment is an exception. This is my turning point. This is the beginning of the rest of my life.

I take a deep breath, turn the handle, open the door, and there is Nick…

…and Bree…

…and they are kissing.

B etween the rain hammering down on the windshield and the
tears blurring my vision, I can barely make out the road in front
of me. Combine that with the fact that I'm going entirely too fast
in extremely hazardous weather, and it's clear that there's a very real
possibility this could end badly. Thank God that Susan's Hybrid
Escape has a GPS, or I would be lost somewhere in the woods, two
states over by now.

Escape. How appropriate.

The irony of the car's name might have been amusing if I wasn't
currently busy berating and despising myself.

Idiot, *idiot, IDIOT!*

They were kissing.

Kissing!

I'm so stupid! What the hell have I been thinking! I knew he had
feelings for Bree; I had seen it from the start. All the signs were there,
staring me in the face, and instead of accepting them for what they were,
I spent my time explaining them away. I could have tried to deal with the
situation, but instead I dug myself into an emotional hole. What the hell
was I thinking? "This is going so well." "He is more friendly." "He needed
me." "He wanted to kiss me." Blah, blah, blah…I'd talked myself into
believing there was a change in Nick, when I couldn't have been more
wrong. It wasn't a change in Nick. I was the one who'd changed! I wasn't
afraid of him anymore, so he *seemed* friendlier. He needed someone to
talk to and I was the first sap to come around the corner, so it *seemed*

like he needed me. I was more comfortable around him, so he *seemed* more comfortable around me. I was *projecting*, for God's sake!

I squeeze the steering wheel and try not to grind my teeth. Eight years! He had eight years to build a life, get married, have kids, and all that other crap, but no! He has to wait and do it all *right in front of me!* He couldn't have planned a better revenge if he'd tried. And of course, leave it to me to make it ten times worse than it needs to be.

Why did I even come on this stupid trip? I'm sure I could have gotten out of it. How could I have possibly thought this would end well? I practically set myself up for disaster.

God damned, blind, stupid idiot...

My internal scolding is cut short by my phone buzzing on the passenger seat. I quickly wipe the tears off my face, grab my headset, and answer the call.

"Hey, Susan." She must have gotten my message.

"Hi! So you are on your way?"

"Yep. GPS says I should be there around four o'clock. Is that okay?"

"Of course! We're cooking out by the pool tonight. You can wear your new suit!"

"Great," I say, trying to match her enthusiasm and failing miserably.

There's a pause on the other end. "Oh no, what's wrong?"

"It's nothing. Same old," I tell her, hoping she will understand without further explanation. If I go into it now, I'll just end up blubbering into the phone and scaring the hell out of her. "I'll tell you about it later."

"Oh, okay. Well, drive safe, and I'll see you in a few hours. Call if you have any trouble."

"Will do. See you then."

I toss my phone back on the seat and take a deep breath. Shameful and lame as it is to run away like this, I have to admit it feels really good. I know it's the definitive wrong thing to do in regard to your problems, but honestly I don't think I could have stayed in that house for three more days without completely losing it. Due to our rescheduling all of Monday's inspections, Margaret and Bree would now have to stay until Friday, and I would definitely have gone crazy by then. Luckily, I've never been the sort of person to miss work or slack off in any way, so when I went to Margaret immediately after "the sighting" and told her I needed to leave right away, she didn't hesitate to let me go. I do feel bad though. She probably thinks I have some major family emergency going on, got evicted from my apartment, or something else horrible like that, when actually I'm just having an emotional breakdown. But hey, personal emergencies have to count for something too, right?

I drive toward Susan's family's ranch, trying to get my mind in a more comfortable, not to mention socially acceptable, state.

So much for being my own fairy godmother. I'm pretty sure my wings have been revoked. Or, at the very least, have been fitted with the fairy wing equivalent of a parking boot.

How could I have let myself get so carried away? Thank God I didn't have the opportunity to talk to Nick like I'd planned. He would have laughed in my face! If there is any good that's come of walking in on them like I did, it's that now the pain and embarrassment I currently feel is private, and no one else, particularly Nick, knows anything about it. That's at least something.

The rain lets up while I dig around in the glove box for something to blow my nose with. So what now? My latest plan has hit the crapper, and all I have to show for it is the undeniable knowledge that my instincts are shitty. Oh well. I'm not going to worry about it now. Later, I can talk to Susan and see if she can give me some of my perspective back, but for now, I have some time to clear my head and make myself presentable. Can't very well show up at Susan's, red-faced and sniffling. I'm going to turn all my attention to having a nice, relaxing time with one of my closest friends. There's always time to be miserable later.

"I am so happy you could come!" Susan's mother, Andrea says, giving me a hug and a peck on the cheek. "It's been years!"

"I know, thank you so much for having me. I hope it's no trouble."

"*Trouble?* Please! How could you even think such a thing? You stay just as long as you possibly can!" She pinches my cheek, and moves on to talk to the next group of people gathered nearby, leaving

Susan and I as she found us — reclining on lawn chairs by the pool, wine in hand.

"I'm glad you came too. It will be great to see you for more than a couple of hours. Plus, there is a serious lack of women here this time."

I look around and see she's right. Susan has four brothers, only one of whom has a wife, and she was unable to make it here for some reason. Susan, her mother, and I make up the entire female population, while the men out number us three to one if you count Susan's three little nephews.

"So," she says after refilling our wine, "you don't have to tell me if you don't want to, but I am curious…"

She leaves her sentence hanging, knowing I would realize what she meant. With a sigh and a swig, I begin my tale of embarrassment and botched plans. I go over everything: the beach, the hospital, all my ill-conceived notions that night, my observations, and everything else that led up to my fleeing the house this morning. When I finish, I let out a shaky breath and take another long sip. Susan doesn't seem to know what to say, and joins me in watching her husband and brothers wrestle with her nephews in the water.

"So," she says after a long moment, "what are you going to do?"

"What is there to do? I'll go back to my life, and try my best to pretend none of this ever happened."

"I'm really sorry. This is kind of my fault isn't it?"

"What?" God, does *everyone* have to try to take the blame for my stupidity? "Of course not. What are you talking about?"

"I'm the one who said you should talk to him."

"Oh, that. It's not your fault. This happened because I got carried away. I thought that I could trust my own instincts for once, and make my own fate, or whatever. My instincts suck, and it was a horrible plan, that's all."

We lapse into silence for a while, and watch the boys have a pool noodle fight. After a few minutes, Susan's stepdad calls over from the grill, and we head for the food. Before I can stand, Susan puts a hand on my arm. "Just one more thing, and I won't bug you any more about it," she says. "For what it's worth, I don't think it was a horrible plan. It might not have worked out the way you wanted, and maybe you had the wrong goal in mind, but I think the basic idea was good. You are the only one who can make yourself happy." She leans in and gives me a quick hug before walking over to dinner.

After we eat, the boys talk their aunt into joining a game of pool volleyball, leaving me to have my dessert on my own. As I watch the match, I can't get Susan's words out of my head. Maybe she's right. Just because my first attempt at fairy godmothering went awry, doesn't mean I have to retire my wings altogether.

In any event, I'm not going to worry about it. I have almost three weeks of freedom, and I'll be damned if I'm going to spend my first vacation in God knows how long being broody and miserable. I'm going to push aside any feelings that aren't vacation appropriate and have a good time.

My first test comes just over a week after my arrival at the ranch. It is 11:32 p.m., and I decide to check my e-mail before bed. I open my inbox and there, glaring at me, is an e-mail from Bree.

Subject: *I'm in Love!*

My throat closes and my eyes burn. After a few minutes and some deep breaths, I highlight the message and hit "delete." Then I go into the trash folder, highlight it again and select "permanent delete." A box appears that says "Are you sure you want to permanently delete *I'm in Love!* from your inbox?" I quickly click "Yes."

There, done. I said I wasn't going to wallow in misery, so I won't. I'm not going to force myself to suffer through a mushy, detailed synopsis of every private moment she's had so far with Nick. Hell, that's exactly why I left. She's one of my best friends, and in some hidden, deep down place I'm probably happy that things are working out for her, but for the time being, I'm not ready to deal with it.

If anything, all this talk of love should make me feel better. No one falls in love in less than two weeks. Not real or lasting love anyway. Well…I did, but that's hardly the point. *Most* people don't, and surely Bree would fall into the *most people* category.

I shut my computer and climb into bed. Somewhere on the outskirts of my mind, I know that Bree has never been the sort of person to fall in and out of love easily. As I hover on the border of sleep and awake, a part of me realizes this thing between her and Nick must be real.

I'm more than a little depressed as I drive through upstate New York on my way back home. The two and a half weeks with Susan and her family was the best vacation I've had in years. Her family was warm and welcoming, and the overall atmosphere was so peaceful and relaxing, that I would have been happy to stay another month. And I'm happy to announce I stuck to my word. I enjoyed myself as much as possible and didn't think about Nick once.

Well, okay, once.

Maybe twice.

All right, I saw him every time I blinked. The *point* is, I didn't wallow. I wasn't mopey, or depressed, or broody. I may have been a bit more melancholy than you would expect a typical vacationer to be, and — after the *"I'm In Love"* scare — also decided to avoid my e-mail entirely, but I did my best.

Susan also kept her word; we didn't discuss Nick or the situation again the whole time I was there. All she said as I left was a quiet, "Keep me posted," into my ear as she hugged me good-bye.

Instead of renting a car, Susan's stepfather had absolutely insisted I drive one of his eight hundred cars back down to Manhattan. He gave me the address of a parking garage where I could leave the car in a spot he owned. He had been adamant that *I* was actually doing *him* a favor, because the parking manager was threatening to rent out his space if he didn't start using it. I knew he was full of it, but reluctantly accepted, flattered that he would make up a story just to save me money. They all really were about the nicest people you could ever meet.

I start driving, still enjoying the relaxing bliss that seems to have come along with me in the car. However, with each mile that passes, the bliss slowly dissolves, leaving behind a strange feeling of foreboding, like there's something waiting for me at home. Something I've been running from and am about to face head on. It feels that way because it's true. I am more than aware that Manhattan holds my own personal hell, just waiting to swallow me up.

Reality.

I have been pushing it aside for more than two weeks, and now I have to figure out a way to deal with it. For some reason, it seems so much bigger than the reality I faced when I arrived at Susan's. Maybe the difference was distance. Like when you see something from far away it looks really small, but as you move closer it seems to grow. You know it's actually the same size it's always been, it's only your perspective that's changed.

Hmm. Maybe that's my answer. I just need to change my perspective. The vastness of my forthcoming reality is almost too daunting to even consider, but who says I have to deal with everything all at once? I can break it all down into chunks, deal with the smaller things up front, and move the larger chunks to the back where they look small again. For instance, there is no reason to attack the Bree and Nick scenario all at once when I can break it down into smaller pieces. Things like watching them at the beach, and dinner, and all their other little flirty encounters can go near the front, as they aren't so big a deal. The whole "seeing them kiss" episode would be in the back; that one would take a little more time.

There, see? I feel better already. All I need is a system, and things don't seem so bad.

I spend the next few hours breaking down and prioritizing my chunks of reality until I cross over the border into the city, and there is only one chunk left without a place in the reality lineup. Bree's e-mail. I don't know what to do with that one. I'm really wishing I had read it, or skimmed it over at least, so I'd know what I'm dealing with.

Oh well. I can file that one away until I actually talk to Bree on Monday. This still may blow over. Not that I'm getting my hopes up or anything. I'm definitely not going to make that mistake again, but I also don't need to panic.

I decide to drive straight to my building and use one of the guest parking spots in our underground parking garage. I'll wait until I don't have bags with me to park the car in Bree's stepdad's spot uptown. Finally, after parking, unloading, and dragging all my stuff to the elevator, then up the twelve stories to my apartment, I step inside and suddenly feel like I have been gone a year.

I drop all my stuff just inside the door, and go straight into the bedroom to change. After wearing the same ten or so sets of clothing for almost a month, I'm ecstatic to once again be able to put on my threadbare pink T-shirt and ratty sweats that I didn't deem nice enough to bring with me on the trip. I grab a can of iced tea from the kitchen, but hesitate just before collapsing on the couch.

With a sigh, I realize it's high time I reentered the technological universe. My phone has been on mute since I got to Susan's ranch, and I haven't even opened my inbox since the *"I'm in Love"* scare. I never go this long without at least skimming my inbox to make sure there is nothing urgent. Margaret could have sent me work that needs to be done before I go in on Monday, or one of our other clients may have written with a request or question. There are tons of reasons for me to log in, but I still hesitate. It's as if I expect my inbox to be overflowing with countless e-mails from Bree giving me the play-by-play on her new love life, even though I can admit that's highly unlikely. Bree has never been the sort to revel in gossip, or feel the need to brag about her personal life or romantic exploits.

I grab my laptop before settling into a corner of the couch. It seems to take twice as long to boot up as it normally does, each second adding to the weight on my chest. Why am I getting so worked up? This is dumb. Soon as I open my e-mail, I won't see anything from her, and I will feel totally stupid. Stupid and relieved maybe, but mostly stupid.

Finally the Internet comes up and I sign in to my e-mail account, fighting the urge to hold my breath. Sixty-three unread messages, which actually isn't so bad considering it's been almost three weeks. Skimming through, I see a few things from work as well as loads of junk—coupons, one day sale notices, and so on—but then I stop short. There, three down from the top, sent only a few days ago, is one from Bree.

Subject: *Big News!*

My heart is stuck somewhere in my throat, and I can't seem to move my eyes.

"Big News"? What big news? Something to do with work? No, Margaret would be the one to tell me about that. It would have to be something to do with…her and Nick. Is it official? Have they told everyone they are dating? I sort of figured that's what was in the *"I'm in Love!"* e-mail from a few weeks ago.

With a shaky hand I click open the message and read.

Jules,

Oh my gosh, I have huge news! I know it's crazy, and so
not like me, and you probably won't believe it, but…I'm
getting married! He asked me last night and I almost died!
You should see my ring! Oh my gosh, it's huge! Everything
has happened so fast it's like a whirlwind, but I couldn't be
happier! I just wish you were here! Everyone is so excited!
Margaret had to leave right after the announcement, but
Nick invited everyone else to stay an extra week so we
can plan. Speaking of, you will obviously be one of my
bridesmaids, so keep the last weekend in October open!
Fast, I know, but when you're ready, you're ready!

I know it is incredibly tacky of me to tell you all this in an
e-mail, but I couldn't get a hold of you any other way. Your
cell has been off for days! Plug it in, girl! :) Anyway, I just
couldn't wait to tell you!

We'll all be back to the city at the end of the week, but I
won't be back to work until the day after you get back from
vacation. Call me if you get this before then, otherwise and
we'll talk when I get back to the office!

Miss you,

- Bree

I barely finish the e-mail. By the second sentence I'm sobbing
and hiccupping, unable to breathe. When I reach the end, I close the
lid of my laptop, set it on the floor, and sink down into the couch. I
bury my face into a throw pillow, and give in to the crushing despair
of a happily ever after that will never be mine.

Several hours later, I lie on the couch in the dark, staring up at the
ceiling. My nose is clogged, my eyes are swollen, and the hair behind
my temples is matted with dried tears. I reach up behind me and
grab the phone from the end table, dial and wait. I get the machine.

"Hey, Lisa, it's me. Do me a favor when you get this…and send
me Zach's e-mail address."

12

I'm at the bar in Marino's, staring down into my wine glass. Zach should be here any minute, and I'm currently trying to shake the urge to run out the door. Everything will be fine; I just need to relax. He's going to walk in any second now, and I can't look like I'm about to have a panic attack.

This is it. My first step into my new life. The night before last had been the worst ever, bar none. Never had I actually had to face the fact that it was really and truly never going to happen between Nick and me. Of course, part of me knew that since I dumped him, but I've always had a flicker of hope. Not conscious hope, but just a dim little light in the back of my mind that glimmered ever so slightly on everything in my life—like the hope you have when you buy a one dollar scratch card lottery ticket, or drop your token in a raffle bucket. You don't really think anything will come of it, but there is still that little glimmer of *what if.*

That was the hope I still had for Nick and me. Now that hope is gone. The little light went out at 7:24 p.m. on Friday night when I opened Bree's e-mail. I had never been lower. It wasn't the same low I'd felt after we broke up, because at that point I was still in denial. I continued to tell myself that it was all for the best and other stupid mantras like that, which made my fall into depression much slower and more gradual. Not like Friday. Friday had been a wrecking ball. Specifically, a wrecking ball made up of all the little chunks of reality I had spent most of that day organizing.

But somewhere in between the bouts of hysterical sobbing, I'd come to a decision based primarily on what Susan had said earlier that day. My life wasn't going to get better unless *I* made it better. This fairy godmother was getting back on the horse, and in a big way. Anything between Nick and me is over now. Really over. And while I know in my heart of hearts that I'll always be in love with him, I can't spend the rest of my life living in the land of what might have been. I'm going to change and take back the life I gave up eight years ago, even if it makes me miserable because, right now, miserable would be an improvement.

I know it's not going to be easy and I'll have to force a lot of it. For instance, tonight I'm out on a date with Zach. Or at least I will be once he gets here. Of the many things in my life that need to be changed, my self-imposed ban of all things male is definitely the biggest. I need to try a relationship, and Zach seems more than willing. Now, I'm not using him or anything. I'm genuinely going to try to make this work, even force it if I have to. Zach is a great guy who has his feet on the ground and, as Lisa is fond of saying, is crazy about me. If I can't at least give it my best effort with a guy like Zach, then there really is no hope for me at all.

"Julia?" I turn to see Zach, looking quite dashing in a navy blue suit, and wearing a big smile. "I'm sorry, have I kept you waiting?"

"No, no. I live right around the corner from here. I was early." Well, he's here. At the very least he didn't stand me up. Though that was a minor worry; I'd e-mailed him yesterday morning, asking him if he wanted to go out sometime to give me a call, and then gave him my number. The phone rang not ten minutes later. Overeager as it was, it's nice to feel wanted.

We walk up to the hostess stand and are seated immediately at a quiet booth near the wall of wine bottles.

"So," Zach says after we have ordered our drinks, "Lisa tells me you have been in Maine?"

"I was, but only for one week. The past three I've been upstate, staying with a friend."

"That sounds nice."

"It really was."

"What were you doing in Maine?"

"My team had a showing." If only that were all.

"A showing?"

I proceed to tell him what that means, what it is I do, why I like it, why I hate it, and all the rest of the typical first date Q&A. It was nice in a "don't let us run out of conversation or this could get really awkward" kind of way. Like I said, typical first date stuff. Or at least I think it is, as I don't have much to go on. He seems to be having a nice time though, so it must be going all right. By the time our meals arrive we have covered just about everything on my side of things, so I figure I should start asking some questions of my own.

"What about you?" I ask, sprinkling parmesan on my gnocchi. "I mean, I know what you do, but—"

"Well, now that you mention it, I might be changing professions soon."

"Really?"

"I've been thinking it might be time to move on to something I'm a little more passionate about. Not that being a copywriter isn't fascinating and all…" He leaves his sentence open with a chuckle.

"What do you want to do?"

"Honestly, I'm not sure yet, but I would like to get into management. Something with a little more power…and a little more money," he adds with a grin.

I find myself wondering what he makes, but even I know that salary is *not* a part of the typical first date Q&A. Though, he must do all right; his suit looks designer, and I'm pretty sure that's a real Rolex he's wearing. Then again, I have no idea what a typical salary is for a senior copywriter.

"I've been working on my resume," he continues, "but I haven't found anything I really want to go for."

"Yeah, it's still slim pickin's out there."

The night rolls on, and even though it's not always the most interesting conversation, thankfully we don't run out of things to talk about. When we finish dinner, Zach suggests walking down to Andy's for gelato instead of ordering dessert at the restaurant. It's a little chilly out but I agree, not wanting to spoil the evening by being picky. We walk to Andy's in silence, the traffic making conversation too hard to attempt, and share a large Peaches & Cream. Afterward, he walks me to my building; we exchange the expected pleasantries, and make plans to meet for lunch on Tuesday. I'm relieved that he doesn't attempt to kiss me, and we say goodnight.

I go up to my apartment, close the door behind me, and lean against it as I kick off my heels. There, it's over. I did it. I officially completed my first step toward happiness, come hell or high water. I shuffle over to the couch and start to flip through television stations without actually seeing any of the programs. After two circuits through the lineup, I give up and lie back against the armrest.

Why does this have to be so hard? Why can't it be the way I remember? I'll tell you why: I'm spoiled. It should never have been as easy as it was with Nick. Normal relationships don't happen that way; you have to work at it. It doesn't just happen like magic. Now that I have to be normal, I don't want to. I want it all to just fall into my lap.

See? Spoiled.

But still, there is something that seems a little off…

Tonight had gone well and all, but I can't shake the feeling that there is something up with Zach. There go my damn instincts again, but I can't help it. Almost as if he's too nice. Like when we—

Wait, what did I just say?

Too nice?

Too nice!

Seriously?

That does it—I have to be certifiable. Am I really criticizing a man for being *too nice?* Is this what I have sunk to? I mean, finding minute flaws in men, and using those flaws to justify ending a relationship with them was bad enough—and God knows I've done tons of that—but to actually resort to criticizing *good* qualities? That's over the line.

No, I won't do this, not anymore! I've made a decision and I'm sticking to it. Zach is as good a guy as any, and I'm going to have to get used to the idea of dating men who aren't perfect. No one is perfect, not even Nick, though I've made him out to be in my mind. If I spend my life looking for perfect, I will die alone. And not only will I stop searching for perfect, but I will stop using the search for perfect itself as an excuse to not look at all. I am giving up all that nonsense. I am going to have the life I should.

Come hell or high water.

I lean back in my desk chair, sipping my peppermint hot chocolate, and look around at the otherwise empty office. I know Bree won't be in today, but Margaret hasn't been in yet either and I start to get my hopes up. Maybe they will both be out, and I can put off talking about the wedding for one more day. If there is any way at all to prolong the inevitable, damn it, I'll find it.

Scheherazade's got nothing on me.

Half past two rolls around, and Margaret still has not made an appearance. I've had more than five solid quiet hours, during which I was able to catch up on all the e-mails, phone calls, and paperwork that had piled up over the time I was gone. I come to the happy conclusion that I will be the only one in for the day when Margaret comes bursting through the door in one of her dizzy-tizzies.

"Julia!" *Damn.* "I'm so sorry! You poor thing, you've been here all day by yourself! I've been in and out of meetings all morning, it's just been crazy!" She tosses her bag on her chair, rambling on without stopping for a breath. "The lease on the Weston Building is about to expire, and we don't have any of the renewal paperwork yet. Then Dana announces she's leaving at the end of the year, which means her group will need a new lead, and I have until the end of the month to compile a list of interview candidates, plus I have to meet with Mr. and Mrs. Braxton about their summer house." She finally pauses, coming over and giving me a hug. "Oh, but never mind all that, we've missed you! How was your vacation? Did you have a nice time? Oh!" Her eyes light up. Here it comes. "Have you talked to Bree?"

"I haven't actually spoken with her, but she sent me an e-mail."

"Can you believe it? Isn't it exciting! I am so happy—"

"I know, me too." I give my best fake smile, unintentionally cutting her off.

Unintentionally…yeah.

"Oh, and while I'm thinking about it, I'm supposed to tell you that tomorrow during lunch you're to meet Bree and the rest of her girls here—" she hurries over to her bag, digs through it, and hands me a note with an address "—to look at dresses, then you are all going to a late lunch. Don't worry about coming back in; you and Bree can both take the afternoon off."

"Are you sure?" I ask, trying to come up with a reason to miss out on the lunch, assuming there is a good chance Nick will be there. "You just got through telling me how busy you are, and I have been off for almost three —"

"None of that, none of that," she says, waving her hand like she is shooing a fly. "I'll be fine! You girls go and have fun! I just wish I could be there!"

Thankfully, her cell rings before we get into anything I really don't want to discuss — the proposal, how cute the happy couple is, things like that. I'm more than sure I will get my fill of that, and then some, tomorrow. Ugh! Wedding dress shopping? Really? I know as a bridesmaid I have to be there, and I do want to be there for Bree, but I'm really not sure that I can sit in a room with a bunch of women, talking about how wonderful Nick is with someone else. I have a hard enough time keeping my composure with just the voices in my head, so how am I supposed to keep it together when the voices are real?

Well, I guess it is fairly common for people to cry while wedding dress shopping, right? If I do lose it, maybe everyone will think I'm just being sentimental or some other crap like that. In any event, I doubt anyone will automatically come to the conclusion that I'm upset because I'm the bitter, depressed woman in love with the bride's fiancé. Though with the luck I've been having lately, it's probably safer not to assume anything.

"Oh, one more thing," Margaret says, making me jump. "We got our invites to the party while you were away. Here." She hands me a blue envelope with the SMS logo on the front. "It's October eighth and it's at the library this year."

"Wow. Fancy." My stomach twists as I skim over the elegant script.

Miss Basham and Guest,
You are cordially invited to the 17th annual SMS Gala
Friday the Eighth of October
at Seven o'clock in the Evening

New York Public Library

Every year in the fall, SMS Financial hosts a huge party for all its employees and clients. Normally I hate the thing, because I always go alone and end up tagging along behind Bree all night like a sad, lost puppy. This year will be worse, because Bree will now be there with Nick, wearing her new huge diamond ring and answering everyone's questions about the wedding, how they met, and so on. No way am I tagging along with the two of them, which means I will either be totally alone, or attached to Margaret and her husband all night. Fun.

Maybe I won't go.

I let out a long breath and rest my chin on my hand. I'm going to have to get used to being around Nick. Bree is one of my best friends and my co-worker. She is marrying Nick, which means Nick is going to be in my life now for as long as Bree is. He will be in the office, at work functions, and loads of other places I will also be. I can't hide forever. I refuse. I have to believe in the magic, dust off my fairy wings, and keep my magic wand aimed at the prize. I've already taken the first step in going out with Zach, and I am not about to lose that ground.

Speaking of…

I grab my phone and dial the number to Zach's apartment. It's almost three in the afternoon and he's at work, so I leave a message. "Hey, Zach, it's Julia. Two things real quick. First, I have to cancel our lunch tomorrow. I have a last minute appointment that just came up and I can't miss it. Sorry. Maybe we can do it later this week. Also, on the evening of the eighth, I have a company party, and was wondering if you are free, and would maybe like to go with me. I have to RSVP by the end of the week so just let me know before then. Talk to you soon. Bye."

There. At least there will be no lost puppy this year.

13

The next day, after a restless night filled with nightmares about the wedding of Mr. and Mrs. Nicholas and Brianna Kerkley, and a morning of work that wasn't distracting, I sluggishly make my way down Fifth Avenue to the address Margaret gave me yesterday.

As I walk, I decide to take full advantage of this afternoon. I will get everything wedding related out of the way as soon as possible. That morning I'd looked up the bridal shop online and saw that they were one of the biggest in the city, selling everything from bridal gowns and veils, to bridesmaid's dresses, jewelry, and shoes. A first class shop, all the way. This is good news, as I plan to find and buy my dress, shoes, jewelry, and anything else I need for this wedding all this afternoon. That way I can go the next few weeks not having to think about the wedding any more than I absolutely have to. That will leave me plenty of time to devote to the fairy godmothering of my life plan, which, I am ashamed to say, I've been seriously slacking on the past few days. My date with Zach was a good first step, but I haven't made any substantial strides since then, and I know if I allow it, this whole wedding agenda will derail me completely. I can't let that happen. I know today will be hard, the rest of the wedding functions will be rough, and the wedding itself—well, I can't even bring myself to think about it yet. But all of the hours I don't already have earmarked for work or sleep will be devoted to creating the life that I should already have by now.

I arrive at Bridal Reflections, step into the entryway, and actually have to remind myself not to gawk. This has to be the nicest bridal shop I have ever seen. In fact, I'm pretty sure the word "shop" is an offensive term to a place like this. "Salon" or "boutique" would be much more appropriate. A short smiling woman in a black suit meets me in the lobby.

"Good afternoon," she says, extending a hand. "Do you have an appointment with us today?"

"Yes, I'm with the St. Charles party."

"Of course, right this way. Miss St. Charles has already arrived."

She leads me past endless rows of hangers all dripping with puffy white fluff. There's satin, silk, lace, pearls, and crystals as far as the eye can see.

"There they are." The woman gestures to a long couch.

Bree sees me immediately and jumps up. "Jules!" She runs over and throws her arms around me. "I'm so happy to see you! I've missed you!" After a moment she lets go, and I have my first actual look at her. She is absolutely glowing. I've never seen her like this, with happiness just pouring out of her. I swallow the lump in my throat.

I remember that feeling…

She takes my hand and leads me over to the couch, where three other women are waiting.

"Everyone, this is Julia Basham. Jules, this is my sister, Jen, my Maid of Honor—" she touches the first woman on the couch "—and you've met my mom, Linda." I had, but I'm glad she reminded me of her name. "And this is Ashley, my best friend growing up."

"Nice to meet you," I say to everyone at once.

As soon as Bree and I sit down, a consultant comes around the corner, pushing a rack of dresses. "Are we ready to begin?" she asks, smiling at Bree.

"Almost, we're still missing one."

Ah, Cathy…I had almost forgotten about her.

"Would you like to wait?" the consultant asks.

"Yes, if that's all right. I'd rather not try anything on until everyone is here, but the girls can start looking through those until then."

"Sounds good. I'll leave these for you all to look through, and in the meantime, I'll start pulling your first set of gowns, so they're all ready to go."

She hurries off, and Bree pulls out two swatches of fabric from her bag. "Okay, you will all choose your own dress in whatever style you like. She brought those ones out for you to look through," she says, motioning toward the rack. "When you pick your favorite, they'll order it in these colors. Jen, you'll be the taupe, and everyone else will have the green."

Hmm, not bad. The green was nice, almost like a sage, and from the looks of it, we had twenty or so dress styles to choose from. We all wander over to the rack of gowns, and start going through them. They're all floor length and satin, but otherwise, each is unique. I can see that about a third of them are out for me already—I don't do strapless. I'm a girl who needs a little more than boning to keep everything where it needs to be.

I have a few dresses hung over my arm to try on when Bree calls us back over to the couch. She's standing with a woman about Margaret's age.

Bree puts an arm around her. "Girls, this is Debbie, my future mother-in-law. Debbie, this is my sister, Jen, and my friends, Ashley and Julia."

Wait…what?

She continues to talk, but I've tuned her out. Everyone greets Debbie with a smile, and Bree's mother steps forward to give her a hug, while I can only stare, totally confused. What does she mean mother-in-law? Nick's mother has been dead for years. This must be a mistake. Could this be an aunt or other family member he was extremely close with? No…as far as I can remember, Cathy is his only other family member. What the hell is going on?

Luckily, Bree steps away from everyone for a moment. I go over to her, grab her elbow, and quietly pull her into the first open dressing room, trying my best to be discreet.

I close the door behind us and turn to face her, dropping the gowns in my arms. "What's going on?"

"What are you talking about?" she asks, confused.

"She's your mother-in-law?"

"Well not yet—"

"How is that possible?"

"Because she's Chris's mom?" she tells me, as though she's not sure what I mean.

My heart skips a beat. One word completely stopped my world from turning. I stare at her, trying to put the universe back in order. "*Chris?* You're marrying *Chris?*"

She smiles, but still looks at me as if I have two heads. "What did you think was going on here?"

"I *thought* you were marrying Nick!"

"What? No! Why would you think that?"

"Because the two of you were all cute and flirty and date-y."

"Well, maybe a little at first," she cuts in, blushing a bit, "but Chris and I have been dating since the day you left."

"And that! The day I left, you and Nick were in the library *kissing!*" *What the hell is going on here?*

"Kissing? No! Chris and I were asking him if he would mind our being together. They have been friends for years, and I'm sort of Nick's employee, so we wanted to make sure he was all right with everything before we told anyone else. Nick said he was fine, and that he was happy for us. I gave him a hug and a kiss on the cheek. Is that what you're talking about? That's hardly *kissing.*"

What? No. No way…I know what I saw.

"Chris was there in the room with us," she added. "Didn't you see him?"

"No…"

I swear they were kissing…Her arms were definitely around his neck and…his hands were on her waist.

"I told you everything in my e-mail, didn't you get it?"

"The engagement e-mail?"

"No, the one before that."

Ah…"I'm in Love." The e-mail I didn't read.

"No, I guess not." At this point my face is a blank stare. She's marrying Chris. Shy, quiet Chris. Nick is not getting married.

He's not getting married.

"Are you okay?" Bree asks me. She seems afraid I might fall over.

I snap out of it in time to cover my short blackout. "Yeah, sure, fine, just surprised…that's all. Chris is so quiet, I never thought… well never mind. It's great, hun!" I smile, and give her a hug. She smiles back, obviously satisfied with my lame explanation.

"Make sure you come out. I want to see them all!" She smiles, picking up and hanging the dresses I've forgotten all about. She gives me another quick hug, and then leaves me alone in the dressing room.

I cover my mouth with both hands, and slowly slide down the wall to the floor.

He's not getting married.

For all of five minutes, I sit motionless, unable to even think beyond those four words. So many emotions crash over me, I can't keep them all straight. Relief that Nick is still single. Shame that I'm relieved that Nick is still single and isn't getting the happiness I know he deserves. Shock that shy little Chris could actually bring himself to propose to someone. Astonishment that all this happened so fast. Excitement for the wedding, now that I can be excited rather than depressed. And incredible embarrassment over what I have needlessly put myself through these past few weeks. God, Susan will get a kick out of this one.

With a sudden burst of energy, I pop up and grab the first dress. It's been a long time since I have felt this wonderfully relaxed, and I'm not about to waste it. True, there is quite a lot to think about, but I am not going to do it now. Nothing kills this feeling faster than thinking. I'm going to hop on this incredible wave of Zen, get in the wedding spirit, and enjoy the afternoon in a way I would not have thought possible an hour ago.

He's not getting married!

I lie in bed that evening, thinking about the unbelievable turn this day took. The rest of our afternoon had been spent choosing dresses, picking out jewelry and shoes, critiquing veils, and discussing wedding plans. Amazingly, we all found dresses. I had chosen a sleeveless, scoop-neck, A-line gown. It had gathered ruching from the bust all the way down, until the ruching turned into pick-up style gathers all over the skirt. The sample I tried on had been ivory and, on the hanger, I thought it looked like a pile of vanilla frosting. Once I put it on, however, it was actually very flattering. The ruching hid some of my own personal frosting, while the scoop-neck made my boobs look good.

Bree looked stunning in everything she tried on, finally choosing a strapless fitted silk gown with crystal beading at the bust, an asymmetrical drop waist, and a big, billowy skirt.

Jen, Ashley, and I decided to get matching jewelry, and Bree bought the three of us matching jeweled hair combs to wear as thank you gifts—though she insisted on taking them with her, so she could wrap them and give them to us at the rehearsal dinner.

Debbie was beside herself all day, drinking in every moment. Apparently, it had always been her dream to have a big city wedding, but since her husband was active military when they were married, she had to settle with a small family affair. After that, Debbie had made it her goal to live vicariously through her daughter, and throw her the wedding she had always dreamed of for herself. Two sons and twenty-nine years later, she had all but given up on that dream. She had really never expected Chris to marry; he'd been shy and backward with women while growing up. Brandon, Chris's younger brother, vowed he would never get married but on the off chance he did, he planned to elope in Vegas. So when Chris called Debbie and told her he was engaged, it took her only long enough to recover from the shock to start planning.

The entire affair is going to be first class all the way. The ceremony and reception will be at the Waldorf, family and friends are being flown in from all corners of the country, and Debbie is paying for it all. Bree told me on the way to our late lunch—which, due to the amount of time we spent at the bridal salon, turned out to be dinner—what a great job Debbie was doing with everything and how she always got Bree's "okay" before she made any big decisions. As excited as I know Bree is, Debbie just may have her beat.

I'm so happy for Bree. I really am. I wanted to be happy for her before, but that was, I'm ashamed to say, hard. She's on cloud nine, and it is nice to finally be able to catch the wedding bug, and be excited with her. Plus, it makes me feel much more like a good friend and less like a self-centered bitch.

The shocker for me is that she fell for someone like Chris! Chris is an outstanding guy, don't get me wrong, but I would never have pictured her with someone so soft-spoken and shy. Moreover, I can't see Chris actually having the balls to go after someone like Bree—or anyone at all, for that matter. But hey, good for them. If she has done for him half of what he has done for her, this is a match made in heaven. She was glowing all through the appointment and dinner, talking about Chris, how they met, the proposal, and all their future plans. It was adorable the way her face lit up any time someone mentioned his name. She really is a different person now; she's always been naturally happy, but now it's something different. Her happiness seems to spring from a new place deep inside. In any event, I am sure those two have found their happily ever after.

Sigh. Which brings me back to the issue at hand: what the hell do I do now? My peaceful, relaxing wave of Zen that I let sweep me away in the dressing room has been slowly but steadily dissolving throughout the day, leaving me now in a state of total indecision and doubt.

Okay, so Nick isn't getting married. It's nice to know, but does it really matter? Am I actually planning do something about this new development? Do I approach him like I'd planned to back in Maine? Really, I don't think I can. Actually getting up the nerve to talk to him about all this was iffy at best then; with the emotional rollercoaster I have been on the past few weeks, I'm lucky to still be functioning, much less taking huge risks with the shreds of mental stability I have left. Besides, I've already come to the solid conclusion that my emotion-based instincts suck and are not to be trusted.

I roll over with a huff, crossing my arms under my pillow. I finally have a plan—a real goal—and have already taken the first steps to achieve it. Am I going to throw in the towel just because I find out Nick is still single? How can I do that? A fairy godmother would never let you give up like that, and since that's the part I have decided to play, then I won't either. Not to mention, I'm forgetting a key factor here. Nick has been single all this time, but has made no attempt to contact me in any way. I haven't gone to him, but I had a reason. If he had any feelings for me, or desire to be with me, wouldn't he have gotten in touch with me? I would think so.

So that settles it. I'll continue on as though Nick *is* the one who's getting married. He will some day, so I had better start getting used to the idea now. I knew this plan wouldn't be easy, but if I ever want to move on, it has to be done. I vowed I would push on come hell or high water. Happily ever afters don't just happen; you have to make them happen. So that's what I'll do: keep moving forward, climbing onward and upward toward my new life, leaving the past behind for good.

I close my eyes, ready to make up for all the sleep I lost the last few nights, determined to stick to my guns. But, somehow I fall asleep to the image of Nick, smiling down at me and holding me close.

Ah well…baby steps.

Three days and countless unanswered phone calls from her later, I sit down to lunch with Lisa at Capri Café, which is only a few blocks away from my office. I've been avoiding her and spent the majority of this morning mentally preparing for the onslaught of Zach-related questions I knew would be coming.

"'Bout time you called me! What's it been, a month?" she asks, pretending to be more offended than she actually is.

"I called you last week."

"Okay, first of all, that was two weeks ago, and yeah, you called… you left a message asking me for an e-mail address, and have been avoiding me ever since! Sorry, but that doesn't count."

She's right. I haven't spoken to her since I asked her for Zach's e-mail, the night I got back from Susan's. What's worse, when she called back to give it to me, I deliberately didn't pick up, forcing her to leave it in a message. At the time I couldn't handle giving an explanation, and since then, well, I just haven't *wanted* to give an explanation. Normally, she wouldn't have been so obliging with the information. If I had called her and asked for anything else, she would never have left it on a voicemail; she would have made me get it from her in person. She's more than capable of waiting me out. But she's been pushing this Zach thing for so long, I think she was afraid that by the time I broke down and got back to her, I would have changed my mind and no longer wanted the address. She knew she had to act fast. So really, it wasn't her doing me a favor, as much as her taking advantage of an opportunity.

"I've been busy. Bree is getting married next month," I slip in somewhat out of the blue, hoping it would derail the conversation for a bit.

"Wait, *what?*"

Mission accomplished.

"Yep, his name is Chris. She met him while we were in Maine."

"*In Maine?* What, like *last month?* And they're getting *married?*"

"Yep." I take a sip of my Coke. Sad as it is, I'm almost challenging her to say something. This is the other part of the day I had been mentally preparing for: Lisa's assessment of their quick marriage. Waiting for her to judge or criticize them in some way, so that I can come to their defense. I know it's mean to set her up like this, but I just want the opportunity to stick up for Bree and Chris the way I never stuck up for Nick and me.

Petty, yeah, I know.

Regardless, I'm thwarted when, "Wow," is all she says.

We order our lunches, after which we sit in a pregnant silence. Lisa looks at me with her eyebrows raised in a you-might-as-well-stop-stalling-and-get-on-with-it look.

"How long are you going to stare at me like that?" I ask, still trying to play dumb.

"Until you break down and tell me all the juicy details." She grins.

"Well, sorry to disappoint, but we've only been out *once*. Any details I have are minor and juiceless."

"Did you have fun?"

"Sure."

"What did you do?"

"Dinner."

"Are you going out again?"

"Yes."

"When?"

"Tonight, actually."

"And?" She makes a circular motion with her hand.

"And...what?"

"Come on, you've gotta give me something. Do you like him? Is it as horrible as you'd thought it'd be?"

"No, it's not horrible" — that isn't the word — "but I never thought it would be. And, yes I like him, I guess." *Sure, why not.* "It's still hard to tell."

"Come on, you're killing me! You've got to give me something!"

"All right! Our eyes met from across the room, and we were drawn to each other. My heart was instantly lost and now I can't look into his eyes without seeing the faces of our future children," I say with as much cheese as I can muster. "There, how's that? Better?"

She glares and I can't help but smirk.

"*Anyway*, for what it's worth, I'm proud of you." She raises her glass in a toast. "No matter what happens, you went for it, and that's what matters."

"Thank you." I raise my glass to meet hers. She was right. I had gone for it, and I was glad someone else could appreciate how big a step that was. I am officially trying, and I'm proud of that.

"Plus, he's being promoted next week."

"Really? He hasn't said anything about it."

"He doesn't know yet. We are waiting until this whole mess with Linda is over."

"The one who's stealing? How's that going?"

"Great. We know it's her, and now we're just waiting to catch her in the act so we can fire her."

"If you know it's her, why can't you fire her now?"

"We could, but if we catch her red-handed, we don't have to deal with any 'he said, she said' drama later on. She'll know she's caught, and won't be able to fight it."

"Will you press charges?"

"Maybe, but that's not my decision. I hope so, though."

"How much did she end up taking overall?"

"Well, that's another thing; we're not sure. It will take some time to backtrack and go through it all. So far it looks like she has been at this for over five years."

"That sucks, but at least you can keep an eye on her now. That has to make you feel better."

"I'll feel better when I can fire the bitch."

"And we all know how good you are at that." I grin.

"Hey, we all have our hobbies," she agrees with a smirk.

Thankfully, that is the end of any and all Zach-related talk before we finish our lunches and part ways. When I get back to work and the elevator doors open on my floor, the first thing I see is Bree, pacing in the hall with a huge smile on her face.

"There you are!" she squeals, practically bouncing.

"What's wrong?"

"Nothing, come!" She grabs my hand, and tows me behind her toward our office. Once we pass through the door, she stops, takes my shoulders, and spins me around to face my desk.

When my eyes focus, my breath catches in my throat. There, waiting for me, is an enormous bouquet of roses. They are absolutely stunning: fuchsia, pink, yellow, and orange, surrounded by white baby's breath.

Bree could barely contain herself. "They were delivered an hour ago. Who are they from?" She had obviously been on pins and needles since they arrived.

"I have no idea," I say, reaching for the card I see hanging on a ribbon tied to the vase.

> Julia,
>
> Something to brighten your day, the way thinking of you brightens mine.
>
> Can't wait to see you tonight!
>
> - Zach

Zach? Wow. That's really…sweet. I feel myself blush as I close the card.

"Well?" Bree begs. I hand her the card. "Aw! That is so cute!" She holds the card over her heart. "Who is Zach?"

"A guy I've sort of…been seeing."

"Oh my gosh! You didn't tell me you were seeing anyone!" She hurries over to her desk and grabs her chair. I sink down into my seat and smile as she rolls her chair up alongside my desk. "So, who is he? What's he do? Obviously he's a sweetheart." She gestures to the roses, "How long has this been going on?"

She's leaning in toward me, biting her lower lip, waiting for answers, and I can't help but smile. After all, this is what it's supposed to be like, right? Having the new boyfriend butterflies, chatting with girlfriends about him, oohing and awing over cute stories, analyzing the details of each date. The only little issue is that I don't have the butterflies. The flowers are very sweet, and they definitely make me smile, but they don't make me want to squeal and jump up and down, like Bree seems seconds away from doing. I just don't feel that way about Zach, at least not yet. I'm sure I will soon; I just have to keep going. I've decided to move ahead with the plan, and this is part of it. Simply because I'm not overly excited now, doesn't mean I can't fake it, and eventually I won't have to fake it at all. Soon everything will be the way it should, so for now my objective is to do whatever it takes to get there. After all, it's working so far, right? I have a gorgeous bouquet of flowers on my desk that says it is.

"We've only been out once," I say, leaning over to her, trying to match her enthusiasm, "but it went really well, and we are going out again tonight."

"What does he do?"

"He is a copywriter for Century PR."

"Is he cute? What does he look like?" she asks, biting her lip.

"He is cute. He's a little taller than me, has reddish-brown hair and blue eyes." Now that I think about it, he *is* a good-looking guy. Funny I had never really noticed before.

"You have to bring him in. I want to meet him!"

"Well, let's see how things go. It's early yet."

We are interrupted by Margaret's entrance. "Afternoon, girls," she says.

"Look, Julia got flowers!" Bree announces, jumping up from her chair.

"Oh, my," Margaret says, coming over for a closer look. "Someone has an admirer!"

She begins asking all the questions that Bree asked, and I go over everything again for her sake, though an enthusiastic Bree interrupts me several times. It's funny how her version is so much more romantic than mine. They each ask a few more questions before we all finally get back to work. I move my bouquet to the floor beside me, so I can get to my desk. Before I start anything however, I take another long look at them. A much as I wish it were true, I know it would be a lie to say I wasn't a tiny bit disappointed that the flowers were from Zach and not…well, Nick.

Stupid, I know.

Nick has no reason to send me anything, much less flowers, but I can't help wondering how my reaction would have differed if the roses had been from him. That's hardly even a question. The butterflies would have been so real they probably would have made me sick; I would have jumped higher than Bree, and I would've gotten absolutely nothing accomplished the rest of the afternoon.

I sigh and turn back to my computer. Sure, that's what would have been. As it is, however, there are seventeen e-mails that need my attention.

A week later I'm at my favorite Starbucks on the corner of 47th and 9th, enjoying a congratulatory peppermint hot chocolate and piece of banana-chocolate chip cake. I'm shocked to even think it, but tomorrow is the SMS party and I'm not dreading it. As of last night, I've been out with Zach four times, and I'm glad to find it really is getting easier. Our second date — the evening after he sent me the flowers — was a movie night and went as well as I could have hoped. This past Tuesday we met for lunch, and last night he tried to make me dinner at his apartment. *Tried* being the key word, as it turned out terrible, and we ended up walking down to a pizza place near his building. But hey, it's the thought that counts. I am congratulating myself today, because I actually let him hold my hand on the way back from dinner — I was even able to ignore the creepy feeling it sent up my arm — *and* let him kiss me goodnight on the cheek.

Okay, he'd been going for my lips, but I'd pretended not to realize it and turned my head. I'm not quite ready for all of that just yet. You have to walk before you can run, and I'm not entirely sure I'm done with crawling. But baby steps are still steps, and the hand holding was definitely more than a baby step, and for that I deserve some props.

Go me.

I finish my cake, decide to take the rest of my hot chocolate to go, and start the walk home. I bring my plate to the trash by the pickup counter as a barista calls out a name and order for a grande Americano. As the man steps forward to claim his drink, I nearly choke on mine.

It's Nick.

His eyes meet mine as he takes his drink and stands in front of me. Meanwhile, I concentrate on pushing my heart back down to my chest and not passing out.

"Hi," he says, with a shy smile.

Please don't let my voice crack.

"Hi."

Whew.

"Are you leaving?" he asks, glancing at the plate I had just put in the dish bin.

Not if you don't want me to.

"Yes."

He looks down for a moment, then turns slightly toward the door. "Can I walk with you?"

Yesss! Ahem…I mean…

"Sure." *Blush.*

Damn!

He opens the door for me, and we slowly make our way up 9th Avenue. It's a nice day out, warm for early October, but you'd never know it with the way I'm shaking.

What's going on? Does he want to talk? Are we friends now? Does he need something? What do I say?

We walk along without speaking for a few minutes, neither one of us looking at the other. Both of us seem to be trying to pretend this isn't as awkward as it obviously is. Just as I begin to wonder if either of us will speak at all, he clears his throat.

"Were you surprised when you heard the news? About Chris and Bree, I mean," he adds, though I know what he means.

"I was." I chuckle in spite of myself. "Actually, I still can't believe it. I met Bree over five years ago, and I have only known her to date like, three or four guys, and even those she was only with for a few weeks." *Besides the fact that I thought she was with you.*

"Chris too," he says, smiling at me with those gorgeous blue eyes. "I've never heard him talk about dating anyone. The only thing he's ever said was that he took one of his cousins to the prom, and even that was only because his mom forced him to go."

We both laugh, and I realize with relief that the awkwardness is gone.

"I can believe it. Debbie is something else. I swear, if you didn't know any better, you would think she's the one getting married."

"I know! Chris is the last person I would picture having a huge, lavish wedding. He and Bree would probably be as happy to go to City Hall. Derek works there, so he could hook them up."

"But Debbie would definitely disown them both!"

We laugh again, then lapse into an easy silence. A few blocks later, we pause just short of the intersection I need to cross to get home. I've had a question on the tip of my tongue for two blocks now, and I'm almost out of time.

Come on, grow a pair and speak up!

"Are you coming to the party tomorrow?" I ask before I can wimp out. It's a reasonable question. After all, as a client, he would have been invited. There is no reason for my heart to be hammering in my chest.

"I wasn't sure," he says, eyes shifting down. "Will you be there?" He looks at me, and I'm suddenly struck by the tender longing in his expression. I try to speak but can't find words. After a moment in a completely helpless trance, I nod.

"Then I'll see you there." He smiles and walks off down the street, leaving me standing in a stupor.

He wants me to be there? He didn't know if he was going, but I am, so now he is too? Did I hear that right? Was that really what he said? He wants to see me?

He wants to see me?

I float home on some lovesick high, and before I know it I'm sitting on my couch, staring blankly at the wall. Nick will be at the party because I will be there. It's almost like the words are from a different language and didn't belong together in the same sentence. Something pops inside me, and I have a burst of energy. I hop up, grab my purse, and head for the door, but not before looking at the time: 6:43. Twenty-four hours and seventeen minutes until Nick and I are at the same party. With a giggle, I pull out my phone and call Bree to see if she wants to meet me down at Macy's. I suddenly have the urge to buy a new dress.

15

My cab pulls up in front of the New York Public Library, and I step out, trying—and failing horribly—to be graceful and ladylike in my new heels. I was an idiot yesterday, and bought cute shoes that were on sale and matched my new dress, failing to consider that they had four inch heels, and I have never worn anything over two. They are currently turning what should be a grand and elegant entrance into something that resembles the first steps of a newborn giraffe.

Somehow I make it into the building, check my coat, and stumble into the restroom without falling on my face. I take a quick appraisal in the mirror and actually like what I see. I'm wearing my new, blue, flowy, Maggy London wrap dress I bought yesterday, which Bree assured me looked much better than the brown one I had also considered. Looking at myself now, I'm glad she talked me into this one. It hugs all the good curves, hides all the bad ones, and the V-neck shows just enough cleavage to be sexy without being skanky. I'd gone this afternoon to have my hair done, something I never do, and I took over an hour to perfect my makeup. I'm happy to see it was all worth it—I look damn good!

I make my way—carefully, on my now numb feet—out to the cocktail reception area. The gala planners have really outdone themselves this year, and everything looks amazing. High cocktail tables with burgundy and gold tablecloths, flower arrangements done in rich fall colors, white-gloved servers passing around champagne and hors d'oeuvres, and a large mahogany bar, stocked with top shelf hooch. Funny how the company could only afford to give me a minuscule raise this year, but bacon-wrapped filet mignon hors d'oeuvres for the gala were a fiscal necessity.

I do a quick survey of the room to see if Nick—*ahem*, I mean *Bree* is here yet. As I scan the bar area, I see a familiar young man ordering wine and a cocktail. It's Chris. I walk up behind him and place a hand on his arm.

"Congratulations, Mr. Langston."

"Julia! I was hoping to see you here!" he says with radiant smile, giving me a hug.

I return the hug, trying to hide my shock. I can barely believe my eyes; he's a completely different man from the one I spent so much time with in Maine. He is smiling, warm, and confident—not at all the shy, timid introvert he had been. Love had obviously done wonders for him, and something about it all suddenly makes me want to cry.

"How have you been? We missed you that last week at the house."

"I've been great, no complaints," I say. "We have been doing so much wedding planning this past week, I'm surprised this is the first I've seen you."

"Well, I'm not really needed for most of that." He grins.

"Has your mother scared you into eloping yet?" I give him a wry smile.

"No, but she's getting close." He laughs. "Can I get you a drink?" He motions to my empty hands.

"Wine would be great, thanks. Whatever they have that's red."

Armed with an exceptionally good Merlot, I walk with Chris over to where Bree, Margaret, and Margaret's husband, John, are waiting.

"Julia, don't you look lovely!" Margaret says, hugging me.

"Yep, that is definitely the one." Bree beams, nodding at my dress.

Their conversation picks up where it left off, and I quietly sip my wine, pretending to pay attention when I am actually scanning the room as discreetly as possible.

Shouldn't Nick be here by now?

Everyone else seems to be here. Maybe he's changed his mind and isn't coming. That would figure. A hundred and twenty dollar dress and an evening of primping down the drain. Wait, is that him? No, too short.

Maybe he's just late.

"Jules?" Bree calls me out of my search. Everyone is looking at me expectantly, and I have no idea what they are even talking about.

"I'm sorry, what was that?"

"Margaret was asking about the dresses."

Dresses? I stare at her blankly.

"For the wedding…"

"Oh, yes! Sorry, don't mind me."

"She won't tell me what they—" Margaret suddenly looks past me. "Mr. Kerkley," she says, stepping around me. "I'm so glad you could make it!"

I turn around to see Nick, looking *impossibly* handsome in a three-piece tux.

Okay, don't blush, everyone will notice, don't blush, don't blush.

Margaret gives Nick a quick hug, then makes introductions. "Mr. Nicholas Kerkley, this is my husband, John Herstein." The two shake hands, and then Nick takes a few steps over to greet Bree and Chris. After the greetings are over and the conversation picks up where it left off, I decide it's safe to bring my gaze up off the floor and take a peek at Nick.

Big mistake.

As soon as I look up I see that he's watching me. Our eyes lock, and he gives me a smile that makes my toes curl. God damn it all! It is *ridiculous* how much I still love this man!

I quickly turn my attention to the person talking, though my peripheral vision never leaves Nick. He slowly makes his way around the parameter of the group; my heart pounds just a little harder and harder until he is right next to me. I wonder if he can hear it.

Okay, now is your chance, say something to him.

I take a deep breath, turn my shoulders toward him slightly. "Hi."

Hi? Dear God.

Okay, say something intelligent next time, idiot!

"Hi," he replies with a grin.

"I'm glad you came," I say before I can stop myself.

"Me too." He really needs to stop looking gorgeous, or I'm going to be on the floor. "You…you look beautiful."

He really is trying to kill me! My cheeks are on fire before I can even try to stop it. "Thank you," I say, or at least try to say. I'm not sure any sound comes out.

"This is nice," he says after a moment, glancing around the room. "I really didn't know what to expect. Do they do this every year?" We're completely facing each other now, and I relax. It's just so easy to be around him.

"Pretty much. It's always at a different location, but just as… grandiose. It's a big company with big clients; they want to make sure they impress everyone. This might be my favorite one so far. I like the library idea. At least someone was being creative."

"I like it too. I didn't even know you could have events like this here. Maybe next year they can rent out Yankee Stadium; that would be fun," he adds with a chuckle.

"It would be, but I'm sure that's much too low brow," I say with a snotty inflection and an eye roll. "Besides, you hate the Yankees." I blush suddenly and look down as I realize that I've just openly acknowledged our past for the first time since this reunion began. Something in his smile tells me he realizes it too.

"Okay, maybe Madison Square Garden then." He grins.

I smile without having to think about it. This feels so comfortably familiar. So easy. The two of us have slipped into our own private bubble, and it happened so fluidly that the rest of the group doesn't even seem to notice. Which is all for the better as I would be happy to stay this way forever. After a few moments I realize that we have fallen silent, but it's not awkward; there's only a strange but relaxing feeling of relief, like taking a breath after being underwater. I sip my wine and look up, meeting his gaze. Our eyes lock and my heart races again.

"Actually, Jules," he says, quieter now, not breaking our stare, "there is something I've been wanting to talk to you about."

The intensity in his eyes makes my heart jump into my throat, and the room suddenly feels like it's a thousand degrees. For a few seconds I can only stare back at him, afraid to blink or he might disappear. I take a breath, but before I can get my first syllable out, something catches my eye from across the room. I glance over, and my heart stops. There, working his way through the crowded room, is Zach.

Oh God, no!

The bubble I'd imagined surrounding Nick and me pops, and my world comes to a screeching halt. Before the word "hide" even comes to mind he spots me and walks over.

As I watch him approach, my throat closes and I can't breathe. How the hell could I have done this? How could I have completely forgotten about him? For God's sake, I invited him! I had told him to meet me here! Yet somehow, it was possible for his existence on this planet to totally escape my mind for the past two days?

Seriously?

I feel completely helpless as he reaches us and, with a big smile, pulls me into a more-than-friendly hug and kisses my cheek. Nick actually has to take a step back to let him in.

I want to die.

"I'm so sorry I'm late," he says, releasing me from the hug but keeping a hand on the small of my back. "I had the slowest cab on earth."

I'm frozen. I stare at him for a moment before forcing myself—in the name of common decorum—to smile and greet him like a person. "No, it's fine." I'm praying I don't sound as uncomfortable as I am. "Zach, this is Mr. Kerkley, one of our clients." I know that the rules of polite society demand I introduce the two men standing in front of me, regardless of the fact that the situation is so awkward that I'm currently contemplating climbing the stairs and jumping off the balcony. "Mr. Kerkley, this is Zach Connoray." I venture a look up at Nick. He's staring at Zach with no expression whatsoever. All the smiles and warmth from a moment ago are gone.

"Nice to meet you," Zach says, smiling and extending a hand. Nick shakes it stiffly and nods once, but says nothing.

"Jules?" I hear Bree call from behind. I turn to see Bree looking back and forth between Zach and myself, and notice that the rest of the group has also taken interest in the new arrival who has his arm around me. I turn and take a step toward them—happily disengaging Zach's hand in the process—and start the introductions.

"Everyone, this is Zach Connoray. Zach, this is Brianna St. Charles, her fiancé, Chris Langston, and Margaret and John Herstein."

"So this is the young man we have heard so much about?" Margaret asks with a mischievous smile.

I could kill her.

I blush hotly, but not at all for the reason anyone suspects. It has more to do with the person standing directly behind me who I can't see, but can feel like a knife in my back. How could I let this happen? Am I really this obliviously one-track minded? Nick tells me he is coming to a party where I will be, and somehow, that conversation equates to erasing Zach's name as well as any plans I had with him from my mind entirely? And could he have walked in at a worse possible moment? What was Nick about to say? What did he need to talk to me about? The look in his eyes told me it was definitely not work-related. I'm dying to look at him now, just so I can try to read his expression. Should I turn and look? That seems way too obvious, plus I don't have the balls for that. I'm terrified of what I will find, because there are no good possibilities. Is he mad? Happy? Indifferent? Better not to know, because it will upset me either way. If he's mad, it will make the situation that much more awkward. If he's happy, that will depress me, and indifference would be worse. Much as I hate to admit it, part of me — the selfish, heartless, bitchy side that we all have but rarely acknowledge — actually *wants* him to be mad. Or at the very least, mildly upset or annoyed in some way.

I really am horrible!

Luckily, or maybe unluckily, the group slowly rearranges itself, and I throw an inconspicuous glance over to Nick. He has his hands clasped behind his back, no expression on his face, and is glaring downward through the floor. He's impossible to read, but my stomach still ties itself a new knot.

I begin to notice a stirring at the other end of the hall as two large doors open and we are welcomed in to be seated for dinner.

"Looks like it's time to eat," Margaret says, stepping out to lead our group forward. As she nears Nick however, he stops her.

"Actually, I'm not going to be able to stay, and I just wanted to say goodnight."

What?

"Oh," Margaret says, putting a hand on his arm. "That's too bad. Are you sure?"

"Yes." He tries to hide the curt tone to his voice, but I can hear it.

"Well then, it was nice to see you. I guess we'll be meeting up soon to make new plans if you're sure you are passing on the Marston Estate."

"You're not taking it?" Chris chimes in, overhearing. "I didn't know that."

Neither did I.

"No, I'm not. I realized I wanted it for the wrong reasons," Nick says, then, turning his gaze to a subtle but pointed glare at me, adds, "and some things belong in the past and are better left there."

I feel like I've been stabbed in the chest, and have to bite down on my tongue to keep from crying.

"All right then, dear, I'll be in touch," Margaret says, patting his arm.

"Goodnight." Nick nods to the group, then walks off without looking at me again.

I stare after him for several seconds, afraid that any movement at all will shatter me into a sobbing heap on the floor.

"Shall we?" I hear Zach ask, putting a hand on my back. I slowly look up at him and see a combination of concern and confusion on his face. I nod and, still lost in my stupor, stagger forward with the rest of the crowd. "Here," he says, taking my glass. "Let me get you a refill."

Yes. Wine. I need more wine.

My eyes aren't open yet, but I can tell the sun is pouring in my bedroom window. The second thing I notice is a pulsing headache. The third is simply the realization of the fact that I am home in my bed and have no idea how I got here.

Dear God, what did I do? Please just let me not be fired.

Sudden movement on the bed makes my eyes pop open. What the hell? I turn over and see…Zach.

Oh my God, what did I do?

Zach is in bed with me! Dear holy hell, please tell me we didn't have sex! We couldn't have, I mean there is no way I was *that* drunk…

I glance down at myself and see I am still wearing my blue dress from the party. Okay, good. Still dressed, underwear…yep, still on. Another look shows Zach took off his jacket, tie, and shirt, but is still wearing his undershirt and pants.

Okay, deep breath.

There was no sex.

No one has sex and then gets redressed just to go to sleep. All is well.

Zach stretches and sits up, glancing over at me to find me staring back.

"Good morning," he says with a sleepy grin. "How do you feel?"

"What the hell happened?" I ask, sitting up.

"You had a little too much wine," he says, exaggerating "little."

"Oh God." I close my eyes, preparing for the worst. "What did I do? Please tell me I'm not fired…"

"No, no, nothing like that. In fact, I think I'm the only one who knew." *Oh good.* "You just got really tired. Margaret thought you might be coming down with something and convinced you to go home. You passed out in the cab, and I brought you up. I knew your building, but had to go in your purse for your apartment number, sorry," he says with a guilty grimace.

"You're *apologizing?*"

"I didn't feel right just leaving you, so I stayed. I would have slept on the couch, but it's way too small." He still sounds guilty.

"Don't worry about it, and thank you. I'm the one who's sorry." I get up and check my balance. Not bad.

"How do you feel?"

"Just a headache, so pretty good, considering. How many did I have?"

"Glasses or bottles?" he chuckles.

I bury my face in my hands.

"Don't worry about it." He comes around the bed and rubs his hands up and down my arms. "Like I said, no one realized."

"How could they have not noticed how many I had?"

"You drink fast. Your glass was always about the same level; what they didn't see were the refills. Besides, you weren't acting drunk, just tired. They're all worried you have the flu. You could probably get out of work for a few days, if you want," he adds, laughing.

I finally smile, relaxing a bit. "I feel gross. If you don't mind waiting for me to shower and change, I'll take you to breakfast, or lunch as the case may be." I feel eternally grateful to this man. I know breakfast is kind of weak, but it's all I can do at the moment, and I have to give him something. "We can stop by your place on the way so you can change."

"Sounds good."

I get in the shower and let the hot water run over me for a few minutes. Thank God for Zach! If it hadn't been for him, I'm sure I would have made a complete ass out of myself. I owe him so much, and I feel really guilty about resenting him for interrupting Nick and me last night. He really is a sweet guy, and as for Nick—

I can't even *think* about that right now.

The fact is, Zach is a great guy who thinks the world of me, and I've been giving him the brush off for almost a week now. It is time for me to get back on track and start learning to want what's best for me. How many guys would have taken care of me the way Zach did? I am lucky to have him. The best way for me to get over what happened with Nick last night is to move forward just like I'd planned.

I wash, dry off, pop two aspirin, and throw on my comfy jeans and hoodie. I find Zach on the couch, waiting for me.

"Okay," I say, slipping on my ratty sneakers. "Let's go." I turn back toward him when he doesn't immediately follow me. He is still sitting on the couch, looking down at his hands. "Something wrong?"

"No, not at all," he says, glancing up. "But can we talk for a minute?"

Oh no, what now?

I sit down next to him on the couch and brace myself.

"Look, Julia," he says, taking one of my hands in his. "I think you know how I feel about you…"

Oh God.

"…but I can see there is something wrong, and I just want you to know it's okay."

Wait, what?

"Huh?" I whisper, my heart beating a little faster.

"It's okay. I mean, we've been out a few times now, and it's been great. Really it has, I'm not complaining. I can tell you are trying, but I can also tell you're a little hesitant."

"You can?" I stare at him, totally dumbstruck. I hadn't thought it was so obvious. Why isn't he running out the door? Honestly, if he has any idea how damaged I actually am, he probably would be.

"I don't know what it is that bothers you, but we all have…you know…stuff…and I just want you to know that whatever it is, it's all right," he says, gently squeezing my hand. "I understand."

Tears are in my eyes before I can blink them away, and I press my lips together to keep them from trembling. I don't deserve this. I don't deserve *him*. How can he be so wonderful after the way I have treated him? He is looking at me with so much warmth and sympathy, which are two things that, as far as my treatment of him is concerned, I'm not worthy of.

Suddenly, before I even realize what I'm doing, I lean over…

…and kiss him.

Maybe it's the incredible gratitude I feel for him right now, maybe it's the tender compassion he's just shown me, maybe it's the horrible and somewhat selfish need I have to be wanted and loved, or maybe it's my inner fairy godmother, who also had way too much to drink last night and probably isn't thinking clearly. I'm not sure what it is, but in the end, it doesn't matter.

He jumps slightly at first, but after a moment he gets over his shock and relaxes, kissing me back. We stay like that for a few moments, lips moving lazily against each other, and I have to say it's… nice. Not earth shattering, not mind blowing, just…nice. And really, I think that's exactly what I want it to be. Zach is the one to break the kiss and when he does he leans back and smiles at me.

"Well, I wasn't expecting that."

"Me either."

He leans back in, but just as our lips touch again, his phone buzzes in his pocket. With a groan he pulls it out, checks the display and chuckles. "Hey, Lisa," he answers, with a smile over at me. "No, I'm not busy." *Oh, Lis, if you only knew.* "Oh, yeah sure, I'm not far. Give me ten minutes. Okay. Bye." Lisa doesn't usually work weekends; something must be up. Zach closes his phone, lets out a long sigh and turns to me. "Looks like we are going to have to make a stop before we eat. For some reason, the reports I sent to Lisa are coded, and she needs my ID badge. It won't take long, sorry."

"No problem," I say, though actually I'm incredibly anxious. What is Lisa going to say when I show up with Zach? It's still early. Will she guess that we spent the night together? Nothing happened, but I know that won't make any difference at all. Trying to squash my discomfort, I add, "There are a few good restaurants over that way. Maybe we could do breakfast over there?"

"Sure," he says, as we make our way outside. "I'm really sorry, I always leave my badge in my desk. Go figure that the one weekend I don't…"

"That's the way it goes," I say as we turn onto 7th Avenue, and I take my second huge leap of the day, sliding my hand into his. I glance up to see him smile broadly, but he doesn't look down.

What has gotten into me?

It only takes us a few minutes to get to Lisa's building, but all the way I'm nervous. In and out, we'll be in and out. I won't even give Lisa the chance to ask a pile of awkward questions, or even give her the opportunity to deduce that we spent the night together. In and out. No questions, no talking.

As we step out of the elevator onto Lisa's floor, I see her sitting behind the receptionist's desk waiting for us. It takes me a few minutes to see the two police officers with her.

That's weird…

One of them approaches us. "Are you Zachary Connoray?" he asks.

"Yes," Zach answers, the color draining from his face.

"Miss," the officer says to me, "if you will step aside please."

I move back a step in shock, as the officer removes a set of handcuffs from his belt.

"Zachary Connoray, you are under arrest for theft and embezzlement. You have the right to remain silent…"

Three weeks, five bottles of wine, an entire bottle of aspirin, six boxes of cookies, two pounds, and two boxes of tissue later, I'm in hell.

Twenty days, sixteen hours, and twenty-seven minutes in hell if I'm counting, but I'm not. That would be pathetic, so three weeks it is. Three weeks since I removed my fairy wings, burned them, and lapsed into an existence seeped in depression, wallowing, remorse, bitterness, alcohol, and sugar. I have no goal or plan. I don't want one. I want to be miserable. And from where I sit, I have every right.

First point of misery: I wasted time, thought, and emotions on Zach, who is now in jail. Well, he was at least, but I'm sure he's made bail by now. He was arrested that morning in Lisa's office, and I haven't seen him since. That's right, I kissed a guy for the first time in almost a decade, and then he went to jail. If there were ever a list of things I never thought I'd say, that would definitely be high up on it.

It was discovered that he was the one stealing from Lisa's company. He had been at it for almost two years and as it turns out, he's very skilled at fraud. He made sure all his actions were traced to the accounts payable/receivable department so it would seem like one of those ladies were responsible—which was how Lisa came to suspect Linda. He even made sure to back date certain transactions, so it would appear whoever was doing this started long before he was even hired. As of the end of last month, he had embezzled over one hundred and sixty-two thousand dollars in the two short years since he began. His only mistake was making a transaction on a day when all three of the ladies in the accounting department were out. He had seen Linda there that morning, but he didn't know she'd gone home sick.

So I've spent a portion of my life trying to force myself into a relationship with a con artist.

Go me.

Point number two: Bree and Chris's happily ever after. Don't get me wrong, I couldn't be happier for them, and I am not bitter at all. That being said, it's extremely hard to get into the whole lovey-dovey wedding spirit when one currently hates their life, and is ready to take a hatchet to anything even remotely heart-, cupid-, or wedding ring-shaped. I want to be miserable, which is difficult at wedding functions. Over the past three weeks I've had two dress fittings, a bridal shower, and a cake tasting to suffer through — though there's never much suffering when cake is involved — as well as several meals and other planning sessions. I fake it well enough; no one seems to notice that my smile is taped on. I am not about to be a downer and ruin everyone else's good time — that's not my style at all. My misery doesn't need company. I do fine on my own.

My final point of misery, which has been occupying the majority of my thoughts, sober or otherwise: the parting between Nick and me the night of the SMS Gala. His words continue to buzz around in my head like an angry hornet.

"Some things belong in the past and are better left there."

"…better left there…"

What did he mean? Okay, I know what he meant, but was he saying he had been thinking of *not* leaving it there in the past — *our* past? Is that what he wanted to talk to me about? Could that even be possible? Not that it matters. There were definitely things he didn't have a chance to say, but what he *did* say was loud and clear.

It's over.

He doesn't want anything from me, not now, not ever. And it's more than likely he never did. Sure, I'd like to think that he had wanted to talk to me about us, and being together, and all of that other stuff, but that was probably not it at all. Odds are he wanted to discuss something to do with the wedding, maybe a surprise for Chris and Bree that he didn't want them overhearing.

That had to be it.

Then Zach comes in and totally interrupts him; he had to be annoyed by that. Then I turn away, and introduce Zach to the rest of the group without even a backward glance, as if Nick and I hadn't been talking at all. I'd treated him like a nobody. Like some random client that I didn't want to be talking to in the first place. God, I even addressed him that way! I had called him "*Mr.* Kerkley"! Not "Nick Kerkley," or even "Mr. Nicholas Kerkley."

Argh!

To make matters worse, I had not seen hide nor hair of him since that night. Every time there's a wedding-related function, I half hope, half fear, he'll be there—but he never is. I guess in the long run that's a good thing. I'm not sure how I would do faking my happiness with him in the same room. So all in all, it has been for the best.

But he will be there tonight.

Tonight he has no choice—neither of us do.

Tonight is the wedding rehearsal.

I am still in my underwear, having just finished my hair and makeup, staring unseeing into the mirror. Tonight there will be the rehearsal, dinner, and maybe even dancing. The room will be filled with love, romance, and every other feeling on my embargo list. If I were still in my delusional phase of being my own fairy godmother and turning my life around, I might look at this evening as an opportunity. I could maybe talk to Nick and clear the air, or perhaps meet someone new and have a dance. Maybe—if I were still delusional, that is.

But I'm not.

I don't want dreams, and I don't want fairy tales. They are not made for everyone, and that's just how it is. My life was fine before I screwed it up by trying to fix what wasn't broken. It may have been far from perfect, but that doesn't equal bad. The only goal I have is to get through this night and tomorrow. After that, who knows.

I slip on my black Prada cocktail dress—a birthday gift from Lisa and the nicest item of clothing I own—and fill my evening bag with the essentials. The *bare* essentials given the size of the bag. As the weather took a cold, depressing, wintery turn about the same time my spirits did, I pull on my boots and a large wool cape-wrap, stash my dress shoes in the oversized pockets of the cape, and head out.

The rehearsal dinner is being held at a restaurant called Barbetta. Up until last week, we were all to meet at the Waldorf for the actual rehearsal first, then make our way to dinner after. However, the room at the Waldorf we were going to use for the rehearsal needs to be used for another event tonight, so the Waldorf's wedding coordinator agreed to give us the rehearsal rundown at the restaurant instead. No skin off her back as she was coming to the dinner anyway, and none off mine, as Barbetta is in my neighborhood. I had been there for a brunch once, but that was during the summer and we were in the garden. I've never seen the private indoor rooms.

It takes me all of five minutes to get there, and I take a deep breath before going in. I switch my shoes, stashing my ugly boots inside the cape as soon as I am in the door. A hostess takes me up to our private room, where I find everyone mingling and drinking. This really is a nice place. Everything is classy and elegant, fitting perfectly with the overall theme of the wedding. Debbie is thrilled, I'm sure.

"Don't you look cute!" Bree says, spotting me and coming over. "I love your dress!"

"Thanks. I'm just glad to finally have a reason to wear it." I turn on my best-practiced smile, preparing to keep it on for the rest of the night. I quickly glance up to locate Nick. Just so I will know where he is, so I don't have to worry about him surprising me.

Yeah, that's it…

I find him with a group of guys near the chapel-like arrangement of chairs by the back wall, where I assume the actual rehearsal will take place. He doesn't so much as glance my way. Good.

"Would you like a drink?" Bree asks.

"No, no, I'm fine." I have adopted a "no alcohol in public" policy after my near disaster at the Gala.

"We were just about to start the rehearsal. We have a makeshift aisle set up over there, and we were just pairing up."

Pairing up?

Let's see. Jen and Brandon will be together as Maid of Honor and Best Man, so that leaves two to one odds I'll be with Nick. Crap! How could I not have thought about this earlier?

"You will be walking with…"

Please, please, please no…

"…Derek."

Thank God!

"Okay, I need the bridal party and parents over here, so we can begin," the coordinator calls out. Bree hurries off, and I make my way over to the chapel area, scanning the room as I go. I have met every-one in the bridal party at one point or another, with the exception of the flower girl and ring bearer. The only other people I recognize, however, are the parents of the bride and groom, and Cathy and Rob, who I see standing over by the tables. Cathy's eye catches mine, and she waves with a smile. I smile back while thinking it was odd to see them here. Though I guess they would be considered out-of-town guests, who are customarily invited to the rehearsal dinner. At any rate, I am glad to see her. It will give me someone to talk to, as my usual conversation keepers — Bree and/or Chris — will be busy tonight.

The rehearsal goes smoothly. There's a little drama when the flower girl drops her basket and cries over the spilled petals, but that is quickly resolved. Throughout the entire rehearsal I try my best not to look at Nick, but fail horribly. I sneak glance after glance, hoping and dreading to just once find his eyes awaiting mine — but they never are. In fact he seems to be totally unaware that I am in the room at all. Not that he should be paying me special attention or anything, but I'm pretty sure I've, at the very least, made eye contact with everyone else in the wedding party at one point or another.

It's okay. Just don't let it get to you. It can get to you later when you're at home, but for now, keep it together.

The evening progresses slowly, moving from the rehearsal into appetizers. I am happy to see that there are no assigned seats and make my way over to where Cathy is seated.

"Julia!" Cathy stands to give me a hug. "It's so good to see you! We missed you up in Maine after you left."

"I know! It seems like I missed the best part."

"So what's new with you? Are you here alone? Bree tells me you have been seeing someone."

"No, that was nothing really," I say, hoping that by telling Cathy, the information will find its way to Nick.

"Oh, that's too bad. She seemed so happy for you."

"Yes, well, Bree made a lot more out of it than it really was. You know how it is when you're in love; you want to see everyone else in love too."

"That's true. I should have added the proverbial grain of salt." She laughs.

I pick up the menu card at my place at the table, and idly toy with it. "I am happy for her, though. For them both. It seems to be a match made in heaven."

"Soul mates," she agrees, glancing over at them, "if you believe in that sort of thing."

"I do actually, but I think most women do. We almost have to, what with the stories we grow up with. I think it's the men who are harder to convince."

"You think men don't love the same way we do?"

"No, some do, it's by no means a rule. But I do think they can get over us much more easily than we can them. And we certainly love the longest. Even when there's no hope left. Men don't have the trouble we do moving on."

"That could be true," she allowed, "but that could have something to do with the stories *they* grow up with. They aren't taught to be as sentimental as we are."

"No. The funny thing is, they're the same stories. Cinderella, Snow White, Sleeping Beauty, they each waited their whole lives for one man: Prince Charming. Are there three separate 'Prince Charmings' out there, I wonder, or is it the same guy, working his way around the kingdoms? You would think if it were three different guys, that they would each warrant their own name. Women are taught to believe they have to look for and find 'the one,' while men are taught to believe there will always be another princess."

"I never really thought about it quite like that," she says, clearly amused by my logic.

"I've put some thought into it, sure, but don't forget that grain of salt. I am just as biased as Bree, but in another way entirely."

She smiles but doesn't comment, which is probably for the best. We turn our conversation to lighter subjects as others join our table.

Dinner comes and goes, and as dessert is being served I hear someone clink a spoon against their glass, calling us all to attention. I look over and see Debbie standing by the bridal party table with a microphone, and standing next to her, holding a champagne glass, is Nick.

Great. Something else I hadn't considered was the possibility of having to sit through Nick addressing a room full of people on the subject of love, happiness, and devotion. This night gets better and better.

"Good evening, everyone," Debbie begins. "As the Best Man and Maid of Honor will be addressing us tomorrow, I have asked Mr. Kerkley, one of the groomsmen, to say a few words before we all enjoy our cake."

As Nick takes the microphone, my palms begin to sweat and my pulse pounds in my throat. I sit rigidly, staring at the spot of empty air where Debbie had just been standing, which makes it appear to anyone who might look at me as though I'm watching Nick — something I absolutely refuse to do. Short of running out of the room like a two-year-old, I have no choice but listen to him give a lovey-dovey toast, but I'll be damned if I am going to look him in the eye while he does it.

I steel my emotions, lock my position and facial expression in place, and brace for impact.

"When Debbie asked me to give a toast I was nervous, because as anyone who knows me can tell you, I am not exactly qualified to talk about marriage. The only marriage advice I could give anyone came to me first hand from my brother-in-law, who is fond of saying that marriage is very much like football. It takes practice, teamwork, and is fun for about three hours each week in the fall."

He pauses for the laughter, and I unclench my fists just a bit. He's joking and light-hearted — maybe this won't be so bad.

"So," he continues, as the chuckles of the guests die down, "as you can see, my personal knowledge of wedded bliss is somewhat lacking. However, what I can say a few words about is love. Love is a word that is overused these days, due to other *lesser* feelings often being mistaken for it. Infatuation, admiration, and attraction can pose as love, and can sometimes overwhelm us and fool us into thinking we have found the real thing when we haven't. Those other feelings may be pleasant for a time, but they are not real love. Real love is rare. It's something that, quite honestly, I believe very few people ever truly experience.

"However, when love — real love — finds you, I believe you'll recognize it instantly. Chris and Bree have gotten something of a hard time about the fact that they got engaged within a month of being introduced. That may seem strange to some of us, but that's the thing about real love: when you know, you know. When you meet that one special person, somewhere deep inside, your soul recognizes its other half. Somehow you know that you have found the person who will make you happy for the rest of your life, the person who makes you the man or woman you were meant to be. It's not easy to come by, and it's easy to be fooled. However, I've always believed that the real thing is worth waiting for."

Fooled. He thinks he was fooled.

I am still sitting perfectly still, staring at the empty space beside Nick. The only difference is that now I can't even blink, because if I do, the tears swimming in my eyes will spill over, and I can't allow that.

"Now, as for me," he continues after a pause, "I'm still waiting. But *as* someone who is still waiting, I can tell you that Chris and Bree remind me of what exactly it is that I am waiting for. And I think I can speak for everyone here tonight when I say that seeing the two of you —" he turns to face Chris and Bree "—and the love that you so obviously share, gives us all a little more faith in love and a little more hope in that age-old idea of happily ever after. Congratulations, and all the best to you." He raises his glass; we follow his lead, drink, and applaud. Nick takes his seat, and as soon as discreetly possible, I steal quietly out of the room and lock myself in a bathroom stall.

After a good fifteen minutes spent blubbering, sniffing, trembling, blowing my nose, wiping my eyes, and fixing my makeup, I emerge from the restroom emotionally battered but composed. When I get back to the table, I see my purse and favor have been moved, and my drink and cake, which I hadn't had a chance to touch, have been cleared away.

Damn!

I decide not to sit — as now I have no cake to eat — and mill around the room, looking for someone to occupy my time and mind. At first I worry that my milling could cause a run in with Nick, which I absolutely could not handle at the moment, but relax as I notice he's nowhere to be found. I see Bree sitting with Jen and Derek, and figure there is no harm in joining them. After all, Jen and Derek are not really guests, therefore, I would not be taking the bride away from her duties as hostess. The four of us talk for over an hour about this and that, occasionally being joined by a passerby or two. Finally, Chris takes Bree away so they can say good-bye to the guests who are starting to leave for the night.

I wander back over to my table, planning to head home my-self—a sad thought on a Friday night. I grab my favor and my bag, but for some reason my bag won't close. I look in to see what is blocking the latch, and pull out a folded menu card. I open it up and find writing on the back.

Julia,

I was planning to speak with you tomorrow, but after what I heard you say to Cathy tonight, I can't wait. Men forget? Men move on? I'll admit I've been a lot of things: mad, resentful, bitter, even vengeful. But I have never forgotten, and I have never moved on. God knows I've tried. I meant every word I said tonight. I am still waiting, waiting for you.

I love you, Jules. I have never stopped loving you. My heart is more yours now than it ever was, and I only pray that what we had isn't lost forever. I am going out to the garden and I'll wait for you until nine. If you don't want me the way I do you, you don't have to explain or apologize. Just don't come out. If I don't see you by nine, I'll have my answer.

Always yours,

Nick

I stare at the letter, not blinking, not breathing, totally motionless.
This can't be…
I read it again.
Could he really…
I read it again.
He loves me…
He loves me!

I am suddenly lighter than air and smiling uncontrollably. He loves me! He still loves me! After everything! After what I did, he still loves me! Part of me is worried I will wake up any minute and this will all be a dream, but the rest of me doesn't care. I jump up and grab my wrap, ready to run outside. Ready to throw my arms around him and never let go. Ready to—

I stop short. What time is it? I grab my phone out of my bag and flip it open.

9:11 p.m.

Oh no...

I bolt out of the room, leaving everything behind. I run through the restaurant, looking for the doors leading out to the garden. Finally finding them, I throw one open, stumble out into the cold night air, and see...

...no one.

17

"Nick?"

The garden is silent.

He's gone.

"…I'll have my answer."

He thinks I've thrown him and his love aside—again—and has left.

I sink down onto an ice cold stone bench next to the empty basin of what, in better weather, would be a pond and fountain. I stare at the ground around my feet, tears running down my face.

Well, I'm here—in a garden, hopeless and crying. It really is perfect. Sure it's the dead of winter and I am freezing, but doesn't that just add to the overall atmosphere? So what is she waiting for? Isn't this the point where my fairy godmother finally shows up and saves me? Come on, this is her chance to fix everything she let me down on eight years ago. She could magically bring Nick back, or even something as stupid and unromantic as telling me, "Oh, he's still here, he just had to run to the bathroom. He'll be right back." That would be fine. I'm not picky.

For an insane moment I actually look around, expecting a grandma with wings, or even the condescending creepy godmother from my dream, to show up. But of course there is no one. The world doesn't work like that. No one is going to hand you everything you need to be happy. That's the real appeal of a fairy godmother anyway—not having to take any risks. Cinderella had it all handed to her, and then after the clock struck twelve and she was on her own, what did she do? Did she march up to the castle in her rags and lay it all on the line, hoping the prince would still love her in the plain light of day? No. She ran home and hid. She made the prince come to her. She took the easy road, and it worked out for her because it's a fairy tale. In real life, there is no happiness without risk.

Nick had taken the leap. He'd laid everything inside him out for me to see—something I don't think I would ever have had the courage to do—and he did it with nothing more than the small hope that I would return his feelings and make it all worthwhile.

And I had let him down.

He took the risk that I couldn't bring myself to take.

And now it's too late.

Too late?

Out of nowhere, a fire sparks somewhere deep in my chest and I'm gripped by a sudden burst of determination. No. It's not too late. It may be too late for *us*, but it's never too late for the truth. Nick was able to lay it all on the line, and I'll never be able to live with myself if I don't do the same. This isn't some imaginary fairy godmother's chance to fix my life—it's mine. If I have to live the rest of my life without him, I can have the one small comfort of knowing I did everything that I could. I can't let this chance go.

I won't.

I jump up and make my way back to the rehearsal room as fast as I'm able on my frozen toes. There are only a few people left, and I scan the room, praying Derek hasn't left yet. I see him at one of the tables, collecting the leftover favors.

"Derek," I pant as I reach him. "Do you know where Nick is staying tonight?"

"He's over at the Waldorf. We all are. Figured it'd be easier that way—"

"Thanks!" I cut him off and run for my wrap and purse. I know he is probably confused, but I don't have time to worry about that. Nor do I have time to fuss with my boots, which I leave under the table. Someone will find them, and if not, who cares. I dart out of the restaurant without saying good-bye to anyone, and frantically look for a cab going the right way. The Waldorf isn't far, but a taxi would still be much faster than running in heels and a dress. After an eternity, I flag one down.

"The Waldorf Astoria, please," I tell the driver as I fling myself into the cab.

He pulls out without a word, and I lean back on the seat, taking a minute to pull myself together. By the time we turn onto Park Avenue, I've caught my breath for the most part, but my heart is still pounding. We make it to the hotel, but get stuck in a line of vehicles waiting to drop off or pick up at the main entrance.

"This is fine, thanks," I say, throwing a twenty over the seat to him, and hop out onto the street. I slip and slide my way over the slush to the salted sidewalk. Once there, I straighten my shoulders and attempt to muster some grace. It'd be best not to run like a mad woman into a world-class hotel.

The doorman greets me, and I make my way inside and up the steps to the main lobby.

When I reach the center of the marble floor however, I hesitate. What the hell am I doing? I have absolutely no plan — not that any have worked so far. I don't know what room he's in, and even if I did, there is a good chance I need a room key to even operate the elevators to his floor. I stand motionless, staring into space as I figure out what to do. I see the check-in counter, and realize I should start there.

There is a small line, but that's okay; it gives me time to come up with a story. Odds are, I can't just walk up to the woman and ask for someone's room number, so I am going to have to come up with something clever enough to get me in without getting me caught and thrown out. After all, there is a wedding here tomorrow that I am very much a part of, and I don't want to get myself blacklisted from the hotel. Maybe I can say I am with him and I lost my room key. No, if that were true, I would know the room number. Okay, maybe I am here to surprise him. Girlfriends and wives surely do that sort of stuff all the time. I could say I'm his…girlfriend? No, wife is probably less suspicious. Wait, but then they might want to see ID. Maybe I could say I didn't change my name. Or I could say—

"Can I help you?" *Wow, that was a fast line.* I snap my head up to see a short, middle-aged woman with a warm smile and thick glasses looking at me. Her nametag says "Mary."

"Yes." I throw on my best smile. "Sorry. I wonder if you could help me. Can you tell me what room my husband is in?"

Wow, that was good. I didn't stutter or anything!

"Certainly, what is the name?"

Yes!

"Nicholas Kerkley."

"Yes, here he is…Oh."

Uh oh.

"He doesn't seem to have anyone listed in the room with him."

"No, he doesn't know I'm here," I try, still smiling. "I want to surprise him."

"Oh, how nice." Despite her smile, her eyes tell me I'm out of luck. "Well, you are going to have to have him come down to meet you, as I can't issue room numbers or keys to anyone not listed as a guest. I'm sorry."

My heart sinks to my knees. "It's fine, I understand."

"Why don't I call his room for you and see if he is there?"

"No, that's…" Hmm, I hadn't thought of that. He might not even be here. "Actually yes, could you? But just to see if he is there. Don't say anything about me." She picks up the phone and dials. My hands start to shake as I wait to hear a voice on the other end.

After a moment, she hangs up. "I'm sorry, there was no answer."

"That's all right, thanks for trying," I say.

My deflated disappointment must be clear on my face, because she reaches out and sympathetically pats my hand. "I'm sorry, dear," she says again. "Do you know where he might have gone? I could call you a cab."

"No," I sigh, "I have no idea where he is." He could be anywhere. I could go back to the restaurant and see if I'd missed him. That's a place to start anyway. "I just have to go look for him," I say, trying to be nonchalant. The concerned look on the receptionist's face, however, tells me that she can see this is a bit more serious than simply a "surprise my husband" visit.

"Go out and look for him? But you have no idea where he is. This is a big city, my dear."

"I don't know what else to do." I try stop my lip from trembling.

"I've always found," Mary says, leaning toward me and resting her arms on the counter, "that when I'm not sure what to do, it always helps to go back to what you know. You know he is staying here, which means he has to come back eventually. Why not wait for him? That has to be a better plan than trying to chase him down in one of the most populated cities in the world."

She's right I know, but I still can't seem to move.

"Why don't you try Sir Harry's," she says, pointing to the doors of a bar just off the lobby. "It's quiet, and you could have a drink and relax for a few minutes. Collect yourself a bit. Don't take this the wrong way—" she smiles "—but you're a mess."

I take a deep breath and realize she's right. "Thank you." I turn slowly toward the doors she referred to.

"Good luck, dear," Mary calls behind me.

As I make my way across the lobby, the idea of a drink sounds better and better. I know I have sworn off all alcohol in public places, but my hands are still shaking, and if I am going to sit here for God knows how long, I'm going to need *something*. When I step inside, I see Mary was right; it is quiet. Not nearly as crowded as I would have expected it to be for a Friday night. I look over to the long wooden bar, and my heart stops.

There, sitting alone at the end of the bar, is Nick.

My stomach turns over. He's facing away from me, hunched over, elbow on the bar, head in his hand, while the other hand holds a near-empty glass. He looks so wretched and broken that it tears my heart to shreds. Worst of all, I know that, once again, his pain is because of me.

I want to go to him but I can't move. After my frenzied rush of the last twenty minutes, I'm stuck to the floor and utterly speechless. What do I say? *I'm sorry?* That seems incredibly inadequate. *I love you?* He probably doesn't want to hear it anymore.

Without a conscious command, my feet slowly propel me forward. When I'm close, I hear the whisper of a voice I almost don't recognize to be my own.

"Nick?"

He turns suddenly, seeing me there for the first time. His eyes widen in shock.

"I'm sorry," I squeak out over the lump in my throat. "I'm so sorry, I didn't know until after...I came right away, but you were gone. I was sitting with Bree, and we were all talking…" He stands and slowly closes the space between us, but I can't stop rambling. "The waiter moved my purse, and I didn't see it until after…I wouldn't ha—"

I'm silenced by his lips crashing into mine. The entire world melts away as Nick wraps his arms around my waist and pulls me into him. I have never in my life felt anything like this kiss. It is so full of love and longing that I don't think I can handle it. Eight years, eight *long* years, I have waited for this kiss, and it's everything I remembered and more.

I tremble, terrified this isn't real, that I will wake up any minute now to find I fell asleep on an armchair out in the lobby. But the terror can't hold a candle to the overwhelming joy that threatens to carry me away.

All too soon he releases me and takes a half step back. Without a word, he slides his hand down my arm, laces his fingers through mine, and leads me out of the bar and to the elevators in the lobby. We manage to get one all to ourselves, and as soon as the doors close behind us, he cups my face in his hands and kisses me again—hard. My entire body feels like it's filled with champagne, bubbling and tingling under my skin, just waiting to explode. We kiss all the way to his floor, almost forgetting to breathe. Just before the doors open, we pause, gasping for air.

"I love you," he says against my lips. There's a catch in his voice, and I wonder if he's as close to tears as I am.

"I love you too," I answer, still struggling for breath.

He takes my hand again and leads me down the hall. The door to his room isn't even shut behind us before I'm in his arms again. If I thought the ride in the elevator was passionate—I had no idea. Now behind closed doors, our kisses grow more and more possessive, and begin to travel beyond our lips to cover our necks, chests, and anything else within reach. His hands work their way through my hair, letting it fall down around my shoulders. A few moments later he lays me back on the bed, and I realize that we're both completely undressed. I have no idea how that happened.

As we melt into one another, it's so much more than just sex. Maybe it's the fact that we have gone so long without each other, or maybe it's a consequence of the intense emotions we've both had to cope with this evening; I don't know for sure. All I do know is that

I've never in my life even imagined feeling the way I do now. There is more fervor, love, and passion pouring out of me than I knew I was capable of. My soul had been starving for almost a decade, yet I hadn't realized how much I had been missing—how much I had given up. Now that I have it back, I can barely believe I've lived so long without it.

We don't speak because there is no need. We just love, on and on, until every shadow of the last eight years is swept away, leaving us both floating somewhere in heaven. Minutes or hours later, while we are both still breathlessly recovering, Nick rolls to his side and pulls me against him. His arms wrap around me so tightly it nearly hurts—not that I would ever dream of complaining, or moving an inch. I lay against him, lost in happiness, breathing in his familiar scent, until I slip into the most peaceful sleep I've had in years.

18

I wake up slowly in a dark, unfamiliar room. The clock by the bed says 12:17, and I can distinctly feel someone lying behind me, and an arm draped over my side. Memories and images of a dream start to flood back to me. A dream about Nick, and Bree's rehearsal dinner, and a letter, and the Waldorf…

It was a dream, right?

It had to be. I have that dream — or at least a version of it — all the time. And then I wake up. Though I will admit, I usually wake up in my own bed. As I'm trying to make sense of all this, lips press into the hollow behind my ear.

"Are you awake?" a husky male voice asks against my hair.

"I thought so, but I guess not." I roll to my back, finding Nick's achingly gorgeous face mere inches from mine.

"I'm pretty sure you're awake," he says with a grin, kissing my nose. I'm not sure he's right, but I'm not about to argue. "I'm also pretty sure you're freezing." He traces a finger down my arm over the goose bumps. I shiver, proving his point — though I think it may have more to do with his touch than the cold — and he rolls out of bed. After locating and pulling on his boxers, he adjusts the thermostat and pulls two T-shirts out of a small suitcase against the far wall. He puts on one of the shirts, and then walks over to my side of the bed. He bunches the shirt up to the neck and holds it out as if he were about to dress a small child. I sit up and give him a questioning look.

"Arms up."

I laugh and oblige, lifting my arms over my head. He pulls the shirt down over me, slides his hands around the back of my neck, bringing my hair up and out of the neck hole, and bends down to kiss the top of my head. "I'll be right back," he murmurs, and then leaves the room.

I gather up the front of the t-shirt in both hands, bury my face in it, and inhale. Something about the worn, faded cotton that smells exactly like him brings tears to my eyes. After another deep breath, I move my legs to lay crisscross in front of me and try to pull myself together.

For the first time since I got here I have a moment to glance around the room, or should I say rooms—this is obviously a suite. Two glass French doors separate the bedroom from the sitting area, which has a fireplace, though it's hard to see. In any case, it's much nicer than any hotel room I have ever seen, much less stayed in.

A door opens, and Nick comes back around the corner, giving me a heart-melting smile. He comes to the foot of the bed and crawls across it, falling onto his side and gently pulling me down with him. He tucks me back into his chest, brings the covers up over us, and wraps both arms around me.

"So, Miss Basham," he says, snuggling his face into my neck, "what am I going to do with you?"

"I don't know."

"We should probably sleep, as there is a wedding to attend tomorrow…or later today, I guess."

"Mmm, probably, but I'm not tired."

"Me either," he sighs. "So, what then?"

I hold my breath as I turn over to face him, anchoring myself in his peaceful eyes. "I'm sorry." As much as I don't want to spoil the moment by bringing up the past, I can't help myself. If we can't talk about any of it, it will always hang over us. But more than that, he has to know.

For a split second he looks confused, but my somber expression explains the statement for me, and realization flashes in his eyes. "Jules, you don't have to—"

"Yes, I do," I interrupt firmly. "I let you down, and there was no excuse for it. You had every right to hate me for what I put you through, and I want you to know that I understand. I failed you—I failed us both, and I'm *so* sorry."

Less than a heartbeat later, his lips brush lightly against mine in a tender kiss. "Thank you," he whispers slowly against my mouth. After a blissfully long moment, he presses his lips to my forehead with a happy sigh. "I'm sorry, too."

"What?" I pull back to look at him.

"It's wasn't all your fault, Jules."

"No, I'm pretty sure it was."

"I shouldn't have reacted the way I did. I should have fought harder—fought period—but I didn't. I can't tell you how many times I've thought about how things could have worked out if I had given myself a day or two to calm down and then come back to talk to you. I shouldn't have let you off the hook that easily." He smiles sadly. "I failed us too, and I'm sorry."

I don't fully agree with him, but I am also not about to argue when his words clearly mean a lot to him. After another kiss I roll back over and snuggle into him as he pulls me back into his chest with a sigh.

"And I never hated you, Jules." He slowly combs his fingers through my hair. "I'm sorry to say it, but I did try. In the beginning, I thought hating you would make it easier." I'm glad my back is to him as I blink back tears. He struggles with some of his words, obviously not wanting to discuss this any more than I do, but he also seems to realize that it's necessary. "Hate seemed like it would be easier to live with, but it wasn't real. I was just lying to myself. So, I moved on to spite. I figured if I focused all my energy on proving the world wrong, then I wouldn't have any left over for hurt. I immersed myself in work, almost to an unhealthy level, but at least I felt constructive." He pauses for a few moments while I try to keep my breathing even. "Once the company was up and running on its own, I decided it was time to try to have a normal life outside of work. I even got engaged."

"What?" I say, turning to look over my shoulder at him. It's ridiculous of me to feel jealous, but I can't help it—though I do my best to hide it.

"Mmhmm, to a woman in London," he says, chuckling. "It was a textbook case of an engagement of convenience. We met at a conference. She had just dumped the guy her parents wanted her to marry, and I was trying to build some semblance of a personal life again. We both thought we needed to be with someone, so we just sort of fell into this mechanical relationship. I didn't love her and she didn't love me, but that didn't seem to matter."

He wasn't in love with her; I guess that's something.

"Looking back now, I think the fact that she wasn't someone I could love was actually the appeal. I was able to be in a relationship which gave me at least an echo of the normal life I wanted, without the emotional weight of actually caring for someone. I felt safe knowing that, since she didn't mean anything to me, she couldn't possibly hurt me."

My heart lurches painfully, but I don't interrupt.

"We did everything we *should* have done, and to anyone on the outside looking in, we were the perfect pair. I proposed when it seemed like I should, and she said yes because she felt like she should, but it was like we were following steps in a manual. In the end, we had no business being with each other. We weren't even friends. Eventually we both realized there was no way we could go through with it, and went our separate ways. I never even told Cathy."

I lie still, totally lost in his story, and as much as it hurts to hear, it is also strangely liberating.

"By the time I decided to move back to the U.S., I was convinced that I had put you behind me for good. I was even able to go full days at a time without thinking about you. During the waking hours, anyway. There was nothing I could do about the dreams."

Oh, how well I know…

"Life went on, and I wanted to think I was happy, but deep down I knew I wasn't. Then I signed up with SMS Financial Planners." I hear the smile enter his voice. "I had no idea you worked with the Herstein Group until I got the welcome packet in the mail from Margaret that had all your names in it. Soon as I saw it, I completely panicked," he says, chuckling. "I called the receptionist so many times to cancel my contract, but was never able to go through with it. I must have hung up on her at least ten times!" We both giggle. "I couldn't do it; I was determined not to run away. I was convinced that you no longer had any control over me, and that I could handle it." He lets out a long sigh.

"And then I saw you. I couldn't believe my eyes; all of a sudden I was furious. I had expected to see the woman I remembered, but you weren't her at all. The Julia I knew was bright and fun, but the one that stood in front of me that first day was pale and submissive. You might as well have been a part of the furniture. I wanted to take you by the shoulders and shake you." He gives my shoulder a gentle shove to make his point. "I was so angry — at you, for letting life run you over, and at myself, for caring. I resolved to do what I promised myself I would — prove that you were no longer important to me, and that I could ignore you just like I could anyone else. So that's what I did."

"And a damn fine job of it too," I say, rolling over to face him, and playfully punching his shoulder.

"I was a petty bastard, I know. And that's not even — " He stops, and looks down at the bed, almost as if he's embarrassed.

"What?"

He sighs. "That's not even the worst of it. There was that whole mess with Bree…"

"Mess with Bree? What do you mean?"

"You and Chris…at the house…" He looks down again, his face red. "You two were getting along so well, and Chris doesn't tend to take to people so fast, and the two of you, being all friendly…I didn't like it." *Oh, my God! He was jealous of Chris and me?* "Bree seemed to like me, so…"

"So…?" I ask, then it hits me. "You were flirting with her on *purpose!*" He squeezes his eyes shut in shame, and I have to stifle a giggle. "You were *trying* to upset me?" Suddenly something else becomes clear. "Oh my God, that day at the beach? *That's* why you called her out to you? *That's* why she got stung? No wonder you felt so bad!" He buries his face down into the bed as I laugh hysterically. Just hearing the truth melts the tension inside me.

"It's really not that funny," he mumbles against the sheets, though his tone tells me he's not as upset as he's letting on.

"Yeah, it kinda is!" I kiss his head, still giggling, and he comes up to meet my lips with his. After a moment we settle back under the covers.

"Horrible as that day turned out, it was actually a weird blessing. It made me realize what an ass I was being, but more than that, it made me realize how much I needed you. How much I still loved you. Though maybe *realize* is the wrong word." He thinks for a moment. "*Acknowledge* is more like it. That night I couldn't sleep, and I decided to talk to you about everything. I was so close to telling you that morning by the side of the house, but Derek showed up. I promised myself I would talk to you later that day, but then you were gone."

"Of course I left! I walked in on the two of you *kissing!* Or…at least I thought I did, but it turns out it was just bad timing."

"Wait, what?"

"You know, when I walked in the library, and you and Bree were in there. I didn't see Chris, though she told me he was there too. You and Bree had your arms around each other, and I could swear to God I saw her kiss you…"

"And *that's* why you left?"

I hang my head as my cheeks flush. "Just wait, it gets worse. Up until I met Bree and the rest of the bridesmaids at the dress shop that first time, I thought it was *you* she was marrying."

Now it is my turn to bury my face in the pillow while Nick howls with laughter. "How the hell did that happen?" he asks, when the laughter dies down.

"It basically boils down to me being an idiot, and always assuming the worst."

"God, we're a pair," he chuckles, wiping his eyes. "But really, you were jealous? You? When I'm the one who had to find out you were seeing some little schmuck named Zach who was sending you flowers?"

"Zach and I…wait, how did you know he sent me flowers?"

"Bree couldn't stop gushing about it! I had to sit through dinner with her and Chris the night you got them. She told us all about how you were dating some guy named Zach, and he seemed so sweet, and he sent you flowers. Then, he shows up at the SMS party and kisses you! I have never wanted to hit someone so badly in my life."

"You should have."

"Oh?"

"Yeah…turns out he's a con artist."

He huffs a laugh, but then sees my expression. "Wait, you're serious?"

"Unfortunately. I met him when he was hired at Lisa's firm almost two and a half years ago. They just found out that since then he has embezzled over a hundred and sixty thousand dollars."

"You're *kidding!*"

"Nope. They arrested him the day after the party, actually."

"Holy hell!" he says, chuckling under his breath. "I'm sorry, I know it isn't funny," he snorts through his laughter.

"Shut up," I giggle, and shove his chest.

"Any other Prince Charmings you'd like to tell me about? Maybe a money launderer or hit-man you've dated?"

He is cracking up at this point, and I continue to laugh in spite of myself. I roll away from him, pretending to sulk, but he hooks his arm around my waist and drags me back against his chest.

"Come on, it is a little funny," he says against the back of my head.

I can still hear the smile in his voice, and I know he is looking for a reply, but my mind starts to wander. I can't help thinking about what he'd said about how driven he'd become in our time apart. How my rejection of him had sparked an intense need to succeed. Sure, it was born of pain and spite, but still it reminded me of something Susan had said that morning at breakfast.

"What's wrong?" he asks, pulling me out of my bubble. I look up to find him propped up on his elbow and gazing down at me.

"Nothing, just thinking," I assure him.

"About?"

"I was wondering…" I roll over on my back. "Do you think you would have been as successful as you were if things hadn't happened the way they did?" It wasn't as descriptive a question as it should have been, but he knew what I meant.

His expression turned thoughtful as he absentmindedly played with a lock of my hair, running it through his fingers. "Well, if you're expecting me to say that the time we spent apart was for the best, then you're going to be disappointed. I'll never agree to that. But I do see your point, and honestly, I have thought about it. Sure, I'd like to think that I'd have been just as successful no matter the circumstances, but who knows? My initial success was almost entirely due to the connections and deals I was able to make in London. If we'd have stayed together, I most likely never would have gone."

He looks down and shakes his head. "I *know* I wouldn't have gone. Maybe eventually I would have had the same luck in New York as I did overseas, maybe not. It's impossible to say, which means it's not worth stressing over. None of that matters. You're here. We're here. That's all I care about." He smiles and rests his hand on my cheek. "This—" he kisses me gently "—is all I care about."

I hold his face between my hands. "I love you," I whisper, brushing my thumbs over his cheeks. He looks down at me with an expression that takes my breath away, before lowering his lips back down to mine.

Ah.

I knew looking for my underwear would've been a waste of time.

19

It's 7:21 in the morning, and the impossible dream that started last night still hasn't ended. I've been up for almost an hour, lost in thought and unable to fall back to sleep. The most wonderful man in the world is still sleeping soundly, his head on my chest and right arm draped across my waist. I stare up at the ceiling and—try as I might to deny it—I am actually starting to think this all just may be real.

Last night had been the best of my life. After our second round of lovemaking, we were both hungry. Not wanting to bother with room service, we decided the mini bar would have to do. After that, the evening fell into a wonderful pattern of intimate conversation and amazing sex. We talked about our lives for the past eight years, and told stories of the things we'd done, his tales far more interesting than mine. He told me about his life in London and about building his company, while I tried to put a good spin on the mundane turn my life had taken. We talked—and loved—over and over until around four thirty, when we both finally surrendered to sleep.

It was perfect.

Well, perfect for us. This night had imperfections galore—Nick cut his finger opening a can of cashews from the mini bar, and at one point I got a horrible cramp in my leg during a, *ahem*, position change—but I didn't mind. I don't want perfection, because that's not real life. The imperfections are what made it real, and the fact that it was real is what made it perfect.

The most surprising part of the evening was hearing Nick's side of all the things that had happened over the past several weeks. I am still in shock at everything I've come to learn, and I've been mull-ing it all over in the dark for the past hour or so. One thought in particular keeps popping up.

I was right.

All along, I've been right.

Every instinct I've had — from not wanting to break things off with Nick all those years ago, to thinking he still had feelings for me in Maine, to the weird feeling I had about Zach — all of them have been right on the money. This revelation should probably make me feel good or give me a new splash of confidence, but at the moment, I'm so pissed at myself I could scream!

If I had just trusted my own judgment and followed my gut from the get-go, my life would have turned out completely differ-ent. I spent all that time bitching about being slighted by my fairy godmother, when I'd had one all along deep inside myself—I just wasn't listening. I was too busy following everyone else's advice, or forcing myself into a version of the life I thought I should have, when happiness was right in front of me. Last night was the first time I'd taken a real, honest risk, and look what happened! I'd always been so afraid to take any sort of leap, but that's what life is! Sure, it's hard, scary, and painful, but hell, so is *childbirth*, and people do that every day. Why? Because the reward outweighs everything else. Nothing worth having is free; just look at my life the past eight years. That was free, and that's about all it was worth.

Well, not anymore.

Nick shifts, and I glance down to see him watching me.

"Good morning," he says, with a sleepy smile.

"Morning."

"You looked deep in thought."

"I was actually."

"What about?" he asks, propping himself up on his elbows.

My heart starts to race as I look into his eyes. This is it. I know what I want, and I'm going for it. I'm in charge of me now, and I'm done with letting other people decide how I should live, and I'm certainly done with not living at all.

I take a deep breath and — jump.

"I want you to marry me."

For a second he is silent. "What?" His brow furrows and he cocks his head, shocked and confused.

I sit up so I can face him, and he follows. "I want you to marry me. I've realized that every instinct I have ever had has been right, and somehow I have ignored or pushed aside every single one of them. I've never trusted my own judgment." I know I'm talking way too fast, but everything wants to pour out of me all at once. "I was an idiot when I gave you up. I knew it was wrong, I didn't want to do it, but I did it anyway, and I've been paying for it ever since. I know what I want and I know what I need, and they are both *you*. I love you, and I want you to marry me. I know this is sort of out of nowhere, and I understand if yo—"

His lips capture mine, hands cupping my face and mouth moving gently until I think I might pass out. When he finally breaks away, I am gasping and dizzy.

"Really?" he asks, his eyes boring into mine. "Are you sure?" There is such an incredible look of joy on his face, that it almost knocks the wind out of me.

"Absolutely."

He quickly kisses me again, then turns and jumps off the bed. He grabs the room phone and dials a four-digit number. I watch him, totally confused. He sees my expression and smiles, hitting the speaker button just as someone picks up.

"Hello?"

"Hey, it's me. Get dressed and come to my room."

"Nick?" It sounded like Derek.

"Yeah, get your ass up, and come to my room."

"Why?"

"Because I need a favor."

"What's wrong?"

"Nothing's wrong."

"Dude, it's quarter to eight!"

"I'm aware. Quit your bitching, and get down here." He sets the phone back down.

"What was that about?" I ask, slipping out of bed.

"Here," he says, tossing me my dress. "Get dressed. I'll call you a car."

"Where am I going?"

"Home to change," he says as if this is all making perfect sense. "Unless you want to wear that." He motions to the T-shirt I have on.

"Where are we going?"

He pulls on his jeans. "You said you want to get married, so let's get married."

"*What?*" I squeal. He's crazy! "Are you insane, I didn't mean *today!*"

"Why not today?" he asks, grabbing a white polo out of his suitcase.

"Well, for starters, there are *other* people getting married today. I have to meet Bree and the girls for lunch at noon!"

"Noon? Oh, well no problem then. We have plenty of time." He glances up at me and huffs a laugh at my expression.

"Nick, you can't just get married in a day, this isn't Vegas! We don't even have a license!"

"It doesn't take long. They process your information there while you wait. We can have a license by ten," he states matter-of-factly.

"Okay, smarty pants, but that doesn't mean we're married, and I do happen to know that you have to wait at least twenty-four hours before you can have the marriage officiated." I feel very smart even though my knowledge consists only of what Bree told me only a week ago when she and Chris had gotten theirs.

"Not with a Judicial Waiver, which is why I called Derek. He works at the courthouse, and I know he has friends in the City Clerk's office. I'm sure he won't have a problem helping us out."

"I…" I am speechless.

Can we really do this?

Nick looks at me and stops dressing. He walks over, takes my dress out of my hands, and lays it on the bed. "Look." He takes my hands in his. "We don't have to do this. If you want to wait and have a real wedding, of course we can."

I couldn't care less about a wedding. I had never dreamed of a big to-do or a fancy dress, and I think he knows that. My sudden hesitation has nothing to do with what *I* want. My worry is the simple fact that he doesn't seem to be taking the time to think this through.

"I don't care about a wedding," I say, looking up into his eyes. "Say the word, and I will marry you right this second. It's just that…" I taper off and look down at his chest.

He lifts my chin with his finger. "What is it, Jules?" he asks, trying to hide the worry in his eyes.

"It's you…are you sure?" I'm being insecure, but I can't help it. I can't pretend like there isn't a little voice in my head saying, *How can he be with me after what I did?* and *He'll never really trust me,* and so on. I hold my breath, waiting for an answer, and I see the worry in his eyes soften as he seems to understand what I didn't say.

"Jules, I love you." He brushes his fingers over my cheek. "Everything that's happened is in the past and doesn't concern me anymore. *Now* is what matters. Last night, when I left the garden, I thought it was over. Through all the years we were apart, I always had something in the back of my mind to hold onto. No matter how mad I was, or how indifferent I tried to be, somewhere deep inside I knew that I had the option of looking you up. I could find you again, and maybe you would take me back. I was never able to bring myself to do it, but at least there was the possibility. But last night it was gone, and I sat at that bar trying to picture the rest of my life…and I couldn't. I'm not going to go another day without you permanently by my side, unless I absolutely have to." By the time he finishes, tears are streaming down my cheeks. He wipes them away, and kisses my forehead. "The only part I'm worried about," he adds with a grin, "is that I will have to spend the rest of my life being the man who was proposed *to.*"

I smile, which I think was the point. "Is that so bad?" I sniff ungracefully.

"Only slightly emasculating." He smiles, then kisses me softly. "But I'll get over it."

Fifteen minutes later, I am in the town car Nick had called to take me to my apartment, then to City Hall where I would meet him and Derek. I made sure to leave Nick's room before Derek got there, thinking it would be best to let Nick break the news alone. I lay my head back on the seat and close my eyes, trying to contain the explosion of happiness in my chest.

I'm getting married!

We pull up in front of my building, when a thrilling but daunting question comes to my mind. What am I going to wear? All the way up to my apartment, I ponder my wardrobe. We had decided to go casual because we would be spending the second half of the day dressed to the nines for Bree and Chris's wedding, and wanted to stay comfortable for as long as possible. Having only what he brought with him to choose from, Nick had decided on a white polo and jeans. He apologized, but I'm fine with his outfit. He looks amazing in anything. Regardless, I wasn't about to make him go all the way to his apartment uptown to change.

I stand in front of my closet, and realize that even with the casual criteria, there are still a lot decisions to make. Luckily, I had just washed my best pair of jeans. I slip them on, put on a bra, and turn my attention to shirts. I go with a flowy, light blue, V-neck blouse. I haven't worn it yet, which makes it feel special, and something about it seems to say *bridal*—"something blue" and all that.

I dress, grab my gown, shoes, jewelry, and purse for the second wedding, and make sure I have the documentation I'll need to get a marriage license.

Marriage license! Eeeee!

I grab up everything in my arms and run back down to the car, trying not to trip over the hem of the gown slung over my arm.

When I make it outside, my driver steps out of the car to help me. "Why don't we put that back here, Miss," he says, taking my dress from me and laying it flat on the floor of the trunk.

"Great, thanks!" I say, climbing back into my seat. A moment later I hear the trunk close and my driver resumes his seat behind the wheel.

"City Hall?" he asks, shifting the town car into gear.

"Ye—" A strange tightening at the base of my throat cuts my words short, and I realize that something is wrong.

I'm sure today is going to be the best day of my life—hell, it already is. I have somehow managed to get the one thing I'd thought was lost to me forever. I can't remember a time in my life when I've been happier than I am right now. However, there is still one little thing nagging at the back of my mind. One thing that I still have to do for this day to be perfect in every possible way. I am proud to become Nick's wife, and I am not going to hide it. Not from anyone.

I feel a strange and unexpected calm settle over me as I look up at the set of eyes peering at me through the rearview mirror. "Actually, I have to make one quick stop before that, but don't worry, it's on the way."

I approach the familiar office door feeling far more relaxed than I would have thought possible. Don't get me wrong, I'm still trembling and my hands are so clammy it's like I've spent the last hour washing dishes, but it's a far cry from the hyperventilating heap on the floor I thought I'd be.

I step through the door without knocking and close it slowly behind me.

"Jules! Don't you look pretty," Lisa says, looking up from the briefcase she's organizing, "What are you doing here? Don't you have the wedding today?"

"I do, but I have something I need to talk to you about first."

"Sure, but I've got a meeting with the Board of Directors and the prosecuting attorneys in ten minutes," she tells me, turning back to her paperwork.

"Prosecuting attorneys? Oh…Zach."

"Yep, so make it quick."

Not quite the intro I'd wanted, but I guess that's the best I'm going to get. "I just wanted to tell you—" I pause until she looks up "—I'm getting married."

A full ten seconds pass before she blinks, while I stand calmly waiting for—well, honestly, I'm not sure what.

"You're getting married?"

"Yes. Today, actually. I'm on my way to City Hall right now."

"You're…*today?*" I doubt it's possible for a person to look more shocked than Lisa does right now. "T-To who?" she stammers.

"Nick."

Her mouth closes and the shock on her face is replaced by something else, though I'm not exactly sure what.

"I love him, Lisa. I have always loved him. I found out that he still has feelings for me too, so we got back together and I asked him to marry me. His friend works at City Hall, and with his help, Nick and I will be married by lunch."

As I'm saying all this, I have the strange sensation of hardly recognizing my own voice, as if there is a new person inside my skin. Someone confident and sure, who can speak her mind without seeming defiant and whiny. She feels like—an adult.

"I'm not looking for approval, or support," I continue, "that's not why I'm here. I'm here because you're my sister and I love you and I wanted you to know before it happened."

I stand silently, waiting for a reply, ready to take it, whatever it may be. Instead of commenting or questioning, she sets the folders she's holding down on the desk and walks over to me, placing her hands on my shoulders and looking me dead in the eye.

"Is this what you want?" she asks slowly, emphasizing each word.

Without breaking eye contact even for a second I answer, "Yes."

She lets out a small sigh as a grin pulls up one side of her mouth. "Then go get married."

I hold back for all of two seconds before I throw my arms around her. "Thank you!" I whisper against her shoulders, tears trailing down my cheeks. Only now do I realize how much I truly did want her approval. She is my big sister, and I will always want her to think well of me and the things I do. And yet, even in this admission, I can still see there has been a change in me; yes I will always *want* Lisa's approval, but I no longer *need* it.

"Okay, okay," Lisa says after a moment, trying to hide a sniffle, "knock it off before everyone in this damn office sees me cry." She turns back toward her desk and briefcase looking torn. Immediately I can see she's thinking of blowing off her meeting so she can come with me.

"Lisa, don't. It's fine," I assure her. "Nick's sister won't be there either." She glances back at me, indecision still heavy in her eyes. "Really, Lis, it's okay. It's just going to be Nick and me. That's what we want."

"Oh, so I'm not invited?" she says, feigning an insult.

"You know what I mean." I smile. "Besides, you know you can't miss this meeting."

"No, I can't," she says with a sigh. "All right, but only if you're absolutely sure."

"I'm sure."

"Wait," she says suddenly, looking me over. "You're not wearing that, are you?"

"What? You said I look pretty!"

"Well, sure, pretty for a Friday, not pretty for your wedding day! You're not even wearing any jewelry! Come here." She grabs my hand and pulls me over to her desk. "Sit," she orders, turning the chair toward me with one hand and unfastening the thin string of pearls around her neck with the other. "Put these on." She hands me not only the pearls, but the matching earrings as well.

I do as she says, all the while listening to the sounds of drawers opening and being dug through. Just as I get the earrings in and make a move to look behind me at the noise, Lisa grabs my head.

"Hold still." She runs a brush through my hair. "I only have eight bobby pins, so we'll have to make the best of it."

Five minutes and a few curse words later, my hair is up in a loose but elegant twist. "Thank you, Lis," I say, turning away from the mirror, pleased with my inspection. Lisa stands a few feet away, a wistful look on her face, holding something in her hand.

"Just one more thing." She comes up behind me and fastens something in my hair. I turn back to the mirror and see a lovely silver brooch that I recognize from the lapel of Lisa's winter coat. "It was Mom's."

"I know," I whisper, tears in my eyes again. I turn and hug her again, but not before catching sight of the clock. "I have to go."

"Oh God, me too," she says, clearing her throat.

We gather our respective things and walk out into the hall together. After one more quick hug, she turns down the hall to her meeting, while I make my way to the elevators. I push the "down" button feeling elated, as though the last little piece of the puzzle has fallen into place.

As I climb back into the hired car and the driver once again asks if we're going to City Hall, I realize that for the first time, there is nothing, not one little thing in Heaven or on Earth, preventing me from saying, "Yes."

20

Debbie has really outdone herself; the ballroom looks absolutely spectacular. With sage green tablecloths, silver chairs with taupe organza bows tied around their backs, tall candelabra-style centerpieces topped with roses dripping with crystals, a seven tiered cake that looks too perfect to be edible, and a head table fit for no less than royalty, everything is perfect.

I'm staring in awe at the room through a tiny window on the door that separates the bridal party from the reception hall. "Spying on the party, Mrs. Kerkley?" a voice whispers just behind my shoulder.

Nick.

My Nick.

My husband, Nick.

I grin without turning. "Just admiring Debbie's handiwork." I feel a brush against my side as he steps up and peers through the window. His breath on my bare shoulder raises goose bumps down my arms.

"Wow…she really went all out." He brushes the back of his hand down my arm, making my breath catch. "Seems like almost too much for just *one* wedding." The smile is evident in his voice.

We had both agreed this morning that our marriage would remain a secret until after today. Announcing your own wedding the same day as someone else's is definitely tacky. Today is about Bree and Chris, and we don't want take anything away from them. So Nick and I had agreed to stay away from each other, and act as though nothing had changed.

But God was it hard!

Our own wedding celebration had been wonderful—though excruciatingly short. I arrived at the City Clerk's office to find Nick waiting for me. Within an hour and a half, we not only had our marriage license, but—thanks to Derek and his connections—we also had a Judicial Wavier allowing us to marry that same day, and a note from the desk of the Honorable Justin M. Turpin, the Judge who had signed our waiver, stating that he had a slot open to marry us at ten thirty that morning. By eleven fifteen, I was sitting in the hired car next to my husband, headed uptown for the start of the St. Charles/Langston wedding festivities.

"Are you happy?" Nick had asked against my ear as we reclined in the back seat. Both of his arms were wrapped securely around me, and his cheek rested against my hair. Derek had graciously called his own car, insisting the newlyweds should, at the very least, have the fifteen minute drive back uptown to themselves.

I turned and smiled up at him, bring my lips up to meet his. We spent the rest of the drive silently kissing, losing ourselves in the joy of love, and probably scandalizing the driver.

That was to be our last contact until we got back to his room tonight, but he seemed to be having as hard of a time staying away as I was. All through Chris and Bree's ceremony he watched me, catching my eye, and making me blush, which he seemed to find amusing. I made a point to not look his way during the photos after the wedding for fear that if I did, I would end up red-faced in every picture. Now he was pushing it even further, and with the whole bridal party only a few feet away!

"You're going to get us caught," I whisper, pulling away from his hand and crossing my arms. I glance over to the rest of the bridal party, but thankfully none of them are paying any attention.

"If you don't want my attention, then you shouldn't look so incredibly beautiful. It's not fair to the other bride you know."

Blush.

God damn it, he's got to stop doing that!

I do admit that I look great. After lunch, all the girls spent two and a half hours in Bree's suite getting pampered, polished, and primped by a team of hair stylists and makeup artists. My hair had been smoothed, curled, and pinned in such a way that looked super glam, yet effortless, and my makeup artist had airbrushed my face to utter perfection. And to think, until today, I didn't even know there was such a thing as airbrush makeup.

"We agreed to keep apart," I whisper, stifling a giggle as he bends forward and pretends to look further into the ballroom while actually brushing his nose across my cheek.

"Did we?" he says, making no move to stop.

"Yes. When are you going to tell Cathy?" I add, trying to distract him. We had agreed not to tell anyone, but Nick did say he would probably tell his sister before the night was out. She was family after all, and it's not like she was going to tell anyone, so we figured it was safe.

"Whenever I have a minute. Probably during dinner when everyone is distracted." His nose tickles my ear.

"You're pushing your luck," I tell him, grinning.

"I love you," he says, ignoring me yet again.

"I love you, too, and now I'm leaving." I turn and walk back toward the group, but not before glancing back in time to see him wink.

I make my way over to a crowd of women and pretend to listen to the conversation, all the while thinking about Cathy. She has been on my mind for most of the day actually, and now my fears were about to come true. She is going to find out about the wedding, and about me. He will have to tell her that I am the one he almost married eight years ago, that I am the one she has hated all these years for his sake. Much as I don't want her to know, I realize it has to be done. After all, there isn't really any other way Nick can justify marrying someone overnight.

What would she say?

Could she forgive me?

She made it abundantly clear that day on the beach that she had no warm feelings for me at all. Would that change now that Nick and I were married? Suddenly a painful knot forms in my stomach.

"Okay, everyone," the wedding coordinator says, appearing out of nowhere. "We are ready to start the introductions. Line up with your partners, please."

Derek appears by my side. "Mrs. Kerkley," he says quietly, offering me his arm.

I take it and give his shoulder a punch with my free hand. "Will you stop calling me that! Someone is going to hear you! God, you're as bad as he is!"

He chuckles as we step into line. "For what it's worth, I am really happy for you two," he says, under his breath, "and that is saying something, considering how bitter I have become over the past few hours."

"What? Why?"

"Because, pardon me, this is bullshit!" he says with something between a grin and a grimace. "I've become the only sorry-ass, single loser left standing, and all in less than eight hours. How the hell does that happen?"

"Oh, I'm sorry." I smile and squeeze his arm. "I'm sure we can find someone for you."

"No thanks, *someone* has to make it to the end of this day with his manhood in check, and it looks like it's gonna have to be me."

"How romantic." I giggle as we step up to the door.

"Yes, one of my many gifts."

"Miss Julia Basham, escorted by Mr. Derek Ross," the DJ announces, and we step into the hall.

We take our places at the head table as the new Mr. and Mrs. Christopher and Brianna Langston enter, looking as happy as two people can be. Brandon makes his toast, and before I realize I've eaten anything, my dinner plate is being cleared away. I'm trying to focus on the wedding and enjoy myself, but my eyes keep going back over to the round table just a few yards away, where Cathy and Rob are sitting.

What if she hates me? What if she thinks I'm using him? What if this ruins her and Nick's relationship? What if—

"Here you are, Miss." A waiter sets a coffee cup down in front of me, breaking my train of stomach ulcer-inducing thought.

"Thank you." I look back, expecting to see him there with an urn of coffee, but he has moved on and is serving Jen to my right. I lift the coffee cup to turn it right side up, and notice something underneath it.

Oh, my God.

My breath catches and I slam the cup back down, looking around and praying that no one else saw. I pick up the set and place them in my lap, glancing around once more to make sure no one else is looking before lifting the cup to reveal an unmistakable, scarlet-red

Cartier ring box. There's a small piece of paper on the saucer under the box, and I pull it out.

You may get to propose,
but I still get to buy you a ring.
Love - N

I place the note on the table, and stare down at the red cube with gold trim, willing my hands to stop shaking. I open the box to find the most beautiful wedding set I have ever seen. I'm willing to bet anything it's platinum, and there are diamonds everywhere! The large square solitaire on the engagement ring was surrounded by smaller diamonds all around the edges, and pouring over onto the swirling filigree setting and band. The wedding band matched perfectly and was also inlaid with diamonds. It's a ring straight from the pages of a bridal magazine, the sort of ring that you see and think "holy crap," and you Google the jeweler just so you can see what a ring like that would cost—you'd never expect you'll have one to wear on your hand for the rest of your life.

I close the lid of the box, and put the coffee cup back over it. I look over to find Nick's eyes on me from the other side of the table. He smiles warmly at my obvious surprise and gives me a quick—and somewhat triumphant—wink before standing and leaving the table.

So you think you're clever, do you?

I reach down and grab my purse from under my seat, thanking my lucky stars I decided to make the stop that I did before lunch this morning. I open my bag and make room for my new red ring box by removing the blue one already in there.

Lunch today was at Trump Grill on Fifth Avenue, which just happens to be right next to Tiffany and Co. When I arrived for lunch I realized I still had more than half an hour until noon, so I decided to make a quick stop to buy Nick a ring. We obviously didn't have time before the ceremony this morning, and I wanted to get him a wedding present regardless. The fact that Tiffany's was a few steps away seemed to be fate.

The salesman I spoke to, Dave, was very helpful, even though I was a somewhat unconventional shopper. I told him I would need the ring today, so it had to be in stock, and that price was not an issue. He showed me my options, and I chose the double milgrain wedding band in platinum. I wasn't sure what most of that meant, but I liked it, and I was sure Nick would too. I bought it in a size ten, knowing his class ring was a ten, and hoping that with any luck his size hasn't changed since high school. Finally, after Dave assured me I would have it by one, I had it engraved. The only problem was that there was only room for three characters, which didn't leave me with a lot of options. I played around with the initial idea, but figured that was redundant, as we know each other's names. Besides, I wanted it to be more meaningful than that. I decided on *F & F*, which stood for *Finally & Forever*. Dave was confused, but once I explained, he thought it was great.

The ring cost most of my savings, but considering I was now married to one of Forbes top ten richest men in the country, I figured cleaning out my bank account to buy him a wedding present wasn't such a big deal. With my slip with a pickup time of one or later, I left to meet the girls, arriving just in time. When I ran back in after lunch, Dave not only had the ring done, but he had printed a small card to go with it that said:

Finally & Forever
F & F

I take the ring box and card out of my purse, look over to his spot at the table, and see that he has left his tux jacket on the back of his chair. I walk over and, discreetly as possible, slide the box and card into the front breast pocket. I hurry back to my seat and look around to see where he went and if he saw me.

I find him — *oh God* — sitting with Cathy. They are leaning into one another in a private conversation, and he is holding her hands in his.

He's telling her.

Suddenly my heart is in my throat and my hands are sweaty. I grab my purse and walk, as slowly as I'm able, out of the ballroom and into the nearest ladies room without so much as a glance back at Cathy's table.

The ladies room door closes behind me, and instantly I feel safer. I step into the vanity lounge which has beautiful puffy couches, a low center table with a large flower arrangement on it, and a long vanity counter on the far wall, complete with lit mirrors and several small embroidered benches.

Definitely the Rolls Royce of public restrooms.

I go and sit at the vanity, staring blankly into the mirror, Cathy's words from the beach all those weeks ago thumping in my mind.

"…nothing I'd like more than to give that girl a piece of my mind…"

God, what must she think of me?

A lump forms in my throat, and I am totally aware that I need a distraction, or I am going to completely ruin my makeup. I open my purse and pull out the ring box. I open it, take out the ring, and slowly slide it on my finger. It's beautiful! Suddenly I'm blinking back tears for a whole new reason. Some distraction.

I take a deep breath. Okay, what's the worst that can happen? She can't forgive me for what happened eight years ago, and she never wants to see or speak to me again. Honestly, I'm not entirely sure that I'd blame her. So what should I do? I could stay away from her if that's what she wants. Though if that were the case, she would probably want me to stay away from Nick too, but it's a bit late for that. Besides, after all this, I could never agree to that. I will stay away from her as much as I can, and be polite and courteous when I can't, and maybe after a while she'll come to see that Nick and I are in love. Love has to count for something, right?

My mind is struck silent as the ladies' room door opens. I look up into the mirror and see another woman's reflection staring back at me.

Oh no…

Cathy.

I flip around in my seat as she takes a few steps into the lounge area, never taking her eyes off of me. My throat closes as I see her face. Her lips are pressed into a hard line, her eyebrows are furrowed together, and every muscle in her face seems hard with strain. She's pissed.

Deep breath…

I stand slowly and take a step out from around the bench. Our eyes are still locked but neither of us seems to be able to speak. *Okay, you can do this. We can't stand here all night, just say what you have to say, and don't cry!* I take a shaky breath and another step forward.

"Look, Cathy, I just want you to know th—"

Before I can even finish my sentence, Cathy comes hurling forward, throwing her arms around me in a hug that just about squeezes the remaining air out of my lungs.

"Thank you," she all but sobs on my shoulder. "Thank you!"

I bring my arms up and return her hug in a daze. *"What?"* I breathe, fighting a losing battle with my own tears.

"You don't know what it means to me to see him so happy!"

I lose it. "You mean…you…I just…I thought you would…!" I blubber, then finally give up, crying outright. "I thought you would hate me!" I sob, unable to stop myself.

"What?"

"All those years ago…what I did to him. I'm so sorry! I love him, I really do! I always have!"

"Shh, honey, don't," she soothes.

We stand there for several minutes, sniffing and hiccupping, trying to pull ourselves together. I feel her jump, and turn to see she has noticed the ring box on the counter behind me.

"Oh," she says, as she pulls my left hand out from behind her. "Oh my goodness! *It's beautiful!*"

"I know!" I squeak, which leads to several more minutes of hugging, giggling, sniffing, and hiccupping, until we have both made total messes of ourselves.

"Okay, okay, okay," Cathy says, pulling away from me and fanning her face. "You have to get back out there. They are going to start the dances soon."

"Right." I turn to the mirror to assess the damage. My face is red and my eyes are puffy, but my makeup is still good. God bless that airbrush! After I throw on some powder and lipstick, I feel more collected, and Cathy and I head back into the ballroom, hand in hand.

We arrive just in time to hear the DJ announce the first dance. As Chris and Bree make their way to the dance floor, Cathy and I part ways. "Have fun, sweetie. We'll talk later," she says, hugging me once more, before turning toward her table. I get back to my seat, and see the rest of the bridal party is gathered over to the right of the head table, watching the first dance, and waiting to be called in. I drop my purse at my seat and join them, only to find that Nick is not there. I glance around and see him standing several yards behind us near the corner, facing the wall. He's looking down at something in his hands. Something blue…

He must have found it when he put his jacket back on for the dance. I hold my breath, wishing I could see his face. After a few moments, he puts the box and card back in his pocket, takes a deep breath, rubs both hands over his face, and pinches the bridge of his nose. The lump in my throat and the tears in my eyes make another appearance.

He likes it!

I turn quickly back toward the dance floor before he sees me, and try to blink away my tears — again. This is getting embarrassing! When did I turn into such a blubbering mess? A moment later, I feel a hand on the small of my back.

"Can I have a quick word with you?" Nick asks me, loud enough for the people near us to hear, but not so loud so they'd take any particular interest.

He turns, and I follow him back to where he was standing a moment ago, but further off to the side, where there is a short hall leading to a service door I hadn't been able to see. No sooner do we turn into the hall, then he pulls me hard against his chest, kissing me breathless.

"I love you! I love you, I love you," he says in the few moments when his lips are free. I simply nod in response, as he gives me no chance to actually answer.

We remain this way until loud applause signals the end of the first dance. We reluctantly separate, and walk back out to rejoin the rest of the party, who thankfully have been too distracted to notice we were missing.

$$21$$

I float through the bridal party dance on a high from the interlude in the service hallway, but unfortunately come crashing down when I return to my seat at the table afterward to see the little flashing light on my phone. I have a missed call from Lisa. Taking the phone, I sneak out into the hall. I start out listening to the message with a smile, and by the end of it, I am crying like a baby—again.

Lisa had called during a break in her meeting to tell me how happy she is for us. She went on and on about how proud she is, and that she loves me, and how she's going to get me back for causing her to be so distracted in front of all the big-wigs in her meeting, and basically everything else that I'm sure she wanted to say this morning, but—being Lisa—she couldn't bring herself to get the words out in person. Even in the message, the tone of her voice continues to get higher and higher, as if she was fighting tears—though she would never in a million years admit it. As the message ends, I lean back and wipe my eyes with a sigh. It seems impossible that things could have worked out this way, but I'm glad they have.

Suddenly, I realize there is still one more person I have to tell about last night—one more person to thank: Mary, the sweet receptionist at the front desk from last night. After all, if it hadn't been for her, I might have been scouring the city until dawn. I take the elevators down to the lobby, hoping she's working. I really want to thank her, plus she seemed interested and I'm sure she'd be happy to hear that everything worked out. As I approach the desk, I don't see her, but there is another woman there who is not currently with a guest.

"Hello," I say, smiling as I approach her. "I'm looking for Mary."

"Certainly, what room is she in?"

"Oh no, sorry, I mean the Mary that works here."

"Works at the Waldorf?" she asks, confused.

"Yes, here at the desk."

"She's not here…"

"Oh, well if you could just give her a message for me—"

"No," she cuts me off, "you misunderstand me. We don't have a Mary who works down here."

A few hours later, I'm swaying slowly on the dance floor with the man I love, feeling totally and blissfully at peace. This evening is something dreams are made of.

I never discovered who Mary was. The woman at the front desk insisted no one by the name of Mary worked there, nor was there anyone who matched the description I gave. However, not wanting to imply that one of their guests was mistaken, the woman finally determined that someone must have borrowed a nametag from a "Mary" that works somewhere else in the hotel. It was easy to see that she only said that to appease me, but it didn't matter. And the idea of persuading her that not only is she real, but she is also my fairy godmother isn't even worth considering, so I let it go. It doesn't matter what they think happened. I'll always know the truth.

After cake and pictures, Nick and I had sat down with Cathy and Rob. We agreed to have dinner with them the next day, so that we could discuss things more openly and without having to worry about being overheard.

Finally, since it was getting on toward the end of the evening, Nick and I decided it would be safe to have a dance together on our wedding day. So here I am, dancing with my husband, trying not to look as wonderfully in love as I feel.

A minute or two into the dance, we are interrupted by Chris. "Nick, do you mind if I cut in? Derek needs to have a word."

"Oh, sure," he says, looking surprised as he hands me off to the groom.

While Nick walks off in search of Derek, I look up at Chris who has a gleam in his eye.

"So, Mrs. Kerkley, I hear congratulations are in order."

My cheeks blaze. "Who told you?"

"Derek," he answers with a chuckle at my obvious chagrin. "It's not entirely his fault though, I set him up."

"Oh?"

"I decided you and Nick would make a great couple, and was trying to get him to help me get the two of you together. He simply let me know I didn't have to bother."

"Oh, God," I groan, squeezing my eyes shut. "I am so sorry—"

"You're *sorry?* Why on earth would—"

"Oh, my God!" I huff, my eyes popping open like someone has just punched me in the stomach. "You can't tell Bree!"

"Umm…"

"Chris, please," I beg, pressing my hands against his chest. "Promise me you won't say anything!"

"Well…I can promise *I* won't tell her…"

He turns and looks over his shoulder, but before I can follow his gaze, Bree comes running out of nowhere and throws her arms around my neck.

"Oh my gosh, oh my gosh!" She lets go of my neck so she can grab my face with both hands, mushing my cheeks together. "How could you not tell me?"

Derek! Going to kill Derek!

"Wacause sweedie, iss yor webing dlay," I mumble through puckered lips.

"Exactly! It's my day, which means I get to know everything! This is so amazing! Oh my gosh!" She lets go of my face, and wraps her arms around me again. Okay, well at least she's happy.

I see that Nick and Derek have both joined us, and throw Derek an icy glare over Bree's shoulder. "I'm gonna kill you!" I mouth silently to him. He seems to find my aggravation amusing, but luckily for him, the DJ interrupts my murder plot with the announcement of the last dance.

"Brunch tomorrow, all of us, and you are going to spill, got it?" Bree demands, holding me at arm's length by my shoulders.

"Got it."

"Eeeee!" She gives me one more quick hug, before Chris takes her gently by the elbow.

As they take the floor, I hang my face in my hands and shake my head. So much for the secret.

"Don't worry about it," Nick says, running his hands from my shoulders down my arms, forcing me to drop my hands and slide them into his. "They're both thrilled, and no one else knows."

"I guess." I smile up at him. "Do I still get to kill Derek?"

"Absolutely." He grins.

"Good. In that case, may I have this dance?" I ask, giving him a small curtsy.

"You may, but first…" Letting go of my right hand, he reaches into his pocket. A moment later he is sliding my new ring—which he must have taken out of my purse—onto my finger. "Mrs. Langston insists," he says with a smile. Only then do I notice he is also wearing his. "Now," he says, raising my hand and kissing my fingers, "shall we?"

We start to dance, a bit closer this time, to the last song of the night. It seems as though almost everyone joins us on the dance floor, and even Derek has a partner. This day has been a complete whirlwind that I can't even begin to wrap my mind around, but still, somehow it all seems perfect.

"So are you sure you don't mind missing out on all of this?" Nick asks me, after a few minutes of comfortable silence.

"Missing what?"

"This. A real wedding. Reception, cake, dancing, all of that?"

"Nope."

"Really? Because we can, you know."

"I know. But really, I don't mind. Today was perfect, and I wouldn't change a thing."

"Well, I'm glad to hear it, but just so you know, we may not have a choice. Cathy is already dropping hints."

I laugh. "Oh, is she going to fix our wedding for us?"

"I wouldn't be surprised," he says, wryly rolling his eyes.

"That would be fine too. I'm just thrilled that she is okay with all of this," I admit, as I throw caution to the wind and lay my head on his shoulder.

"So, where are we going to be living, Mr. Kerkley?" I ask after a few more quiet moments. "You passed on the Marston Estate, and I seem to recall you didn't see yourself living there regardless, so where is it you see yourself?"

"I'm not sure." My head still rests on his shoulder, but I can hear the smile in his voice. "The lease on my apartment uptown is about to expire, so I guess I will need to find somewhere new. I wouldn't mind staying right here in the city, but I'll have to check with my wife."

"Oh, I'm sure she'd be fine with that."

"Although, I guess I'm going to need a new financial team, as I don't know how appropriate it is for one's wife to work as his hired help." He chuckles.

"Actually—" I look up at him "—that may not be a problem after all."

"No?"

"There's a position open in our firm as a group leader, and I have asked Margaret to submit my name." Margaret had been beside herself with excitement, almost hugging the life out of me when I asked her.

His face lights up. "Really? That's great!"

"We'll see. It would mean I would run my own team, choose my own clients, and make my own hours. It would be great, but I have to get it first. Though Margaret seemed pretty confident. Her recommendation might be all that I need, but you never know. We'll see how it goes."

"I'm sure you'll get it, but even if you don't, something else will come up. You are amazing."

Could he be any sweeter?

As the song draws to an end, Nick looks down at me with warmth in his eyes that makes my knees weak. "Well, Mrs. Kerkley, I do believe it's our wedding night too."

"I believe it is."

"Shall we?" he asks, bringing a hand up to cup my face.

I rest my hand over his and turn my face to kiss his palm. We gather our things, lace our hands together, and make our way out of the ballroom hand in hand, down the hall toward the elevators.

About half way there we come across a large ornate mirror. As we pass by, I look in and see, not only my present, but my future—Nick and I, together, in love, walking forward, forever. That may be the only thing I can count on, but that's enough happily ever after for me.

And, just as our reflections step out of the gilded frame, I can swear I see the shimmering silhouette of fairy wings behind me.

Love and Sincerest Thanks to:

My amazing husband, Scott, for his encouragement, his ideas, his patients, and endless support;

My mom and mom-in-law, Cathy and Mary, for fixing my mistakes and making it appear to the world that I spell better than I actually do;

Julia, Brianna, Cathy, Susan, Matt, Justin, Mary, Dave, Jill, and SMS for your names and inspiration;

The team at PS Literary for their tireless work and support of my writing, and especially to my fabulous agent, Carly Watters, for taking a chance on me;

Liz, Sam, Ondrew, Julie, Patti, Felicia, Yelena, Beth, Jill, Cathy, Mary, and Scott for reading me and helping to make Once Upon A Second Chance what it is;

QueryTracker.net, not only for being an amazing resource and introducing me to my agent, but also for introducing me to one of the best online support systems for aspiring writers out there;

All the wonderful editors, staff, and authors at Omnific, each of whom I am honored and humbled to have the privilege of working with.

About the Author

Marian Vere is a twenty-eight-year-old writer of Women's Fiction. Born and raised in Pittsburgh, Pennsylvania, she received her degree from Edinboro University of Pennsylvania in — oddly enough — vocal music performance, only to later discover her love of writing and storytelling.

Marian is represented by Carly Watters of PS Literary, and currently lives in the suburbs of Chicago with her husband and two daughters.

Young Adult

Shades of Atlantis and *The Ember Series: Ember* and *Iridescent* by Carol Oates
Breaking Point by Jess Bowen
Life, Liberty, and Pursuit by Susan Kaye Quinn
Embrace by Cherie Colyer
Destiny's Fire by Trisha Wolfe
Streamline by Jennifer Lane
Reaping Me Softly by Kate Evangelista

Historical Romance

Cat O' Nine Tails by Patricia Leever
Burning Embers by Hannah Fielding

Erotic Romance

Becoming sage by Kasi Alexander
Saving sunni by Kasi & Reggie Alexander
The Winemaker's Dinner: Appetizers by Dr. Ivan Rusilko & Everly Drummond

Anthologies and Singles

A Valentine Anthology including short stories by Alice Clayton, Jennifer DeLucy, Nicki Elson, Jessica McQuinn, Victoria Michaels, and Alison Oburia

It's Only Kinky the First Time by Kasi Alexander
Learning the Ropes by Kasi & Reggie Alexander
The Winemaker's Dinner: RSVP by Dr. Ivan Rusilko
The Winemaker's Dinner: No Reservations by Everly Drummond
Big Guns by Jessica McQuinn
Concessions by Robin DeJarnett
Starstruck by Lisa Sanchez
New Flame by BJ Thornton
Shackled by Debra Anastasia
Swim Recruit by Jennifer Lane
Sway by Nicki Elson
Full Speed Ahead by Susan Kaye Quinn
The Second Sunrise by Hannah Downing
The Summer Prince by Carol Oates
Whatever it Takes by Sarah M. Glover
Clarity by Patricia Leever
Glimpse of Light by Jennifer DeLucy